THE WITCHES OF WHITE WILLOW

ANGELA ADDAMS

ABOUT WITCHES OF WHITE WILLOW

Even destiny can't get in the way of what is meant to be.

Hazel Knight is a Promised One—a witch born with unique magic abilities. As a result, her future is laid out for her. She is to join the Circle and spend the rest of her life meditating, chanting and devoting her healing magic to bolster her fellow witches. It's a commitment Hazel is proud to make, and she's just one internship away from fulfilling her destiny.

But just because Hazel's committed to her destiny doesn't mean she can't have some fun before she takes the final step. For the past year, she's enjoyed many clandestine nights with a man who has given her a lifetime of memories to take with her. A mysterious lover whose name she's never asked, whose face she's never fully seen.

Yet when her internship begins, she has no trouble recognizing Healer Duke Hart, the exquisitely sexy witch whom her mother has handpicked to serve as her mentor.

Hazel only meant to have a little fun before she devoted herself to a life of servitude, but Duke is bound and determined to prove that nothing, not even destiny, is written in stone.

For my daughter, Teagan, who introduced me to the TV show that started it all and to my son, Warren, who colored quietly all summer while I was writing this story.

Humans still do this thing where they celebrate the old ways. They touch the magic, only a wisp of it, but enough to leash them to devotion. They honor the rituals and pay tribute to the Mother, bolstering her power and, by extension, ours too. Most of the time, these humans are better witches than we are. Every once in a while, they're stronger than we are too.

Hazel Knight, Promised One Designate

"So you're slumming it tonight? For real, Haz? You're going to ditch me?"

Hazel snorted lightly as she held up yet another wispy gown. "It's not slumming, Mahdyia, and yes, I'm definitely going. Wouldn't miss it. You should come." But she knew before her cousin barked her disdain that that would never happen.

"Hang out with the humans?" She made a gagging noise. "Not on your life." Her voice echoed, the phone on speaker suddenly amplifying in an obnoxious way. "It's our last night of freedom! How can you do this to me?"

Last night of freedom. The night of the Spring Moon Festival she'd attended every year since she'd been old enough to get into trouble.

"What would your mother say?"

Mahdyia would never say a word to Hazel's prudish mother and they both knew it. All the same, the threat was enough to make Hazel gasp.

"*Mother* won't find out. She never finds out. She has no interest in human rituals. Besides, I've been going for years and

I'm not missing this one. It's fun, Mady. Seriously. A night of drinking, dancing—"

"And fucking. Yeah I get it."

"Making love, under the stars," Hazel corrected. "You're acting like I'm some angsty teenager. I'm a grown woman, about to embark on the next phase of my predetermined life. I'm allowed to have a little fun." She sighed. "I know you had big plans for our last night of freedom but I have to go."

"To see him."

Hazel's heart squeezed. *Him.* He'd texted her to tell her he'd be there. In town for work, he'd said. "It'll be the last time. Forever. And then you'll have me by your side, training, working, for the next year of our witchly lives."

A silence hung between them. One year was all they had left together.

"It's dangerous to play with humans. They could mess with your destiny." Mahdyia's tone was mocking, but not in a biting way.

Hazel knew Mady felt the same about Hazel's destiny, forged in stone on the night she'd been born, as Hazel herself did at that moment. Shit luck that she had been born into the Knight clan and to one of the most powerful white witches of all time.

"But it's such fun," Hazel tried to keep her voice light. Every moment she got to spend with him was delicious torture because she knew it was fleeting. "I have to say goodbye to him. I can't leave him wondering forever."

"Oh Haz." Madhya scoffed. "Such a romantic. Fine, go, spend time with your human. See if I care. I'm going to have the time of my life tonight anyway. Don't be late tomorrow. We have to make a good impression." She gave a little harsh laugh. "Or at least, I do."

"Reputation is everything, darling," Hazel chirped, mimicking her mother's tone.

"Easy for you to say." Mahdyia made a kissing noise that

sounded more like a squawk. "Love ya. Don't do anything I wouldn't do."

"Love ya too. And I plan on doing all the things you wouldn't do." She waved her finger and disconnected the call.

Hazel went back into her closet and pulled down the dress she'd been avoiding. It was stunning with its sheen of gold and slips of gauzy material. It dipped low on her chest, almost showing her nipples, and cinched at the waist, leaving her back exposed as the rest of it cascaded to her toes. And if it caught the right light, like when the ritual fires flickered against the dark night sky, yeah, it was damn near see through.

Was she bold enough to pull it off?

It was hardly practical, the chill she'd feel when she danced away from the flames would be unpleasant, especially if the wind was whipping like usual. She'd get it tangled on the low hanging branches and brush as she ran through the woods, chased as a part of their fun and games. He liked hunting her. She liked being hunted. Her dress would snag for sure. But what did it really matter? Before the night was through, he'd have her in his arms and they'd both be naked on the grass, her dress forgotten somewhere along the way. And she wouldn't need it after tonight.

She had a year to prepare her body, mind, and skill for her inevitable journey to her destiny. There would be no time, no room, for romantic fantasy, especially not under her mother's watchful eyes.

With a sigh, she held the dress up to her frame once again and examined herself in the mirror, a small smile creeping on her lips. Yes, for him, it was worth the snags and chills. One last time.

THE CITY WAS OFF IN THE DISTANCE, BLAZING WITH THE LIGHT of typical modernization. Much of its inhabitants still clung hard to the old ways, with over eight hundred practicing witches among them. Human witches. The city was nestled in woods so thick you wouldn't even know it was there if it weren't for the massive highway connecting it to the rest of the world and the big billboards advertising its existence. A tourist attraction that boasted all sorts of enticing and accessible forms of magic: love spells, fortune telling, crystal healing and perhaps a few curses here and there. They catered to the curious of their kind— humans who wanted to learn about witchcraft and all things Salem. Including the notorious witch trials that had almost ended Hazel's kind. The humans, even the non-witch ones, paid tribute and honored the fallen. The human witches were harmless dabblers in natural magics, making fistfuls of cash on the tragedy. She didn't fault them for that. Everyone and *everything* had a price.

Hazel felt a chill from her vantage point on the grassy hill, looking down at the twinkling lights of the city. It was the only appealing thing about Salem—the city and its believers, the pulse she got from their worship made her almost giddy. Her mother didn't value it—the humans were hardly worth her notice, even though they did provide a boost to the Healer's magic. Her mother felt their power was minor and insignificant, but she'd never ventured outside of the walls of White Willow Hospital, other than to come home and instruct Hazel in all the ways to be a proper white witch. She was a strict woman with high standards, expecting much, maybe too much, from her only daughter.

Hazel turned, scanning the horizon for White Willow itself. There, off in the distance, it stood, muted lights hazy in the darkness. Only witches of the non-human variety could locate it. A haven for those in need of magical healing, and soon to be her place of residence for the next year. There she'd train before ascending to her role as a Promised One, designate for her mother who was far too important, far too powerful, to ever give up her role as the Great Mother of all Healers.

Music wafted toward Hazel, floating on the breeze, pulling

her from her dark thoughts. Away from the city and from White Willow was a small ceremonial valley where a cluster of cottages stood. She called it The Village—it was where the human witches assembled to celebrate their faith. Only the elders of their kind actually lived there but it was mecca to the city witches and to Hazel as well. The bonfires were already burning in the center of the village. She could see the wisps of flame calling to her.

Her dress billowed behind her, the wind tickling her thighs. He was waiting for her. Somewhere down there where the fires were warm and the music was loud, where the wine flowed and the food was laid out. He was there, she knew it by the flutter of her heart. She lowered her mask, covering most of her face, as was the custom for the festival. With a jolt of excitement, she picked up her dress, freed her legs, and ran down the dirt path, her feet barely touching ground.

"YOU ARE THE MOST BEAUTIFUL WOMAN I HAVE EVER SEEN." His breath on the back of her neck made her shiver in a delicious way.

She swayed backward, feeling the warmth of his body just behind her. "You've never actually *seen* me," she teased.

He chuckled softly as he lowered his lips to her neck, sending another sweep of pleasure over her. Goosebumps rose all over her body. Somehow, even though he was barely touching her, he noticed. "Are you cold, sweetheart?"

On a sigh, Hazel turned, closing the small distance between them as she wrapped her arms around his waist and pressed her face to his chest, inhaling his scent. Sandalwood, mint, maybe a bit of vanilla. "No, not anymore."

His long dark hair was tied into a ponytail, the tips swishing against her forearms. "Mmm." She could feel his heart hammering as he wrapped his arms around her, encircling her with strength and warmth. "Your dress is very impractical for this weather."

She pulled away just enough to look up at him, his face shielded by his own mask. He had a wry smirk on his lips.

"Would it be better if I was covered in dowdy cotton?"

He licked his lips. "It would be better if you were covered in me."

She could have giggled with giddiness. His mask only revealed full lips, a strong chin and dark sparkling eyes, glinting with wicked intentions. "So you missed me then?" she teased again. He made her feel so alive. So cherished.

"I think about you every day. All day." He leaned into her, his lips brushing hers so tenderly. "Yes, I missed you."

And then he really kissed her. His tongue lunging deep, stroking her, loving her, making her want to gasp and moan. He gripped her ass, urging her to lift her legs to wrap around his waist as he hoisted her up. Her breasts pressed hard against his chest, nipples aching, heart pounding.

This was how it always was. A flame that never seemed to diminish, no matter how many days passed between their visits.

How she would go without him for the rest of her life, she didn't know.

He moved them away, to their secret spot shielded in the woods, and worshiped her body. Licking her every inch as he slowly dismantled her dress, slipping parts away to expose her flesh to his roving lips and tongue. Every spot he touched tingled with pleasure. When he sucked hard on her nipples, laving them then nipping, cupping her breasts with his palm before flicking with his fingers, she was on fire. He slipped the dress down her body, then nestled between her thighs to lick and stroke there too, sucking so hard on her clit that she exploded with a loud cry of pleasure.

And she did the same to him. Wound him up, rung him out. His cock was long and thick. Her lips were barely able to wrap around the width and no way was she taking his shaft all the way down. He was a big man in general—six foot four at least, with a broad muscled chest, like he worked out, or worked hard. His skin was olive, sun-kissed with no tan lines. Dark hair curled lightly around his nipples, trailing down in a line to that fine cock. She liked to take him down to the back of her throat, not all the way down, he was much too big for that, but as far as she dared while cupping his balls. She loved to make him moan and writhe beneath her. Especially when she replaced her mouth with her pussy, riding him hard and fast under the blanket of stars.

They made love for hours, her orgasms shattering her each and every time, making her forget, if only for a bit, that she was meant for greater things. Things beyond human understanding. Heartbreaking things that demanded sacrifice, great sacrifice. For those blissful moments, she couldn't think what could possibly be greater than this.

She lay panting in his arms, her body feeling light, a sheen of sweat making her shiver. "It's always so amazing with you. You make me feel really good." She knew she shouldn't gush, that it made her sound young and inexperienced. Which she was, really, since the encounters she'd had with him were the only ones she'd ever had—the only ones she *would* ever have. He had this way with her, making her feel cherished and exotic, beautiful and loved, just with his body. With his penetrating eyes and his tender lips.

He sighed deeply, running his fingers up and down her arm. "I feel the same way. I wish we could stay like this forever."

Her heart clenched. They didn't have forever. What a stark reminder. She opened her mouth to speak, then closed it again quickly. What would she say? What could she tell him? Despite the fact that he was a practicing Pagan, and wore a forearm tattoo that branded him so, it was forbidden for her to tell any human about her witchy status. It could put White Willow at risk. Humans had turned on them once before. Even though she believed he never would, she couldn't confide in him about being the Promised One. Not that. Not ever.

"I'm in town for a while. The coven is preparing for a solstice celebration." He gripped her tight and pulled her almost on top of him, his cock growing hard at the slight touch. "You could just stay here until then."

Summer Solstice was in a matter of days. Despite the fact that she would be so close, hidden away at White Willow, she wouldn't be able to get away, not even for a few hours. Disappointment crushed her. He'd never stayed longer than one night at a time usually. "I'm sorry. I won't be able to get away again for a while." It felt like her heart was shattering.

His fingers stilled, he released his grip and her body slid back down to his side. "Sweetheart, I know that something is wrong, I can feel it. Be honest with me. Is there someone else?"

Yes. My mother. "No." She raised her head and turned, propping herself on her elbow so she could look down at him. "I have..." She searched for the right words. "A family obligation."

"Your mother again?"

She'd told him only a little about her mother's controlling ways, trying to paint herself as a normal human girl. It was often her mother who prevented her from attending various ceremonies anyway. She could only sneak out unnoticed at certain times, when her mother was consumed with other very important things. Otherwise she kept her life very secret, like her identity. She and her lover didn't even know each other's names, texting only when they could sneak away to see one another.

"You should tell that woman to shove her obligation up her—"

"Let's not talk about her." Hazel leaned down and gave him a soft kiss.

"She's controlling, manipulative, from what you've told me—"

She opened her mouth over his, licking him, stroking him, silencing him. He moaned. She reached down to stroke his growing erection, his tip slick with a mixture of her cream and his.

As she pulled away from the kiss she felt a tug on her mask. "Let me see your face."

She gasped, flung up her hand to stop him. "No!" And then she said more quietly, "You always say the mystery is what keeps you coming back."

"That's not what keeps me coming back." He smiled wickedly. "For once, I'd like to make love to you without any barriers."

He started to lift his own mask. Hazel caught a glimpse of high cheekbones. "No!" She stopped him once again. "Not this time. Please. I'll find a way to come to the solstice. We'll reveal ourselves then." How she would do that she didn't know, but she'd have to find a way. There had to be a way. She needed to see him one last time.

He sighed, lowering his mask. "As you wish, sweetheart." There was such disappointment in his voice.

"I think we can make better use of this time." She slid herself on top of him, slipping him inside, enjoying the feel of him filling her, consuming her, making her feel something more than obligation, duty, and the overwhelming press of her destiny.

2

"Healer Hart, can I have a moment?"

Duke cringed at the tone of that familiar voice. He took another sip of his latte and turned slowly to greet his new boss. "Mother Knight, good morning." He'd come late and hoped to slip into rounds without being noticed, but given that it was his first day of obligatory residency, locking him at home base for the next year, it was inevitable that *she* would want to speak with him.

"Yes, good morning indeed," Mother Knight said, her tone clipped, a stiff smile parting her lips. Her brown hair was pulled so tight against her head it looked painted on, piled into a bun at the base of her skull, and severely yanking her eyebrows into a permanent state of surprise. "So good to have you with us. I've heard great things about your Medic team and trauma tours. You come highly recommended."

Which surprised him greatly. While he was a damn fine trauma Healer, he was also a risk taker, a rule breaker, and on the road for a reason. As his Commanding Officer, Rook Havenbridge, often said, he was a giant pain in the ass with an ego that barely fit through the door. He *was* good—the ego was definitely justified—but

Mother Knight had never been a woman to flatter or praise, and the fact that she didn't even remember who he was bruised him more than he wanted to admit. He had trained under her many years before, had taken every barb she'd thrown his way, had been the top of the class and had left as soon as he could. Out of sight, out of mind as far as the Great Mother was concerned, no doubt.

Mother Knight demanded order and conformity, something that Duke was prone to challenge. This was the last step on his path to Master Healer, which would give him the ultimate freedom to pursue his own interests. He wanted to work in the field as a Medic with his own budget, commanding his own team, and not anywhere near home base or the Great Mother.

"I haven't been back here since I was an intern." He scanned the foyer once again. White Willow was ancient, a sprawling mansion built at the turn of the century. Touches of modernization had not diminished its grandeur. Electric lights and forced heating and air conditioning, or so he'd heard, were now part of the infrastructure, but that was just function. The true beauty of the place was in the ornate details, starting with the sprawling double staircase, all hand-carved wood railings, which bobbed and weaved around a grand pipe organ to the second floor and then again around an angelic fountain to the third floor. White marble everywhere else. It was a spectacular entrance, and was a testament to the rest of the rooms found at the mansion—all one hundred and twelve of them. As much as he hated being under Mother Knight's thumb, he did really love being back at White Willow, if only for the architecture.

The foyer had been upgraded over the years, a small coffee bar added for the comfort of the patients and their families. For all her rules, Mother Knight had done good by the place, taking over, raising tremendous funds to update and renovate, restore and improve the hospital. He'd heard she was a real bulldog when it came to squeezing money out of the board and old wealthy families alike... Also when it came to running her staff. She didn't take no for an answer and expected great things.

"Yes, well, that's what I've come to speak with you about. We have a new crop of interns starting today," Mother Knight started.

Duke moaned into his cup, then coughed when Mother Knight raised her eyebrows, somehow, higher.

"One of whom is my daughter, Hazel, and I want you to be the one to mentor her."

Duke choked on his coffee. "What? Uh, I don't think...I mean..." *Hazel?* Who named their kid that these days? It sounded old. Just like her mother. Ancient and orderly.

"She's a gifted witch and a strong Healer. More importantly, she's only here for a year, set to take her place as my designate in the Circle of One."

And then it clicked. Ah yes, the prodigal daughter, destined to unite the Circle as a Promised One. He'd heard the stories, the conspiracy theories too. Many of the old world witches abroad felt that the Great Mother was taking advantage. That no one should condemn a youth to a life of servitude. That's why the Promised Ones were typically from the older generations—mature witches with years of training to hone the skill it took for that kind of magic manipulation. Her daughter had reportedly been quite powerful from birth, natural raw power that came from her superb pedigree. That she was willing to go along with her mother's wishes meant that she was obedient as well. And loyal.

"With all due respect, Mother Knight, I don't think I will have time to mentor. As you know, I have my own set of skill assessments to complete, ones that I have been remiss to wrap up. I only plan to be here for a few months at most. There's great work yet to be done in the field. Witches are—"

"Yes." She raised her hand for silence. "Healer Hart, I am aware of your goals as well as your compassionate pursuits. We both know, however, that you are consigned to your place here for no less than one year." The way she said it sounded like she was spitting out something bitter. She paused, then softened her tone. "But please consider this a request only. I don't intend to burden you with added work. My daughter is here already. You can meet her and decide if she is worthy of your time." A bustling noise came from the back hall. "Ah, everyone has assembled for morning salutations. I will introduce you afterward."

Duke knew that he really didn't have a choice. If Mother Knight wanted him to mentor her daughter, he would have to damn well do it or risk being challenged continuously on his assessments. Ultimately, it was up to Mother Knight whether or not he was elevated to the rank of Master Healer. If he pissed her off, he was a goner. And with the way he usually did things, of the rule-breaking variety, he was bound to piss her off repeatedly. Better to do her a favor now and use it as a bargaining chip later.

He had hoped, foolishly apparently, to get in and out as quickly as possible, his Commanding Officer promising to pull some strings to have him fast track through his assessments. After all, it was just a formality. He should have known better with her running the show, though. No shortcuts would happen on Mother Knight's watch.

"This is going to be a long year," he mumbled.

He took a few steps to the side, watching as the Healers assembled. It was a grand staff of at least a hundred witches and aides, all varying ranks. A hierarchy that denoted not only respect owed but magical potential and power. The interns stood at the front, dressed in long black robes that marked them as trainees. They all had their hoods up. It was a formality on day one; by the end of the day, they'd be in more comfortable attire, depending on the direction and wishes of their mentors. He didn't pity them—a gruelling five-year apprenticeship was ahead, theory classes, labs and rotations in the hospital to build their power, knowledge and skill, also to determine where their strengths lay followed by rigorous testing. Some would falter and fail and others would rise to the top. Everyone had their place.

That Hazel Knight only needed a year of training suggested that she was not only powerful but being fast tracked by her mother, who had probably done much of the primary book and basic spell casting training herself. The hands on stuff wouldn't come out of a book though; that kind of learning you could only get on the job, so to speak. Duke could only imagine what the poor girl's life had been like. Constant study under her mother was no doubt unpleasant and unrelenting and all so she could spare the woman a place in the Circle. With her daughter there instead of her, Mother Knight would extend her own life and power for decades, perhaps even a century, to come. It was cruel by anyone's standards and he felt pity for the poor kid.

His thoughts shifted to his lover, the village girl with a similarly complicated relationship with her mother. Seemed to be a thing around here.

"Is that you, Duke?" A hearty slap on the back almost made him spill his coffee.

He turned toward the voice. "Ty Cooper." Wow, he had aged. "You have hardly changed a bit."

It'd been ten years since he'd left White Willow to work on field missions, leaving behind the cohort of Healers that he'd been training with since childhood. Ty had come closest to being a best friend to Duke back then, but they'd fallen out of touch when their paths deviated. Not everyone understood Duke's need to be on the road.

Ty was smirking like he knew Duke was full of shit. "I was cursed, man." He chuckled awkwardly as he ran a hand over his balding head. "Literally got hit with a nasty spell a while back. Shaved a good ten years off my life from what I can tell."

"No way?" Duke noted the dark circles under the man's eyes and the hard lines that marked his face. Stress and magic, working in this place was eating him alive no doubt. Any time you were exposed to the confines of a power hub like White Willow, you risked exposure taking its toll. Ty had never been the brightest or the quickest but he didn't deserve to be cursed. "Next time you should duck."

Ty laughed. "Yeah, don't think I haven't thought of a millions ways I could have avoided it. I was young, stupid, dare I say, cocky." He smirked then shrugged. "You do what you gotta do though. Still out fighting the good fight? Saving all those wayward witches?"

"Yeah. Fresh air suits me." Which wasn't really what being in the field was all about. He did spend a lot of time hiking through woods to get to remote villages and covens, but there was an equal amount of time in some damn good hotels, negotiating acceptable medical policy and instructing witches in healing technique and spell casting. He'd admit, his Commanding Officer was good to him, spoiling him with five star accommodations whenever he could. Either way, he wasn't around the magic surges long enough for them to have any ill effects. Another reason why he didn't want to stay at White Willow longer than he needed to.

Ty leaned closer, lowering his voice as he did. "Hey, you still meddle with the humans... The ones who dabble?"

Duke snorted, shook his head and pointed to where Mother Knight had taken her spot at the podium in front of the grand organ.

"My fellow witches." Her voice was amplified, a trick of magic that any good witch could do. "Today we welcome our newest Healers to White Willow, sent to us from various academies and home instructors to begin their internship, unquestionably the most important part of their journey in becoming Master Healers in their own rights. While we encourage innovation and exploration, we must all remember that the foundation of our practice is rooted in tradition and tried and tested methods of spell casting that have proven most invaluable to healing magic. New ideas, fresh power and viewpoints invigorate us, but be cautious of the temptation to let your egos go rogue, for every triumph you will have, there will be great moments of disaster. Your mentors, whom you will meet today, will guide you through this exciting time. Young Healers, be open to absorb all that you are offered, be brave enough to accept any challenge that comes your way, and be compassionate in all that you do."

A tittering rose among the crowd. A giddy rush of excitement. Duke remembered it, vaguely. They were so naive to think the next five years would be anything but painful and exhausting. Even he had struggled.

"As all of you know, today is the day that the interns and their mentors will…"

"Hey, Ty." He pointed his coffee cup toward the group. "You know which one of those black robes belongs to the Mother's kid?"

Ty made a face. "Hazel?" He scanned the crowd. "I've heard she's tall."

"You've heard she's tall?" Duke scoffed. "What? As in, you have no idea what she looks like?"

"Nah, man, Mother Knight has kept her locked up tight at their clan house since birth. Her precious Promised One hasn't been seen by anyone but family. She's got a cousin though, Mahdyia, who's pretty hot, stands to reason—"

"Healer Hart." Mother Knight's voice sent Ty beating a hasty retreat.

"Catch ya later," Ty said before beelining into the quickly dispersing crowd.

Duke turned toward Mother Knight and the dark robe that followed meekly behind.

"Healer Hart, I'd like to introduce you to my daughter, Hazel. I've told her a little about your skills, but perhaps you can give her an idea of some of your worldly experiences."

Duke opened his mouth to once again suggest that there might be a better choice as mentor—a last ditch effort. But then he couldn't speak, because a pale white hand with delicate fingers and manicured nails lifted the black hood from her head and let it fall to her back, revealing a face that, although he didn't know fully, he knew quite intimately.

Those full pink lips.

That quirk of a smile.

The dimple he caught glimpses of when the mask slipped.

When her green eyes locked on his, recognition flashed, then doubt, then shock. She darted her gaze to his arm, his forearm where his clan mark was visible and, if possible, her eyes grew wider.

This was his lover. The village girl who had stolen his heart and bewitched his soul. He'd thought she was human. He'd thought wrong.

He opened his mouth again.

Hazel shook her head.

He spoke anyway. "I thought—"

A screech echoed through the foyer.

"The dead have risen! Oh goddess, there are zombies afoot!"

3

OF THE WITCHES LEFT IN THE FOYER, THERE WERE ONLY A handful who could probably handle the risen dead. And Hazel was one of them. Shoving aside her shock at seeing *him* right there in front of her—and if she had any shred of doubt, the tattoo flashing on his forearm confirmed it—Hazel stepped into the melee and began to cast.

Her mother stepped back, a smug smirk on her face. She always wanted Hazel to prove her worth.

Necromancy was tricky and hard to manage. The decaying corpses ambling toward her reeked of magic gone wrong. The horde of ten locked in on her, sensing the magic building around her. They were drawn to her power. She called them closer, beckoning with her finger. "Come and get me, you rotten things."

Other witches were trying to help. The interns were scattered behind them, looking like they wanted to run but couldn't let their pride slip that much.

Hazel took control.

She cast quickly, siphoning the original spell that clung to the things, pulling the thread away and snapping it until it unraveled. It was a trick she'd learned when she was a child. Sometimes, instead of battling magic, all you needed to do was pull it apart by the seams.

A jolt of magic rushed through her, amping her up, almost making her giddy. *Where'd that come from?* Her spell jumped, moving like it was on fast forward. Making each pass of her magic go ten times faster than she'd expected. She fought to stay in control, marvelled at how efficient it was and wondered if White Willow was the cause of her sudden power surge.

As quickly as it had come, the chaos ended. The corpses fell, some limbs actually clattering away from their bodies. Lifeless once again. *Gross.*

She sucked in a deep breath. She was powerful. Highly trained. But that—*that* had left her breathless. She'd never felt a surge like that. She looked down at her hands, frowning. *What the...* She glanced beside her.

And there he was, at her side, his hands out as if he'd been about to push her behind him. Frozen, with the dumbest expression on his face.

"My daughter, Healer Hart." Her mother's words dripped with pride. "Someone come and clean this up." She snapped her fingers at the orderlies. "I want a report in five minutes. How did this happen? Who is responsible?" She moved past Hazel, doubling back quickly to peck her on the cheek. "My darling, do abide by your mentor. Supposedly, he is quite good. You may actually learn something." The look she shot him suggested she'd believe it when she saw it. And then she was gone. A whirlwind of direct orders and purposeful hand gestures.

Everyone was scrambling to get ahead of her, anticipate her wishes before she barked them. Hazel knew that impulse intimately.

"Where'd you learn that?" Healer Hart asked. He'd wiped the stupid look off his face and replaced it with skepticism. "That's a year five skill."

"I'm sure you've heard the stories," Hazel said. "Destiny

etched in stone, Promised One." She turned to face him, coming in close so that they wouldn't be overheard. "You never said you were a Healer."

"You never said you were a witch."

"You know I can't be your intern. It's highly inappropriate."

"We've already been highly inappropriate—many times." He quirked his eyebrows. "I'd say this is the perfect opportunity for us to get to know one another on a whole other level."

"Shut up!" she hissed, her cheeks burning. "My mother can't know about..." She waved her hands around, feeling flustered and embarrassed and mortified. "She can't know! And I can't be your intern. I'll get myself assigned to someone else."

She tried to walk away. He followed her. His body pressed close, his hand gripping her arm, his head nearly touching hers as they walked together.

"Oh yeah? Well, your mother specifically requested that I train you. She came looking for me because I'm the best. You want to explain to her that you can't be my intern—*why* you can't be my intern?"

Hazel gasped. "She can't know." She pulled him toward the staircase, and nestled them behind a statue, out of sight. When she looked up at him, she had to stifle her reaction. His eyes were dark, brown, and deep, easier to see in the light of day. Mesmerizing. His cheekbones high, he had a widow's peak and his hair was parted in the middle, hanging loose and out of its usual ponytail. She wanted to put her hands on him. Run her fingers through his hair, breathe in his scent, eat him alive. Instead she wrapped her arms around herself. "I am a Promised One. My destiny isn't my own. It belongs to the Circle. You've heard the stories. You know. Nothing can jeopardize that."

"Like me?" He smirked. "Why Hazel, are you saying that your feelings for me could put your devotion to your mother and the Circle in danger? I'm flattered."

"Shut up, you know what I mean. Listen, my mother doesn't

know I've been sneaking out... If she found out." Hazel shuddered. "She doesn't like humans."

"She doesn't like humans?"

"She doesn't believe they are worthy of anyone's time. And if she found out what I've been doing, going to the rituals, seeing you, she would be dishonored. Disappointed. I would ruin her."

"She's making you take her place—"

"It is my *destiny*. She's not making me do anything. I can't work with you. I won't. Please don't make this harder than it has to be." Fate could be cruel and perhaps this was punishment for the indulgences she'd had all year with him. Putting him there, with her, uniting them in this way, it was beyond what she could tolerate. If there were a way to get out of it, she'd have to find it. For both of their sakes. If her mother found out that he'd sullied her or threatened to harm the family name, she'd bury him. Figuratively, perhaps literally. Her mother was a powerful woman and feared for a reason.

"I just don't see what the harm—"

The conversation was going in circles. Hazel sighed, then zapped a disorientation spell his way with the snap of her fingers. It was cowardly, she knew, but she needed to get away from him to regroup and figure out a plan.

He stumbled back, frozen by her spell. She took off at a run. It would be a good few minutes before he figured out what had happened, or at least registered her skill level, and regained the ability to move.

Fifth year spells, my ass.

She barged into the intern lounge where she knew Mahdyia would be waiting for her. She had to change, then find her mother, then figure out how to tell her that she couldn't work with Healer Hart in a way that it didn't mess with his reputation, or hers.

"Whoa! Slow down!"

In a tangle of arms and hands, she tackled the guy who'd just been trying to exit the lounge. They both tumbled backward, her landing flat on top of him, his wide blue eyes full of shock. With their arms and legs entangled, their position was nothing short of awkward.

"Oh shit, Hazel, you okay?" Mahdyia was there, hooking her under the arm and hoisting her up.

"I'm so sorry," Hazel breathed. "I should have been watching where I was going."

"No worries." He rolled himself to his knees, grunting a bit. He was rather hefty, and dusted his legs as if there was dirt. He held his hand out as he stood. "Tate Martin."

"Hazel Knight."

"As in, The Promised One, Hazel Knight?" A tall dark haired girl who was standing at a locker sounded incredulous.

"Yeah, what of it?" Mahdyia snapped. "She's an intern, just like us. Get over it."

"She's doomed!" the girl said. "Sorry, that slipped out." She closed her locker. "I'm Chanda Raj. Sometimes things fall out of my mouth. Some people think it's endearing." She pointed her apple at Hazel. "I've heard things about you."

"Everyone has heard things about her," Mahdyia snapped again.

"No, I've heard things about *you*!" Chanda continued moving her apple until it rested on Mahdyia, then she poked out her finger. "You're the cousin right?

Mahdyia stood taller. Hazel knew she loved it when people recognized her. "You've heard of me?"

"Yeah, I have." Chanda nodded slowly, a smirk spreading on her lips. She took a bite of her apple and spoke between chews. "You're the crazy girl who was at the keg party last summer, who put her mouth on—"

"Okay, enough!" Hazel raised a hand. "I need to speak to you." She pulled Mahdyia toward the bathroom. "Privately."

"Wait, what?" Mahdyia pointed toward Chanda. "I want to hear the rest of that story!"

"You were there, you know what happened."

"Yeah, but it's always more epic when someone else tells the story." Mahdyia beamed.

Hazel shoved her through the door then followed and locked it behind them. "I am in serious trouble!"

"What, did your mother tell you that you had to wear that hideous cloak for the rest of the day?"

Hazel sighed, unclasped the cloak and let it fall to the floor. "No! Will you shut up and listen to me? I am in serious fucking trouble. Big eff trouble!"

"Oh my!" Mahdyia perched herself on the closed toilet seat. "You're swearing. It must be bad. Do tell."

Hazel leaned back against the door, her eyes burning like she was about to cry. "You know that guy I've been seeing?"

"The hot human who's been slipping it to you—"

"Stop!" Her cheeks were on fire once again. "Please, just stop..."

"Haz, what the fuck?" Mahdyia chuckled. "You look like you're ready to burst into tears.

"My mother... She arranged for me to be mentored by this Healer, Hart."

"No shit? Healer Duke Hart? You lucky little shit! I've heard he's super hot and—"

"He's the guy!" Hazel tossed her hands up as she paced the room. "My human, except he's not a human at all! He's a powerful fucking witch and my mother wants him to be my mentor! *My mentor*! For a whole year!"

Mahdyia whistled. "Now, that is the best thing I've heard all day! Again I say, you lucky little shit."

Hazel turned to face her. "It's a nightmare! Mady! Come on! I can't work with him! I can't even be near him without wanting to...well...wanting to..."

"Jump his boner?"

"Mady!"

"What? I don't see a problem here."

"You don't see a big problem with me being mentored by the man I've been having a secret affair with? Who I thought was a harmless human? Who, if my mother found out I'd given my virginity to—"

"Wait... Whoa... He was your first?"

"How do you not know this?"

"Geez, I thought maybe Henry..."

"Cousin Henry?"

Mahdyia shrugged. "What? Grosser things have happened in our family."

"Mady, what am I supposed to do here? I was going to say goodbye to him—the human him. I was going to give him one last night at the solstice celebration and say goodbye. Devote myself to my year of internship and then be on my way. Chaste, regrow my virginity, or whatever, and forget all about him."

"Honey, that's *so* not how it works."

"I know not technically, but I thought with enough time and devotion to my studies, I'd forget and be back to the way I was. I'd move on. Close enough to purity."

"There's no way that was ever going to happen." Mady sighed. "Not with the way you've talked about your human...er, Duke."

"I can't work with him and keep my promise to my mother. Not with the way I feel."

"Well, you're going to have to."

"What? No! Why?"

"If you refuse to work with him, she's going to want to know why, and if he doesn't tell her, then she will get it out of you. We both know when she wants something she gets it, including private information. *Especially* private information."

When Hazel opened her mouth to argue, Mahdyia put her hand up for her to stop.

"You have no backbone with that woman whatsoever. So this is either the hill you die on or it's not. And I'm thinking not, because what's more important to you is pleasing that woman and obliging some duty you feel you owe her."

"She's my mother."

"She's sending you off in her place so the Circle can suck the life out of you." Mahdyia moved to her, taking her hands in hers, her scowl deep, her tone fierce. "You'll age a decade for every year you're there. She is literally stealing your youth."

"Not this again." Hazel sighed. "It's my destiny. Etched in stone, remember?"

"That's bullshit. Destiny is what you make it."

"Destiny is destiny. Now, will you help me figure a way out of this mess?"

"Nobody but your mother has actually seen this stone."

"Mady..."

"What?" She threw her hands up. "Okay, fine. I'll help you. I love you. I want what's best for you. So I'll help you."

"Thank you." Hazel felt relief flood through her. Mady would come up with a plan. She always had a plan.

Hazel flipped the lock, then opened the door.

"I'm looking for my intern, Hazel Knight."

"Oh shit." Hazel slammed the door shut. "You have to distract him, get him out of here. Tell him you're his intern now or something."

"You want me to lie to Duke Hart?" Mahdyia crossed her arms and smirked.

"Yes, what's the big deal? You lie all the time! Tell him I left. Went to speak to my mother or something. Please, Mady, I can't do this. I can't be partnered with him. Not after what we've done together. Not when I have to cleanse."

"I can't lie to him."

"What the hell do you mean? Of course you can!" Hazel tried to shoo her to the door.

"No, honey, I can't. Oh my, how do you not know this? You and your sheltered life. Duke Hart is known for his uncanny ability to detect bullshit... He has a built-in lie detector. He's an empath, you dolt! A renowned one."

"An empath? Holy shit."

And then it all made sense. How he made her feel, how her guard was always down around him. Why she couldn't get enough. Empaths were like honey. They fed you power in whatever way you needed it. Bolstering, amplifying, layering. The perfect companion. Something a witch like her would crave without even realizing what was happening, how an addiction was building. He'd give her everything she needed or wanted. That was his nature. And he'd read her like an open book the more time they spent together.

Sweetheart, I know there's something wrong. Her mind drifted to their last night together. How he'd known. *He'd known.* She groaned. "What am I going to do?"

"Run away. With him." Mahdyia winked. "Fuck destiny."

Hazel's eyes grew wide; she looked at the door.

Mahdyia yanked it open. "She's right here, Duke. Ready to get a thorough internship from one of the greats."

"Mady!" Hazel hissed, eyes wide.

"I told you, I love you. I want what's best for you." She kissed Hazel's cheek. "And he, my friend, is exactly what you need."

4

Duke only saw a glimpse of Hazel before the bathroom door slammed shut, practically in his face. He could hear furious but hushed arguing happening on the other side.

"I think she wants some privacy," one of the interns said, his voice quavering slightly. He coughed when Duke shot him a raised eyebrow. "I mean, she seemed upset."

Upset? She wasn't the one who had just been dealt a dirty spell, frozen in place for anyone to see. To think a first year had gotten the better of him. "This is ridiculous." He shook his head, then raised his hand to the knob. "Haz—"

"Duke Hart? Is that you? Can't be... Duke?"

Yet another voice he'd thought he'd never hear again. "Bridget Rose." He didn't totally have to force the smile that pulled on his lips. Bridget Rose. Although she had a good ten years on him, she was still and would always be a striking woman. "It's been a long time."

She had him in one of her bear hugs before he could think about a next move, her arms gripping in a way that was only slightly emasculating. She was a brick house of a woman, trained for Battle magic and a hardened explorer—lean, fit, powerful and damn sexy. Aggressive as all hell too. Her way or the highway kinda woman. He returned her hug. She felt the same as she had ten years before. Soft in all the right places, welcoming, interested. Very interested.

His hand automatically dropped to her hip, a familiar grip that had his mind going other places. Forgotten places. Not unwelcome places, if he was going to be honest. At least not where his body was concerned.

"Okay fine! I'm going!" The door behind him whooshed open. "You listen to me, Duke Hart...oh..."

Duke loosened his grip on Bridget and glanced over his shoulder, letting a lazy smile show and giving Hazel a wink before turning back to Bridget. He planted a kiss on her cheek before letting her go.

"Duke, you smell the same. Sweet and spicy," Bridget said, her smile wide, like she was genuinely happy to see him, somewhat surprising given how they'd parted all that time ago. "I'd heard a rumor, wasn't sure it was true. So you're back to complete your assessments? Ready to be anointed a Master?"

Duke chuckled. "Yes. Havenbridge said it was either that or I'd be pulling Scrub duty for the next ten years."

Scrub duty—a dirty and painful magical fix for the worst of the worst of their kind. If they broke too many universal laws, put too many witches in danger, they were scrubbed. Washed of their magic for a period of time. It wasn't overly complicated work, but it was torturous for the giver and the receiver, just for different reasons. There were only so many times you could hear a fellow witch scream in that kind of agony before it got to you. For a Healer, putting time in at the Scrub was a fate worse than death. Tending to the magically shackled, caring for their wounds, mostly emotionally, was very unpleasant. He didn't relish the idea of ever going back there.

"Sheesh, I've seen him follow through on that threat." She laughed with a shake of her head. "Your talents are better served elsewhere." She gave him a once over. A very suggestive once over. He could have sworn he heard Hazel make a muffled sound that might have been a jealous harrumph.

"I've been following your career here and there. You've mastered a few things yourself."

"Oh well." She brushed down her lab coat, a pretty blush rising to her cheeks. "Mastered, hardly." She waved him off. "It will take a lifetime to learn everything from the Hags."

"The Storm Hags?" one of the interns, a tall brunette blurted. "Master the humans' magic?"

Everyone heard the tone. The typical discriminatory tone of that most witches had toward humans. It was inbred from birth, taught to them by old school thinking and traditionalist families. At least the chubby kid had enough sense to wince.

Bridget narrowed her eyes, snapping her head so she could address the intern with a hard stare. "Those humans and their magic could obliterate your sorry witch soul. They have more combined power, more natural control, than most witches in this building. Innate talent like that should be revered, cherished, and honored."

Duke stifled a snicker as a look of dread flattened the intern's incredulous expression.

"Oh no, no, no, don't get me wrong, you misunderstood," she sputtered, her face going paler, her lips quivering. "I love the humans... Really...I'm all about the human love."

Bridget turned away, dismissing the intern with an eye roll. "And so it begins." She lifted a hand to squeeze his shoulder, then to run down his arm, appraising his muscle tone to be sure. "So what about you? Are you taking on one of these"—she waved her hand around—"unformed vessels of promise?"

She was mocking the words of the Mother. Seemed uncharacteristically cynical. He quirked an eyebrow. "Actually, I was asked to mentor her daughter, Hazel." He nodded over his shoulder, adding a sarcastic bite to his next words. "But I think she's perhaps too good for a teacher like me."

Bridget scoffed. "Indeed, she's too good for *any* teacher if the rumors are true." She glanced over Duke's shoulder, narrowing her eyes at the girls behind him. "Are you two planning on getting dressed in your uniforms any time soon? Training started twenty minutes ago and we have places to be."

"Unifor—" Hazel started.

"Move, now," Bridget barked, her tone brokering no argument.

He'd always admired that about her—she had the ability to make you jump to action even if you weren't under her command.

One of the other interns waved the girls over, frantically motioning to a box behind her. It was then he noticed the military attire. Black fatigues, standard issue, tank top, cargo pants, steel-toed boots. The tanks had a white willow embossed above the heart. There had been no such uniforms when he was in training. "Are you taking the interns out?"

Bridget crossed her arms and shifted so that they could survey the interns as they scrambled to locate correct sizes. "Too easy." She laughed. "So anyway, yes, I'm taking them out to the field. Got clearance from Mother."

"A problem with the Hags?"

"Mmm, maybe. Hard to tell. I got a message, well, a series of garbled messages from one of my contacts at a remote witch village in the hills. Humans with limited magic mostly, Storm Hags too though. Powerful people. Mother thought it would be a good crash course for the new interns. These ones are with me." She shrugged. "I hadn't realized Hazel was going to be with someone else though. Mother hinted that she had a special request with an experienced Medic. I will admit, I felt a bit miffed that she didn't entrust *her precious* to my care, but seeing that it's you she's given the sacred duty to, I'm less so. You're a fine addition to our team. Speaking of which, you interested in coming along?" She turned her stormy blue eyes on him, batting them like she needed to convince him to go on a field trip. "Your expertise would be greatly appreciated and perhaps badly *needed* if things go sideways as they sometimes do. And it would give us time to catch up." She winked. "I know how much you love the forest."

Duke laughed, delighted that Hazel had heard that, equally delighted that she'd frozen in her frantic search for a tank top to stare at Bridget... No, to glare at her. She wanted him to believe that her feelings had vanished the second he'd walked into her world when it was obvious they hadn't.

"So Mother is behind this? Agreed to the idea of taking her only daughter out there?"

"One hundred percent. We try to get the interns out in the field at some point in their training. As you know, a well-rounded education is a cornerstone of this program. Mother endorses it and knows she can't exempt her daughter from the trial. And besides, my grant money is tied to my publishing. These trips offer me a lot of inspiration for papers. There's always a discovery to be made. I like to introduce the interns to human witches at some point, try to crack some of that old world thinking."

"A worthy pursuit. Does it work?"

"Meh, sometimes." She nudged him. "Sometimes they never come back."

"Hey now, I'm back. It just took me a while to get here."

"You were a fast learner. Eager too, from what I remember." She nudged him again then stepped forward, commanding attention of the interns with just a wave of her hand. "You four are mine. I own you for the next five years. You"—she pointed at Hazel—"belong to Healer Hart and will follow his command." She turned back to the rest of the group, ignoring Hazel's sudden seething glare. "All of you, when we say jump, you jump. When we say duck, you duck. You will remain vigilant. You will absorb our teaching. You will listen and you will be open to whatever magic learning comes your way. From me, from Healer Hart, from the humans. All are above you in this hierarchy. If you ignore that simple rule, you will probably die...which is a better fate than failing this trial."

One of the interns scoffed, a surly-looking guy who was leaning against the lockers, arms crossed, appearing all the badass troublemaker in his uniform.

"And if you have a problem with that, we can arrange for double duty in the Scrub. Healer Hart has direct access. We might even venture there for a side trip if you don't behave."

That got them all wide eyed and standing straight, even the tough guy. Duke had to stifle a laugh. The fear of the place was not undeserved.

"Get dressed, grab a pack, meet us on deck in fifteen."

"Are we going somewhere, Healer Rose?" the chubby one asked. The nametag now featured on his chest read Tate Martin.

"Scotland, highlands. You're getting your field training early," Bridget said, arms folded, expression stern. "Get to it, people! We leave in fifteen."

Duke didn't wait for Hazel to protest. He didn't even look at her as he followed Bridget out of the lounge. "That got their attention."

"I'm not joking either. I've never lost an intern, but I have had some close calls. It can get crazy out there with the Rogues roaming. They seem to be increasing in numbers lately. Joining forces and luring white witches in innovative and devious ways. We've lost three Healers in the last six months. Good witches, promising but inexperienced." She shook her head, clearly distressed.

"I hadn't heard anything about that." Duke found it equally as surprising that Mother Knight would let her daughter out there if things were as dangerous as Bridget said.

"The Trappers know. They're doing their job, hot on the trails and all that." She waved her hand. "But it's best for us to be vigilant, not let ourselves get too distracted." She leaned in close, her lips almost touching his neck as she angled up to his ear. "I'll bring my big tent though, the one with the soundproofing and the down floor. You remember that one? You liked it a lot, if I recall."

Duke stopped her hand from trailing down his stomach. Now that Hazel was out of sight, the ruse seemed pointless. "Oh yes, I remember. It's where you left me fast asleep, spell induced, while you took credit for something that belonged to me, a rather precious gem." He gave her a sly smile when she pulled away.

"Oh, Duke, you and your gems. It was a necessary strategy. You and I both know that I had to be the one to bring it home. Besides, you got me back, remember?" She slipped her fingers into her blouse and shifted it to the side, showing the three-inch scar that bubbled over her breast. "Magic scars can't be removed, you know?" She ran her finger over the marred flesh. "But I don't mind. When I touch it, it reminds me of you. I can still feel your magic there." Her smile turned sour as she let her blouse fall back into place. "It's good to see you again. Been too long. You remember where the deck is, right?" She didn't wait for him to respond. "I'll see you up there in ten."

Duke watched her walk away. He noticed the way the other Healers and aides heeded her space, moving out of her path even subconsciously while they were preoccupied by file folders or conversations. She'd always been commanding. Always demanded respect. And he had unconditionally respected her, right up until the moment she'd betrayed his trust. Then his feelings had changed.

He rubbed his hand down his face. But that had been ten years ago and he'd gotten over it. Mostly. As much as he enjoyed teasing Hazel with Bridget's proximity, he had no intention of leading either woman on. Hazel might not have been the woman she'd claimed to be. She wasn't the sweet and not-so-innocent village girl he'd thought she was, but that didn't diminish his feelings for her.

He'd fallen in love with Hazel months ago and nothing had

changed since then. If anything, the idea of her being Hazel, the Promised One, intrigued him more than anything. The girl with a destiny he'd been hearing about for most of his adult life. The mythical witch with such raw talent that she could unite the Circle in a way that would ensure unending power to all Healer-kind. And she did have that raw power. He'd felt it when she'd taken out the zombies. She was gifted. Those rumors had been true. But her power was untested mostly, rough, still needed refinement and with his help, he could shape her into a formable witch. More powerful than her mother even.

He started toward the back staircase that would take him to his room. He'd need to pack quickly if he was going to make it to the deck in time to catch his ride. Hazel's loyalty to her destiny was admirable, and insane. To give up her life to the Healers... That was hero status, to be sure. She'd be sacrificing more than just the relationship she had with him. And he could see that she really believed it was her only path. The role her mother played in her devotion was problematic, but it was a challenge he was certain he'd overcome.

Nobody's fate was predetermined, etched in stone or not. What he'd learned about destiny, what the human witches had taught him time and time again, was that destiny was fluid, a multitude of threads that strengthened and broke, that grew and twinned. By choice, by nature, by chance, it could be altered. Hazel Knight was a thread in Duke's destiny and he was going to prove to her that it was a thread he wouldn't let her cut. Not until she understood just how much power she actually had over her own life, her fate, and her future.

His heart belonged to Hazel and only her. This field trip was just what he needed to remind her that her heart belonged to him as well.

5

"THIS IS TERRIBLE." HAZEL HELD A PAIR OF ARMY FATIGUES IN one hand and a black tank top in the other. *What just happened?* One minute, she'd been sure she had it all figured out. Stand up to Duke, tell him how things were going to be—namely not being in his vicinity for the next year, and wham—Bridget "The Enforcer" Rose was making it impossible to get away. What her mother had been thinking by agreeing to a field trip like this, she could not guess.

"The uniform?" Chanda smoothed her hands down her body. "I don't know, I kinda think it looks hot."

"Not the uniform!" Hazel sank down to the bench, feeling defeated. "I can't go on this trip."

"Too good to get your hands dirty?" Tough guy, Bas Frank, blurted. His arms still crossed, his lips pulled into a sneer. "I've heard about you, Promised One. You're probably not used to the idea of hard labor, are you? Or slumming it with the rest of us. The horror."

Hazel blinked, hard, at his tone. She'd lived a privileged life, she knew, venturing out with her mother only ever resulted in praise and respect. But even when she slipped out under her mother's nose, she was never treated with hostility. So she wasn't totally prepared for the vibes she was getting from a complete stranger. Most people she'd encountered in her life either didn't know who she was and treated her at face value—which was never a bad thing—or knew exactly who she was, what she was meant to be, and treated her like a cherished, delicate piece of art, which was not always a good thing. Disdain was unfamiliar.

"Hey, asshole," Mahdyia snapped. "Check your attitude. There's shit going on here you don't understand."

"Nah, I've heard the rumors. The Promised One, destined to save all our asses. Yeah, I got it. She's important. *Very* important. I mean look at her, she's already been given Prince Charming as her mentor while the rest of us have Queen B—"

"That's enough!" Mahdyia moved closer to Hazel, taking a seat on the bench next to her. "Hey, this isn't a bad thing. Being out in the world. Travelling more than you've ever done before. Among the humans... The Hags! Your favorite." She nudged Hazel. "You sure you don't want anything more to happen with...Prince Charming? I mean...really sure?" She'd lowered her voice further for the last part, but it was still loud enough for everyone to hear.

Hazel gave her a dark glare. "I can't, Mads, you know that. Mother would—"

Mahdyia sighed. "Okay, listen, we'll use this opportunity to get Duke off your back. Make sure he understands that you're not interested."

"Last time you said that, you pushed me out the door and tried to turn me over to him." She wasn't saying she didn't believe her cousin had her best interests at heart—or at least what she perceived her best interests to be—but she wasn't completely convinced they were on the same page where Duke was concerned.

Mahdyia opened her mouth to argue when Tate cut her off.

"Wait. Are you being harassed, like sexually, by Healer Hart?" Tate took a step toward her, a deep frown on his face. "Because I've heard things about him."

"What kind of things?" Hazel asked. All of a sudden, that feeling from earlier returned. Seeing Duke's hands all over Bridget made her want to barf or scream, or cry or punch something.

"Yes, that's right. He's taken an interest in Hazel, you know, because she's like a freakin' unicorn," Mahdyia's voice had an edge.

Unicorn? "I'm not—"

"And he won't take no, right?" Chandra sighed, shaking her head. "Been there, too many times to count."

"I'm sure you have," Bas said before pushing himself off the lockers. He lifted a hand to stop Chanda's next words. "Listen, I'm all for using your assets, but if you're not interested in advancing your career, then just tell him to fuck off and be done with it." He nailed Hazel with a look that made her want to shrink to the floor. "You're not a child. You're some big deal, right? So just tell him that *you'll* send him to the Scrub. We all know you can do it, right? Your mother is *the* Mother. You don't even have to tell him off yourself—just get mommy to do it."

"Shut up, Bas," Chanda said, shrugging him off in dismissal. "Ignore him, Hazel. He's got a chip the size of a boulder on his shoulder. We'll run defense for you. The way Healer Hart was flirting with Healer Rose... Well, I bet he's used to getting all the women. I've seen it before. Scumbag." She motioned toward the door. "I mean, with a body like his, those muscles, did you see them? Mmmm—"

"Yeah, okay, got it." Hazel stood up from the bench, her cheeks heating at the thought of Duke's body...which led to thoughts of his hands and what they could do...as well as his tongue and his mouth...*oh goddess*. "It's unwelcome," she whispered. Even though she wasn't thrilled with the direction

Mahdyia had taken things, she could see the benefits. Duke had to be the villain in this little story, right? That was the only way for her to stay sane for the year and to keep her promise to her mother, to all Healer-kind, to fulfill her duty.

So why did that make her heart clench so hard it felt like she was dying? "I don't want this."

"What a waste," Bas mumbled.

"She's lived a sheltered life," Mahdyia said. "Completely innocent, if you know what I mean."

"I'm not—"

Mahdyia winked at her as she stood. "Shhh, dear. It's okay. These guys will help you out of this mess."

"Nah, I'm not helping," Bas said, then turned as if he was going to leave. "I'm here to get my training, not to participate in anyone's drama."

Tate stood in his way. "Yes, you are." He crossed his arms. "Hazel needs our help, so we'll help her. We stick together."

"Oh yeah, tough guy? What are you going to do about it if I don't?" Bas clenched his fists, looking like he was ready to unleash at any moment.

Tate smirked. "Go ahead. Hit me. See what happens."

Bas snorted. "You got it." He pulled back his fist.

Hazel winced, taking a step toward them as if she could somehow tamp down the testosterone overload.

"Guys—"

The door whooshed open. Hazel's mother walked into the room, narrowed her eyes and scrutinized everything, as she usually did. "What's going on here?"

Bas dropped his hands, took a step back so he was pressed against the locker, fists still clenched but Hazel imagined for an entirely different reason. Some tough guy.

Tate turned to greet Hazel's mother. "Good morning, Mother Knight. We're just getting to know one another as we prepare for our first duty."

Hazel's mother looked from Tate to Bas, her brow furrowed for a moment. "Yes, well, get on with it. You're not ready, by the looks of things. Bags aren't packed."

"Yes, ma'am," they chimed in unison.

"Being in the field," she began, halting anyone from going anywhere, "is a great responsibility. You represent White Willow in all that you do, but most importantly in how you treat those in need. We do not normally interact with the humans. However, Healer Rose has gained much unique information from the Storm Hags, who are descendants, in some capacity, from the great Elemental witches. Rudimentary magic—practical, not always predictable or reliable, but worth seeing in the flesh, which you are about to do. Represent White Willow with your best thoughts and actions. I expect nothing less than exemplary behavior."

Her mother stopped her lecture, looking expectantly at the interns, who suddenly realized she was done.

"Yes, Mother Knight, of course," Chanda said. "Better get dressed, Hazel. We leave in five."

While the others scrambled to gather their things, Hazel clenched her clothes to her chest and moved to the bathroom. Her mother followed, closing the door behind her.

"I know that this is probably an overwhelming prospect for you, dear. Out among the humans. But Bridget is a highly capable Healer, my right hand if you will. Healer Hart as well—this is his area of expertise. I wouldn't entrust your safety to anyone but the best. Although it is unfortunate to have to use our talents on the magically inclined humans, we do owe them some compassion, I suppose. I believe Mahdyia calls it slumming? Apt description."

"Mother, I don't think—"

"Field time is a requirement." Her tone had taken on a stern edge, like she was revving up for another lecture. "Better to get the hours out of the way. An opportunity has presented itself, giving your field time purpose. Sometimes we have to wait for months before we have a need to venture into human territory." She shuddered. "It's dirty work, but best to keep the Hags under watch. If they are experiencing trouble, illness or guidance, we need to see to them. Bridget values their skills."

"I have some reservations...some concerns about—"

"Be brave, daughter, I know that it's not what you were expecting on your first day. I did secure you with a talented mentor and this will be an opportunity to show your peers your value." She winked then ran her fingers through Hazel's hair, coming around to her back so she could pull it into a pony tail and secure it at the base of her neck. "You are very important to me. To all Healer-kind. Show them what you can do."

She snapped her fingers and suddenly Hazel was dressed in her army fatigues. "Mother, you know I hate it when you do that. I can get dressed myself."

"I know, dear, just doting on you. I know you will prove your worth to all of the witches here in your actions. I believe in your gifts. You are my special witch. My Promised One."

And there it was, her mother's pride, which normally made Hazel's stomach flutter. It was the closest thing to love that she'd felt from the woman and she'd spent most of her life chasing it. This time though, it felt hollow. False. Hazel frowned.

A heavy weight fell against Hazel's chest. She looked down, her fingers touching the gem she now wore. It sparkled on its own, crystal with hints of blue. A summoning stone. Very rare. "Mother..."

"You left it on your dresser. You know how I feel about you taking this off." She came around to Hazel's front.

"The shower..." Hazel had removed it the night before, not wanting her mother to have access to her whereabouts.

"Nonsense. You know I've warded it. It's waterproof. I'd prefer you kept it on you at all times."

"I know, Mother, it's just that it tangles in my hair." She could totally lie to her mother. Mahdyia would be impressed... Actually, she'd roll her eyes, but whatever.

She placed her hands on Hazel's arms, giving her the look that brokered no further argument. "It stays on from this moment forward. If you need me...well, I can bring you back here with a snap of my fingers. Rest easy, daughter. I will never let you venture too far without my assistance at the ready."

Hazel gulped. She was taking the damn thing off as soon as she was out of her mother's sight. The gem was her mother's attempt to shackle her with her version of love. She didn't need to wonder about her mother agreeing to the trip. It had to happen, fine, but it would be on her mother's terms. No way she'd let Hazel go without a means of retrieving her. Out of sight—maybe; out of mind—never.

"You know I'd go with you if I could but I must stay behind to deal with this zombie mess." She sighed. "One of the families tried to raise their deceased daughter and the spell went the wrong way. Not the first time we've dealt with something like this. Necromancy is not for the average witch but the grieving families just don't understand sometimes. I need to be here to make sure the family is dealt with properly." Her mother smoothed down Hazel's hair, her hands moving to the sides of her face. "Make me proud out in the field, darling. That's all I've ever asked. You are destined for great things. Everyone saw that today when you stepped up to take care of the problem. I expect you to rise to this occasion as well, as challenging as it may be."

Hazel nodded, that familiar feeling of obligation nudging her. "I will Mother, always."

"I know you will."

And Hazel heard the underlying message there...*because if you don't, you will be such a bitter disappointment to me.*

"Better get going. They don't call Bridget 'the Enforcer' for nothing." Her mother chuckled as she exited the bathroom, leaving Hazel to stare after her.

She reached up to finger the amulet once again with one hand and pulled her hair from the tight elastic with the other. "I live to serve, Mother."

Destiny demanded it.

❧ 6 ❧

TRAVELLING ALONG TIME LINES WAS AN ART RATHER THAN A science. Only a few witches could navigate successfully that way, though many had tried. Bridget Rose was one of them. Duke, not so much. It was a dangerous bit of magic. Only the strongest could survive the journey, let alone master the art. All Healers needed to have the experience, if only to weed out the weakest.

"This is so exciting!" The interns were tittering off to the side. All hiding their anxiety, which Duke could feel amplified with each second that passed. They didn't grasp what was about to happen, the cost for convenient travel.

Duke was standing by the launch pad, waiting on Hazel. She was late. Had she figured out a way to get out of it after all? Had her mother decided at the last minute that her precious prodigy would get her field hours in another, safer way? The interns had said that Mother Knight had paid them a visit, had reminded them about the importance of making a good impression. So where was Hazel? Being coddled? Hugged? Seemed unlikely. From what Duke remembered of Mother Knight, she was not actually the mothering kind.

"Create a circle," Bridget commanded, motioning for the

group to round up and fall in line. "You're all familiar with the chant? In theory, at least?"

Even with his back to her, he could sense Hazel's approach. She was moving quietly, a cloud of heavy thought surrounding her like an aura. He had to wonder at the level of devotion to her mother's grand plans that would cause her such feelings. An encounter with her mother garnered pensive eyes, a closed expression, no smile.

He couldn't help but feel that this mother-daughter bond was hard on Hazel, harder than she realized, that the devotion alone was costing her bits of her personality, certainly her free will. That she would deny her feelings for him, the chemistry they'd had—still had—was enough to tell him of the battle that waged in her head. What they'd experienced over the last year had not be a mistake or a tryst. The feelings he'd developed for his sweet village girl would not be dismissed because of duty—not without a fight, anyway. The fact that Hazel was so torn, that he could practically feel the battle waging, boded well for him. It meant she wasn't completely devoted to her destiny, or at least there was enough dissonance to give her pause. The field trip was a perfect opportunity for him to show her a different destiny.

He leaned into her as she stepped up toward the group, closer than was necessary for sure, but he wanted to touch her so badly and this was the next best thing. "We need to talk, I'd say."

She looked up at him, her eyes wary, expression still guarded. She worried her bottom lip.

"I miss talking to you—"

"Mind if I slip in here?" The chubby kid Tate bullied his way between them, his bulk and proximity taking Duke by surprise, parting him and Hazel. "The sun's in my eyes over there, can't concentrate."

Duke did mind. He was about to blast the kid when Bridget spoke instead.

"You need total focus for this to work with such a large

group." Bridget held a blade in her hand, lifting it to show the group. "We need blood so ante up."

Duke glanced at Hazel, watching as she drew her own small blade from her leather forearm sheath—standard equipment for all Healer-kind. Hers was ornate from what he could see, jewelled and bearing filigree that would help channel her power.

Quite a bit of magic required witch blood. It was a catalyst but also an adhesive, binding the words, the magic together. A few spells couldn't withstand the magic if they were performed dry and would cause skewed results. Or no results, which could be deadly given their line of work.

Duke pulled his blade out as well. It was nothing special. Gifted to him by his father, it had been in the Hart family for centuries, passed down for initiation purposes. Since Duke had no one to pass it along to, he'd kept using it. It was practical, if ugly, or rather plain compared to Hazel's. The blade was perpetually sharp and the cut true. He had nothing to complain about.

Everyone made their cut. A few probably cut too deep, the men wincing as they pumped their fists, trying to get the blood really flowing. Tough guys, including himself.

"Join hands," Bridget said again.

Duke wanted to be next to Hazel. He wanted to feel her flesh again, even if it was just a benign touch. Instead, he was stuck holding hands with Tate, who gave off a surprising jolt.

Duke leaned in. "You pack a punch, eh?"

Tate cocked an eyebrow and curled up one side of his lip.

Not as friendly, or as timid as he would have expected from a lowly intern. Duke suspected that Tate had been underestimated a lot in his life but the kid was concealing a ton of raw power. It made him more intriguing to be sure. Something for Duke to investigate when he had the time.

"Is anyone here familiar with time shifting?" Bridget surveyed the group, her expression suggesting that she already knew the answer.

No one spoke at first, rather looked at one another. It was more than likely that none of them would have had experience with this—typically a procedure reserved for Healers who needed a quick form of travel to get to the injured. It demanded a lot of power from the Circle so it required special permission from the Mother.

"I have," Hazel said. "Once."

A few of the interns gasped.

How am I not surprised? Mother Knight had taken Hazel's education *very,* seriously it seemed.

Bridget narrowed her eyes, taking Hazel in like she would an annoying insect. "Do you remember the words?"

Hazel nodded.

"Very well. You'll lay down the base for me. The rest of you will focus your magic on us. Bolster, don't distract. Remember your training. If one person deviates, it can send us off in different directions entirely. We'll be shifting approximately five hours to the left. You'll feel the time lines as we pass them, you may even see a bright, colorful rope of light. Do not touch! Or reach out or even stare too hard. You could send us off course. I will guide us. Understand?"

The interns nodded. Hazel appeared to be readying herself, her shoulders squared, her face set into an expression Duke was coming to recognize meant business. She might be the Promised One, but she clearly didn't take that for granted. She was ready to work—he could see that in the tension across her shoulders, her steady gaze, her mouth moving oh so minutely as she presumably rehearsed.

She was exceptional. He knew this already. Her sweet voice, her lithe body, her moans, the love she'd given him: understanding, acceptance, comfort.

"Healer Hart, you with us?" Bridget's words were edged with sarcasm. "Perhaps you can bolster too? Give Hazel something to draw from? Show these interns what a strong partnership of magic can really do."

Ah, those words. Duke smiled.

He saw Hazel startle. She shifted a quick look his way, eyes narrowing. Just a coincidence, nothing meant by it. Bridget didn't know. Right?

Duke grinned wider. "I'm ready." He was already feeding her some of his power, letting it roll off him, move through Tate to tickle along Hazel's arm.

She felt it amplify; he could tell by the sudden widening of her eyes, the flush on her cheeks. She licked her lips then turned her gaze away before closing her eyes. Shutting them all out. She didn't shut his power out though. Instead, she pulled from what he was offering, giving him the sensation of fingers plucking at him, not in a bad way, but it was like nothing he'd experienced before.

A low hum of magic enveloped the group. A pulse that started like a vibration, a subtle rattling of the air. Hazel was laying the foundation, building the base for Bridget's spell. Any witch could do it for most spells. It was a basic skill you learned as a child, but the way Hazel was doing it was like an intricate web. He could feel its intensity and marvelled once again at her talent. And for this spell, it took extra talent. Extra care. If Hazel messed up the base, Bridget wouldn't be able to get the time shifting to take flight.

Minutes began to stretch. Literally. An odd sensation to experience and one that Duke didn't relish. As the spell started to take hold, a feeling of slowness descended on them. Like an elastic that was being pulled slowly, so slowly, creating tension, building momentum.

Until, with a swell of power, they catapulted forward.

One minute they were there, on the deck, open air all around, then next they'd slipped into the time stream. Dark but for the wisps of time lines swirling all around. He kept his grip firm, didn't want to lose any of the interns on the trip. It had happened once or twice in the history of time travelling—famous cases of witches lost to a time period or trapped in the time stream. But they were legends mostly, the last one having happened over fifty years ago and not on Mother Knight's watch.

Unlikely to happen now, what with the powder keg of witches binding the spell together. Still, he didn't want to be the one to lose an intern on his first day. That would be bad.

Bridget's voice echoed in his head, snippets of the spell. It wasn't an overly complicated bit of magic but it did take skill to recite it and navigate the time lines. Despite the danger, the expense of power this would take, it was the best method of travel, especially since they needed to get to the Hags sooner than later. A distress call had been received, more severe than Bridget had let on, according to Ty Cooper. Traditional travel would have taken a day or more—this would only cost them an hour. That and some time to rest.

Oh, and they'd all be without their magic.

The consequence of using a spell like this, going against the natural order of things, meant a magic sacrifice. They'd each be without power for however long it took to recover. Some maybe a few hours, some possibly a day. The more experienced the witch, the less trauma travelling this way had. It was a good lesson to learn.

Duke remembered his first experience with time shifting. He'd been laid up in Bridget's tent for half a day...moaning and disoriented, completely unprepared for dealing with magic deprivation. Bridget had soothed him of course, taking pity on the intern. Perhaps taking advantage with her expertise. He hadn't complained at the time. Being favored by an instructor of Bridget's magnitude had its perks. Many of them, in fact.

Would Hazel be as open to some coddling? Would she be so sick she'd look to him for some compassion? Some soothing touches? He'd be ready if she was. He hoped that she would be—

sick that was, which was a horrible thing to think, right? Being this close to her, all he wanted to do was resume where they'd left off the night before. Body against body, her warmth making his desire hum in all the right ways.

They landed with a gentle impact that was consistent with a trained spell caster. Not a sound, not jarring—smooth, gliding, leaving them all on their feet, still holding hands. Duke scanned the group, noted the dazed expressions, the sallow skin, the wobbly legs.

They fought valiantly, held up for maybe a minute at best and then one by one, they each fell down, eyes rolling back, faces slack, sliding to the ground like lumps. Leaving Duke and Bridget to smirk at one another...and to look with mirrored shock at the only other person who hadn't fallen.

Hazel. Of course.

"We'd better take a look at them," Bridget said as she turned to the intern on her left, crouching to check vitals.

"You okay?" Duke shook off the disorientation he felt. Mild, somewhat uncomfortable, not life threatening. His magic would maybe spark if he really needed it but it was better to let it rest for a while, give his body time to gather energy from the magic stores that came naturally from the Earth, the humans and from the Circle back home. "Hazel?"

Hazel blinked a few times, seeming to zone in on him as he sidestepped Tate's prone body and moved closer to her. "Yes."

He ran his hands over her arms, flipping her left hand to inspect the cut she'd made. It was closing rapidly, a good sign. "You don't feel dizzy? Disoriented? Nauseous?"

"No." Hazel pulled her hand away and wrapped her arms around herself, shuddering a little as she did.

"Not at all?" Duke scanned her again. "How's your power? Feel drained?"

She should have. For such a young witch. She should have been on the ground like her peers.

"I'm fine." She leaned into him, her hand on his chest. His breath caught. He moved closer to her, raising his arms to embrace her. And then he felt it. Her touch growing warm, hot even, for a second or two. Like a match to a wick, her magic ignited his power, washed away any fatigue, disorientation and gave him back what he'd lost.

"What the..."

She didn't wait for him to finish the sentence and instead moved around him, that intense look of concentration on her face. Crouching down, she did the same with each of the interns. A second, maybe two at their side and she'd move on to the next, leaving a trail of rousing witches behind her. All sitting up, shaking off their disorientation, marvelling after her as she moved.

Bridget stopped what she was doing, watched like the rest of them, a look of awe on her face that she couldn't seem to hide. He knew the feeling.

Hazel stopped at the tough guy, Bas, the last one and ran her fingers through his hair first, tenderly stroking his cheek and then laid her hand on his chest. Did she know this guy? Why such familiarity? Jealous reared. Until he realized that Bas wasn't rousing like the rest of them had. He wasn't moving, in fact.

"There's something wrong with him." Hazel locked eyes with Duke. "I don't feel anything inside of him. No spark. I've given what I can but there's something missing."

"Duke, didn't you check that one?" Bridget bullied her way past him to crouch at Bas's other side

"No, I..." He'd been too preoccupied with Hazel. He hadn't noticed the way Bas's mouth hung open or how limp his body seemed. "Is he breathing?"

Hazel's cousin pushed past him as well. "Here, let me see." She knelt down next to Hazel, sharing a look of concern as she put her hands over his torso, her eyes sliding closed as she did. "There's something wrong with his heart. It's barely beating."

"I can help," Tate said. "Everyone needs to take a few steps back. Give me some room." He positioned himself above Bas's head, straddling him so he could lean over his chest.

Duke felt the air around him crackle, the hair on his arms rose. He took another couple of steps back, mirroring what the others were instinctually doing. This kid...he had an impressive Elemental skill.

With fingers splayed, Tate zapped Bas's chest, jolting him once and then twice before Bas sprang upward looking like he'd been electrocuted, which he kind of had. His blond hair was almost standing on end and smoke wafted off his clothes.

"What the fu—"

"Your heart wasn't beating properly." Chanda offered her hand to help him up.

He ignored it and instead looked up at Hazel. "You were in my head. What the hell did you do to me?"

"I...uh..."

"She restored your power, dickhead," Mahdyia said. "She restored all of our powers. Lucky for you that she did, or you'd be dead right now."

"No way she could do that," Bas scoffed. He pushed himself to his knees, brushing away dirt as he moved. "Only the most—"

"—powerful witches can do that?" Bridget finished for him, her eyes locked on Hazel. "Yeah, well, behold. Now you know why the Promised One is so revered."

"Once you join the Circle..." Chanda said with awe.

"That kind of power..." Tate shook his head. "Well, it's impressive."

"It's freaky if you ask me," Bas said, rubbing his chest and pointing at Tate. "You zapped me."

Tate shrugged. "You kinda deserved it."

"Remind me never to piss you off," Bas mumbled as he walked away. "I need a minute." He disappeared into the trees, trailing his fingers along the bark as he did.

"I've never seen anything like that, have you?" Bridget was next to Duke, watching as Hazel chatted with the rest of the interns.

They were excited, giddy, peppering her with questions. Hazel's face was crimson, her hands out in an attempt to calm them down or stop them, or get away.

"She's something else," Duke admitted. "It's amazing Mother Knight has kept her so contained for all these years. With power like that." And amazing that she'd been able to sneak out all those times to see him.

"Mother has a vested interest in keeping that kind of power a secret." Bridget didn't say it with any kind of tone. She wasn't normally a political woman. Everything she did was to service herself first, and staying neutral on the topic of Hazel and her Mother was the best way to ensure an elevated position at White Willow and the confidence of the Great Healer. "It will be interesting to see what more she can do. What a boon for us, if only for a limited time."

Before she joined the Circle went without saying. Before her power was shared with all of Healer-kind.

Duke nodded. Even without his magic bolstering her, Hazel's power was impressive and also scary. That kind of magic could feed generations of witches, could help harness powerful spells. He could see the allure. He could see the sacrifice too. And why the Mother thought it was best to give her daughter over to the Circle instead of herself. Hazel's power was unmatched. It was intoxicating. Any smart leader would recognize that potential, even if it was self-serving at its core. Mother Knight was not only doing this for all of Healer-kind—she was doing this for herself too.

Hazel would lose her youth and vitality with each year she spent in the Circle. They'd drain her dry until she had nothing left to give, certainly nothing left for herself. They needed her. He knew that. Especially since the Promised Ones in the Circle and most Healers in general ignored the power that the human witches could provide. And natural magic, well, it just didn't give enough of the kind of power they needed or wanted. So Hazel was the answer. The Circle would keep her alive, sucking from her for centuries. Like a rechargeable battery that slowly loses its ability to regenerate over the years. Hazel would give everything she had. Willingly. For her mother, for the Healers.

The idea of that scared the ever-living shit out of him. It made him more determined to convince her that staying with him was the better option. What they could do together, for witch-kind, the humans included, was much more important than what she would do for the Circle. Her talent, matched with his powers, could save many lives. Lives Mother Knight didn't think were worth saving. She had such a distrust of the magical humans whose power stores could bolster the Circle. If only Mother Knight would act as the conduit she was born to be, rather than rejecting that side of her powers and forcing her only daughter, a powerful witch in her own right, to take her place. And besides, if that's what Hazel wanted, like really wanted, to join the Circle, she didn't have to do it now. She could do it once she'd lived her life to its fullest because even as an elderly witch, she would likely still have so much to offer all Healer-kind.

Duke was beginning to understand all the different ways Hazel Knight was being pulled and why such a battle waged within her mind. It didn't make him want to stop his pursuit though. No way. Hazel was a treasure, sure, but she deserved a chance to choose, really choose, what her destiny should be.

❧ 7 ❧

OKAY, SO, DUKE'S EMPATHIC POWER WAS VERY INTOXICATING. She could identify it now that she understood it was coming from him. The boosts of power she always felt, the buzz along her skin, weren't her feelings for him getting out of control like she'd come to believe over the past year. It was his power. He'd been feeding her his magic, making her think it was all about the romance...

She sighed. *Yeah...right...keep telling yourself that, honey.* He hadn't known she was a witch, so he couldn't have been doing it maliciously. Did their magic speak to one another? Hell yeah. Had it been the entire year of their affair? Most definitely. But convincing herself that it had been the only thing going on between them was delusional. And she wasn't into distortions of reality.

She winced. Okay, so plan keep-Duke-away-from-Hazel was a based on a lie...but that hadn't been her idea in the first place.

Hazel slowly chewed the granola bar Mahdyia had given her, resigned to the turmoil of her thoughts.

Her life had suddenly gotten super complicated and it was only ever meant to be simple. That's what her mother had planned for her, anyway. If she hadn't disobeyed by venturing out into the human world, answering to the magical call that had spoken to her all those years ago, then she wouldn't be in the mess she was in. No Duke either. As much as she wanted to convince herself that the simple life was a preferred life, everything about the man was very un-simple, and attractive, intriguing, deliciously tempting.

She'd wandered off from the group, seeking solitude so she could gather her thoughts, recharge her power from the trees around her. The rock she was on was covered in a soft moss that hummed to her as she ran her fingers over it. All around her was lush greenery, twittering birds, buzzing insects and magic, so much magic. Unfiltered, natural waves that pulsed around and through her. She called to it. Soaked it up. It wasn't a skill unique to her—every witch could call the power from the air, the water, the earth. Most didn't, though. They undervalued it...including her mother. Human magic, natural magic, was not as potent as magic that came from the Circle, drawn directly from the Promised Ones.

A branch cracked, a sound made on purpose so she wouldn't startle—that was obvious. She wasn't surprised to see Duke come around a large tree. She felt him just on the periphery of her awareness, his power complementing what she was taking in from the forest around her.

"We need to talk," he repeated his statement from earlier. Before Tate had intervened.

"No, we don't." Talking would lead to more complications. Talking would lead to other things too. Touching. Kissing. Lusting... She gulped down another bite of her food, trying to keep her emotions in check.

He plucked some of the hanging moss from a branch before leaning against the tree. "You can't avoid me forever."

Just his leaning was sexy. The black T-shirt he wore was tight enough to define his muscles. A chiselled chest she'd licked many times before, thick biceps that were flexing just the right way as he reached up to pull some more moss down to twirl around his fingers. He looked good in those pants too. Jeans that were a dark wash, form fitting enough to show off his ass—ets.

She shoved the rest of the granola bar into her mouth and washed it down with some water.

"I can try." She laughed bitterly. And fight every urge in her body to run to him, let him embrace her, take her away from it all. *Wait, where did that come from?*

"You're pretty special." He was mocking her, his tone light, a smile tugging on his lips. "Extraordinary. I can see why your mother has pinned so much on you."

"Stop." She rubbed her hand over her eyes, pressing with her fingers until her eyes hurt. "You don't know what you're talking about."

"Everyone knows your destiny, Hazel. We've all been led to believe that some all-powerful heir would be stepping to the Circle, providing unlimited power for centuries to come. This special witch who we would draw from, who would give us bolstering like we've never experienced before." He scoffed lightly. "I don't think anyone ever really believed it, the mythical Promised One of all time. I sure didn't. Not until today. Not until I met you for real." He took a step away from the tree, the smirk gone. "She's using you. You know that, right? Probably has been using you since you were born. Siphoning power from you to bolster her own and now she'll use you again when you're forced to take her place."

Hazel frowned. Was he talking about her mother? *Wait...* "What?"

"No one thinks it's valiant on her part. Even without knowing you, most witches don't agree. They think your mother should be taking *her* destined role, not foisting it on you."

Her mother had prepared her for this kind of talk. Witches who lacked the ability to envision a future with her in the Circle. Unable to see what her power could do to help Healer-kind. She couldn't blame them; as her mother pointed out, they'd never experienced a witch like Hazel before. Once she became one with the Circle and they felt what she could give them... Well, then they'd understand.

"I don't expect you to get it." She sighed, pity behind it. "I don't require you to, either. I have to complete this trial, this year of testing and training and then I'm going to be doing my duty. I'm going to fulfill what I was born to do. You'll see. It's what's meant to be."

So Mr. Perfect wasn't so perfect after all. He was just what her mother had described—a man lacking vision.

"You're throwing your life away. Your talent."

"No, I'm not. I'm sacrificing it for the greater good."

"The greater good?" He flipped his hand up. "Propaganda. You don't really believe that, do you?" He closed the distance to her, yanking her up from the rock, not releasing her hand once he had her at eye level. "Hazel, after everything we've shared, you don't really believe that you only have one destiny, do you? One that would take you away from all this." He waved his other hand around while pulling her closer. "From me? You say sacrifice, but I say slavery. And I know that's hard for you to see right now but it's true. No one should be asked to give this kind of sacrifice. But that's just it—you were never asked were you?" He lifted his hand to touch her cheek, his tone softened. "Sweetheart, I don't want to lose you. Not when I just found you."

Hazel frowned, not at all liking the feeling she had in her stomach. Those butterflies. That anguish. His words affected her. *I don't want to lose you...* The look in his eyes, such passion. A feeling she shared. The romance of it all tormented her, knowing that what her heart wanted couldn't be.

What did her heart know anyway? Stupid heart.

She tugged her hand away then skirted around him, ready to use magic to keep him away.

"Stop running, Hazel. Stop pretending that you don't know

what I'm talking about. Your mother isn't here. Let your guard down. Be with me like before, in the village. I know that's the real you. Show me that girl again."

She froze, let a shudder run through her. And when she turned, she made sure he saw the truth on her face. "You should be angry with me. I lied to you. I misled you. I just wanted to experience something a little different. I wanted to experience life a bit before my training at White Willow began. There was never any possibility of a future with me. What we had... It was fun, but it wasn't ever going to go beyond the village. I'm not hiding anything from you. My guard, as you put it, is down. See for yourself. I'm putting my time in here because it's required and then I'm joining the Circle. It's better if you move on. Find someone else and forget about me."

She let her words sink in, saw the flicker of emotion cross his face. Disbelief maybe, sadness, perhaps, and then a flash of anger. That's where it needed to be. Enough anger so that he would leave her alone.

"Hey, Haz...oh....right..." Chanda came to a crashing halt just in front of them. She took in the scene, then grabbed Hazel by the arm and tugged her back. "I'll get you out of this." She put herself in between Hazel and Duke. "Listen, buddy, she doesn't want your attention. She isn't interested. Got it? If you don't back off then I'll report you to the disciplinary panel and it'll be you going to the Scrub!"

Hazel opened her mouth, shock rolling through her. It was like a train wreck she couldn't stop from happening... And yet, she wanted it to happen, didn't she?

Duke's face was a mask of real anger now. "What the fuck are you talking about?"

"She told us all about your propositions, your grabby hands! Speaking as a woman, it's appalling that in this day and age, witch-kind hasn't done away with men like you. Using your position of authority on someone like Hazel. She isn't interested, okay? She's freakin' special. Exceptional. And she's destined for greater things than you. So back off, mister."

"She told you..." Duke gritted his teeth. He wasn't looking at Hazel any longer but she could tell by his expression that he was seething. The air around them changed, charged perhaps with his mood swing. "Well, no worries there, sweetheart. I understand Hazel's destiny as much as the next witch and I would never dream of derailing her from that path. Especially if it is *unwanted* attention. My mistake. I was only after a bit of fun. No hard feelings." He gave Chanda a heated once over, pulling a startled giggle from her in the process. Hazel was intimately familiar with that look. "I certainly hope her feelings aren't shared by everyone. Not that I would think of abusing my power, but with a willing partner? Well, I'm sure you could see the benefit of such an arrangement."

Chanda moved a little closer to Duke, giggling again as she did.

Hazel shook her head. So childish. And yet...why did she feel like she wanted to push Chanda out of the way? Knock her aside so that it was Hazel getting one of those heated looks from Duke. Better than the burning hatred she saw now flashing her way.

Ugh. Men.

Instead of indulging the behavior she walked away, leaving Duke and Chanda to pursue whatever would come. She'd told him to move along, right? That there was no future with her. So that's what he was doing.

Moving *right* along.

SHE STUMBLED THROUGH THE FOREST, NO PATH THERE TO HELP her out as she tripped and trudged back to the small clearing they'd landed in earlier. Quiet talking stopped her up short and she circled a large tree. She saw Bas and Bridget lounging on the forest floor, nestled on a bed of moss that cascaded from a rock. Most of their clothes were on but looked dishevelled, like they'd hastily put them back on recently. Bas had his head resting in his crooked arm, looking smug, or at least satisfied. Bridget was running her fingers up and down his bare torso which had an impressive display of abs. Hazel moved backward a step, concealing herself behind the tree.

So this is the way things were for the interns? Sexual trysts with their superiors?

If Mother only knew.

"I don't care what anyone says, that chick is seriously freaky," Bas's voice wafted toward her.

Hazel frowned and leaned closer.

"Hazel can't help it, Worm. She's been blessed with a powerful gift and has also been sequestered her whole life. She doesn't know what proper witchly interaction is. Showing off is just something she was raised to do. Her mother... Well, from what I know, she encourages flagrant displays of prowess. I'm sure it's not the last we'll see this year. But you should feel indebted to her in the end, right? She's going to do great things for all of us when she joins the Circle. Just look at what she accomplished here, now, without harnessing the Power of One."

"Indebted to her? Nah, I feel sorry for her. She's obviously whipped by her mother if she's willing to devote herself to that kind of servitude. It's creepy. She's creepy."

Servitude, slavery. What was with the men around here thinking her sacrifice wasn't worthy of praise?

"Oh, get over it. So she was in your head, who cares? You scared she's going to see something dangerous in there?"

"To her, yeah probably," Bas grunted. "Highly inappropriate shit going on up there, especially where you're concerned."

"Shut up, Worm," Bridget said with a laugh. "There will be none of that."

"Oh yeah? How about some of this?"

Bridget moaned, then laughed.

Hazel used the opportunity to move away, Bas's words circling in her head. She was creepy? She didn't understand how to interact with witches? How could that be? She'd been sneaking out of her house since she was a teen, meeting new people all the time, mostly in the village, mostly human witches. But she'd gotten along with all of them. She even had some friends...well, people who she talked to regularly. She knew what was going on in their lives even if they had no clue what was going on in hers. Even Duke—she'd gotten along with him, up until that morning. She wasn't that strange. And everyone had needed her help earlier. Their powers had been completely depleted and she was capable of restoring it. Should she have not done that? Should she have let them suffer?

She frowned as she reached into her pocket and fingered her mother's amulet. She could use some counsel. Had she overstepped? Hadn't she done what was required of her? She hadn't meant to slip into Bas's head. He was just so...open.

And she hadn't seen anything in there that was bad. Quite the contrary. What she'd seen, what she'd felt was an affinity with magic that she envied. The man could manipulate magic in a way that she would never be able to. Sure, she could absorb it, but Bas... He could change it, speak to it, unify spells. It was a nurturing method of spell casting, one he'd probably learned at his mother's knee, perfect for a team of Healers. To have a witch capable of unification was a boon for their group. If she had to guess, she would say that he had strong spell mixing abilities as well. Taking natural ingredients to manufacture potent spells in interesting ways. A lot like the humans did. That was nothing to be ashamed of. Sure, it wasn't the most glamorous skill, nothing flashy about bringing people together. But proficiency with unification to the degree that Bas seemed to have would make him an asset to any department in the hospital. Not a superstar probably, but the backbone.

Hazel sucked in a deep breath. Yeah, okay, she got it. He felt emasculated by his power when compared to others in the group. His insecurity was speaking back there. She could understand why he didn't want anyone poking around in his head, especially her.

"Hey, Haz." Mahdyia came out of the tree line. "You get lost or something?"

Sight for sore eyes. Hazel finally understood that sentiment. She gave her cousin a hug.

"You okay?" Mahdyia held her at arms' length, concern all over her face.

"Yeah, I'm okay, or I will be. Tell ya later." Hazel leaned in closer. "You will not believe what I just saw, or rather, who I just saw...together...barely clothed."

"Oh, do tell." Mahdyia linked arms with her. "Do tell it all..."

8

"WE'VE GOT TWO OR SO DAYS OF HARD TREKKING TO GET TO the Storm Hag village. Thanks to Hazel, we didn't lose a day to recovery so we can get moving sooner than I'd planned." Bridget was standing over the crowd of them on top of a boulder, looking commanding as usual. "Be vigilant and aware. There are Rogues in these woods who scout for innocent Healers to capture."

Duke smirked at the commonly believed myth, and the reaction of the interns. Bridget had them scared, as they should be. He'd done some travelling over the years in the highlands, visiting different remote clans and tribes so he had some familiarity. The woods could be treacherous. Especially these woods. The magic from centuries of concentrated spell casting had given them a haunted atmosphere, which at times could be deadly.

"Eyes on anything that moves. Even if it looks innocent," Bridget continued. "And be wary of cries for help. There are creatures that live close to the Hag village that feed on witch blood and can mimic human noises. They will drain you dry in minutes."

"But the Rogues..." Chanda said, wringing her hands as she looked fretfully around. "I've heard that they've ramped up their attacks lately."

"They have," Bridget confirmed. "Which is why I'm telling you to be vigilant."

Rogues were indeed in the woods, roaming, scavenging, sometimes hunting. But they typically didn't attack large groups. They weren't organized enough, their parties were scattered, not unified and their magic was equally so. Not much practical training, no theory at all. The Rogues were known for chaotic bursts that could be deadly for sure, but were more likely to be misdirected and self-harmful. It was a lot of hype and for all his time spent in the field, Duke hadn't encountered any Rogue he couldn't handle.

Duke surveyed the group again, keeping his gaze from settling on Hazel. Her words earlier had hurt him. The truth behind them had hurt more. She wanted him to believe that she was fully pledged to her destiny. He could see that she was...except for thud of her heart that spoke differently to Duke. He wasn't the type of man to try to impose his beliefs on others. While he didn't agree with Hazel's choice, he wouldn't try to change her mind if he didn't hear a different story from her heart. It called to him, longed for him, just as his did for her. She wasn't being true to herself, not completely, and he needed her to open her eyes to that before she made a final decision that could keep them apart for the rest of their lives.

So he wasn't going to give up on her, no matter what she said. Was he mad at her? Hell yes. Furious actually. She'd misled the other interns to believe he was lecherous. A dirty game to create distance between them. It wasn't what he'd expected from his little village girl, it wasn't something he really liked much either. But he understood why she'd done it. In her mind, he was dangerous. He created dissonance and she was going to do whatever she could to correct that. Rocking what she'd accepted as truth her whole life. He knew how scary that could be. When the foundation of your beliefs were challenged at a gut level.

So he was going to keep his distance for now. Give her time to acclimate to the trip. Stop pushing for conversation and let her come to him. That didn't mean he was going to take a back seat. No. It meant he was going to be smarter about his plan of attack. No matter what, he wasn't ready to let Hazel go, not when he hadn't had a chance to prove to her that there was more than one way to look at a situation. More than one path to a destination. And more than one way to play the game.

And so they trekked. There was a clear path, well beaten and wide enough to accommodate pairs but moving with such a large group was slower than he was used to. Duke kept himself busy by studying the interns. People watching was something he liked to do. You could learn a lot about a person from quietly observing them.

Like Chanda, the pretty dark haired one with the full pouty lips and pale blue eyes. Her easy smile and flirty words didn't match the hard edge in her expression. The way she flinched at every little twig crack or howl from the woods. Tension ran high in that one; he could feel it with every breath she took. He wouldn't be surprised to learn she had some deep dark story with tragic twists and turns. She was smart—all the interns were, the best of the best—but she was also sassy, independent in a loner kind of way. She walked close to the pack of them but not too close, listening like he was and interjecting a comment here and there as she weaved closer then pushed herself away. Tentative of getting too entrenched in the group. She would see danger before the others.

Tate, the mysterious Elemental. Elementals were usually female, descendants of Storm Hags, another mythical story that ran as truth among Healer-kind. The Hags they were travelling to see now were an off-shoot. If you were one to believe in the purity of witch lineage, Elementals were one of the original sects. Endowed with Earth magic that could transcend barriers, the Elementals got to the root of all spells with their innate ability to talk to the Earth. Tate's skill with electrical impulses suggested that he was gifted in only that aspect, which meant he wasn't of a pure line necessarily. Or it could be that he just hadn't gotten the proper encouragement yet. With the right kind of mentor, that kid could be a super power among the interns. Not quite as powerful as Hazel—he didn't really know of any witch who could touch her in terms of magics—but Tate could get close if he could manipulate more than just electrical pulses.

Tate was also keeping close proximity to Hazel. He was chatting quietly with her, making her smile. Duke tamped down the rise of jealousy that came. It was immature but surprisingly sharp. Just the night before, he had been the one to make her laugh. He had been the one she'd shone that smile at, those dimples of hers to die for. When she stumbled, Tate wrapped his arm around her waist and helped right her. Duke didn't particularly like that either. In fact, he thought the intern needed to keep his hands to himself.

"Hey, Healer Hart." Hazel's cousin, Mahdyia stepped to his side, preventing him from moving to Hazel on their awkward path. "I've heard some things about you."

Duke cocked an eyebrow in her direction. "Oh yeah? All good I hope."

Mahdyia gave him a once over and smirked back at him. "Yep. Mostly fan-freakin-tastic." She coughed as her gaze slid to Hazel. "So anyway, I've heard you've worked extensively with the humans, like with the outreach program that never really gets talked about at school...because, you know...humans...*ick*." She snickered at the disapproving look he gave her.

"Mahdyia," Hazel snapped without looking back at them. "Be quiet."

"What? Like it's a secret. You human sympathizers are rare. Don't get me wrong, I'm not a hater, but I don't totally get the point. It's not like we can help them at White Willow, right? Their presence is strictly forbidden. My medical training interests rest solely in speciality arts, like counter curses. So no human interaction for me." She winked at Duke and he frowned in return. "But, I digress. Like I was saying—or rather, asking— *you've* been working with humans, right?"

"For ten years actually," Duke said, confused by the attention. It wasn't often that Healers willingly started a conversation about human witches and clearly Mahdyia wasn't interested for her own pursuits. It was a taboo subject at the best of times. Even if you weren't traditionally minded, or a purist, polite conversation didn't have room for the humans. It stemmed from the Burning Times, when the humans had hunted and killed witches without compassion, and although Duke didn't think it was ever a good idea to forget what had happened then, he didn't feel that forgiveness was out of the question. "Humans, magically inclined humans, have a lot to offer. Not only for the magic worship but they are innovative in how they approach spells. They aren't bound by the traditional teachings we are. They haven't been conditioned like we have so their minds are free from those burdens. Working with them is always rewarding."

"That's what my cousin says all the time," Mahdyia said. "Right Haz? The humans you know—they've given you some unique spells, haven't they?"

Duke studied Mahdyia's face, her expression appearing earnest while her tone suggested something else. He frowned, glanced over at Hazel.

"Right Hazel?" she persisted. "She insists that they have so much to offer. That they can bolster our power with theirs. As if they have anything to offer a witch like me. I find it hard to believe but she's so insistent sometimes."

"They can!" Duke and Hazel both said at the same time.

Hazel locked eyes with him, her cheeks red, a look of exasperation on her face. She quickly moved her eyes to the others. "They have so much to offer!" Hazel said. "I've seen humans do miraculous things, manipulating magic in a way that witches couldn't fathom because we're so locked in to the right way. The *proper* way."

"Oh right, you expect us to believe that humans can wield magic like you do? Miss Superstar?" Bas scoffed. "Or wait, better than you?" He screwed up his face and Duke kind of wanted to punch him to straighten it out.

"Yeah, I've seen it too. Maybe not as direct as what we've seen Hazel do, but humans look beyond the boundaries," Duke said. "Just last night we...er...I saw a human use an alchemist's spell that transformed human blood to something very close to witch blood."

"Great, so the humans are manipulating their blood now? For what purpose? To hunt us better?" Bas sneered. "Think of what that can do. Dangerous magic with no one to monitor it. Humans have no right playing with spells."

Bridget snapped her head to look at him. "You're not serious, are you?" Her frown deepened. "I never took you for a purist."

"I'm not, but like Mahdyia, I just don't see the point in wasting our time on humans at all. I mean, I get it, we have to put the hours in for a well-rounded internship and appease whatever tender-hearted witch made the requirement, but I have no interest in spending any more time with them than I need to."

"You lost family to them, didn't you?" Hazel blurted, her expression softening.

Bas growled in her direction. "You pull that out of my head when you were snooping around?"

"No, I...just... I mean..."

"Everyone lost someone during those times," Duke snapped. "You don't have the market cornered on loss, my friend. Besides, it was hundreds of years ago. Don't you think it's time to give the benefit of the doubt, meet on common ground?"

Bas stopped walking. "It wasn't hundreds of years ago for my family, Healer Hart," he said with a sneer. "It was my mother and it was ten years ago and they watched her burn, so fuck you very much. Me and the humans, we have no common ground."

He stormed off as best he could, moving through the thick foliage and disappearing within seconds.

"I'm going to make sure he's okay," Bridget said as she started after him. "Don't want to lose an intern this early in the game." She nodded at Duke. "You got the coordinates for the stones?"

Duke tapped his watch to project the map he'd downloaded before they'd left. "Got it."

"We'll meet there at dusk. I'm going to educate young Bas with some human lore."

Duke nodded. Fuck him into the right state of mind is what that meant. She had a way with words when she was in the zone. He didn't think she'd be able to conquer this particular case, but Duke knew from personal experience that when she set her mind on a task, she was dogmatic about completing it.

Good riddance to that one for a while.

"Any other strong opinions regarding humans?" Duke moved to the head of the group and continued onward, not bothering to look back at them for answers. "Because I have to say, that kind of attitude, a display like that could land us some trouble with the Hags. The humans, they're not always proficient with magic but when they are, they can floor you with their powers. Even if it's just with insight. Soothsayers in particular—they're really good at getting to the truth of things."

And perhaps that was the way to go with Hazel. Let her sit down with one of the soothsayers in the village, get them to dose her with a bit of reality. Their understanding of destiny was very different than the majority of witch-kind. Not something to be revered but something to be consulted, judged and altered or discarded as necessary. Nothing was set in stone.

"Just the usual prejudice," Mahdyia said from the back. "No closed minds though, right guys?"

A mummer went up from the group.

"We're here to learn from the best. Human or witch, doesn't matter. Some of us weren't born to *be*, you know? We need some educating." She chuckled. "Hazel's been playing with the humans since she was a teenager. She can help us adjust."

Oh really? Duke glanced over his shoulder, eyebrow cocked.

"Enough, Mads," Hazel said, blushing again.

"Her mother thought she had an invisible friend but really it was a human girl she used to visit—"

"Enough!" Hazel stomped to her cousin and yanked her back a few more paces, leaning in close to whisper at her furiously.

"What? We're all friends here, right? Right?" She was waving her hands toward the others. "Code of silence, right? It's not like I'm going to spill the beans about your love affa—"

Hazel knocked Mahdyia off the path, garnering a startled gasp as they both rolled down the small hill.

Duke laughed. He was beginning to really like Hazel's cousin. She was just the right kind of shit disturber and, he realized, maybe not completely in line with Hazel's version of destiny.

9

"So what's it like, being the Promised One?" Tate asked as they walked.

It was midday, the sun streaking through dense foliage in concentrated beams of light. It wasn't hot in the forest, not much of a breeze penetrating but that didn't make things stifling. It was nice. Pleasant even. Except for the bugs. The bugs were kind of a pain in the ass.

"It's the only thing I've ever known." Hazel didn't look at anything but the ground, keeping track of where she was putting her feet, swatting away whatever buzzed in her face. She was still finding pieces of twigs and leaves in her hair and clothes from her tumble with Mahdyia earlier. She didn't want that to happen again and tried to keep Tate in between her and the slope of the hill.

"The only thing you've ever known?" Duke's voice was kind of like a razor blade down her spine. "Really?"

The others probably wouldn't pick up on the tone. She did though and she winced, wanting to curl up into herself.

"But isn't it a burden? Knowing that you have such a heavy destiny to fulfill?" Chanda was walking parallel with Duke. Occasionally her arm brushed his. Hazel noticed every single time it happened.

"It's an honor to know that I will be serving Healer-kind." Hazel could practically hear her mother's voice in that statement. It was the mantra she'd memorized from the time that she'd been a child.

"So there's a destiny etched in stone," Chanda continued, glancing over her shoulder at Hazel. "And that's how your mother knew it was meant for you?"

"My mother sought out a Mystic once she learned she was pregnant with me."

"A Mystic?" Duke asked, then snorted.

Chanda smirked at him, and her arm brushed his. Again.

"The Mystic gave Mother a prophecy as well as a prediction. When the prediction came true, Mother knew that the prophecy would as well."

"What was the prediction?" Tate asked.

"That I would possess exceptional powers from birth."

"And from birth she has. It's all I've ever known," Mahdyia said, her tone challenging. She was walking behind the group, keeping her distance from Hazel.

They'd probably both be black and blue from the roll down the hill they'd taken and Mahdyia was limping a bit. Hazel had offered to take care of it but Mads was sulking. She thought she had a right to tease Hazel with her secret life; Hazel didn't agree. She'd threatened to cast a silencing spell on Mahdyia if she spoke about it again. And Hazel would—she'd bind her to her promise to keep her secret if she must. She was tired of everyone thinking they knew what was best for her.

"The story goes, when Hazel was born, her mother was haemorrhaging and the midwife Healers couldn't seem to control it. Baby Hazel was crying and making such a fuss that they laid her on her mother's chest to try to calm her while they tended to the bleeding. Once there, Hazel's whole body heated, as my aunt says, like a little furnace and her magic just pumped out, healing her mother's tearing, repairing the damage and stopping the bleeding. A miracle from birth."

Silence.

When her mother told that story it didn't sound so preposterous. It *did* sound like a miracle. All of the midwives who were there attested that that's what had actually happened. For most of her childhood, that story had been Hazel's favorite.

"That's pretty amazing. What does the prophecy say?" Tate asked, nudging her a little with his arm.

Hazel hesitated for a moment, feeling a jolt of anticipation mixed with trepidation. This was always the exciting part.

"A Healer child born of the Great Mother will come to learn sacrifice and great devotions when she commits herself to all witch-kind. Uniting the Circle with powerful purpose," Mahdyia said, her tone bland.

Hazel had it memorized from the time she was a child—their whole family had. She'd cherished those words, feeling so special because she had been chosen as a Promised One from birth and now Mahdyia was tainting it by sharing it like this.

Everyone was quiet for a few minutes, the sounds of the forest suddenly amplified. Hazel's normal bubble of excitement at the reception of the prophecy had turned to a weird kind of anxiety. Why weren't they saying anything? Why wasn't there a reaction? This was the punch line, the thing that always got the gasps, the *ewws* and *ahhs*

"Well, as far as prophecies go, that one is typically cryptic." Chanda chuckled. "I mean, I guess, in combination with the prediction, it is somewhat clear—"

"Clear? Oh come on!" Duke said. "That's about as clear as muddy water."

"What about it isn't clear, Healer Hart?" Hazel snapped. "I am a child born to the Great Mother, I will commit myself to witch-kind and unite the Circle. It's as clear as day to me and to everyone else in my life. Everyone with a vested interest in our future, anyway. I plan to sacrifice my life so that all Healers can benefit from my power. I will do that willingly, selflessly. It's my destiny."

Everyone got quiet again, the tense kind of quiet. Hazel felt her cheeks warm. She looked at the back of Duke's head, wishing he'd give some kind of retort, to snap back. Instead he made a comment to Chanda that Hazel couldn't hear. And Chanda had the nerve to giggle. *Giggle!*

Hazel growled.

"Well I appreciate your sacrifice," Tate said weakly. He touched her hand, squeezing quickly in a show of solidarity. "It is selfless."

Chanda gave a sympathetic nod toward Hazel but her eyes didn't convey the same emotion. Her eyes were laughing.

Hazel suddenly felt like she was an inch tall.

Mahdyia was silent.

Way to go, Hazel. That's the way to win friends.

She'd overstepped. She'd forgotten her place. Duke was supposed to be her mentor and there she was talking to him like they were friends, which they were not. Not any more anyway. And bragging to the rest of them, as if they owed her something... *Ugh, such a dolt.*

Hazel curled in on herself emotionally. She'd always been introspective, spending a lot of time alone in her room, studying, practicing, researching. Being in her brain was comfortable. Safe. For the first time in her life, she wondered just what she'd missed out on by being so isolated. She'd had Mahdyia growing up, when she was given free time, that was.

Mads and her family lived on the same property, the family estate with sprawling lawns and an equally sprawling mansion. Mahdyia's mother was Hazel's mother's sister. Younger, not as accomplished, more like a wild child who had gotten herself pregnant at the same time as Hazel's mother. Mahdyia's father had died in some kind of magic skirmish and her mother had come home to live with them in the guest house while she awaited the birth of her daughter... then, as Hazel's mother put it, had never left.

Hazel had never seen them as anything but immediate family but sometimes her mother acted like they were there to serve her. Like they owed her something. She reminded Mahdyia often that it was only because of her generosity that Mahdyia had her *very expensive* private witch training, rivalling what Hazel had received to some degree. Same instructors, not the same number of hours. Hazel was definitely favored in that department. Mads had gotten a lot of days off that Hazel hadn't.

For her whole life, Hazel had felt sorry for Mahdyia, thinking she was being spoiled and her cousin was getting the scraps. But Mahdyia had had a life, with friends, and parties, and other normal things while Hazel had been honing her skill in preparation for her *sacrifice*.

Despite the difference, they were close. Like sisters. Which meant the hits dug deeper, were harder and lasted longer.

Hazel suddenly felt very alone.

Thankfully, no one else spoke to her because she was pretty certain if she got any more prodding, she'd probably burst into tears. Self-pity was a vortex of darkness and she was quietly spinning in the middle of it.

Poor little Hazel. A Promised One with no friends. All alone and suffering while her lover flirted with another woman right in front of her.

Snap out of it. Alone is better. It's safer. Alone means your heart doesn't explode with lust or jealousy or love.

They kept walking. The forest was alive with noise. Strange noises that seemed unnatural. As Bridget had pointed out earlier, the forest leading to the Storm Hag village had been imbued with magic purely because of proximity to such powerful human witches. The bird sounds were deeper, sometimes mimicking human voices like a parrot would. The buzzing bug noise sounded slightly more sinister, and the bites she was getting were definitely itchier.

"We're going to detour for lunch." Duke broke from his conversation with Chanda with a beaming smile. "There's a small tribe of witches who live nearby. They're known for their hospitality and I've been meaning to check in on them for the past few months."

"Where are they? How far off course?" Mahdyia asked.

"See that hill there?" Duke pointed just ahead. "They're up there."

"I don't see anything." Tate was squinting at the hill, just like the rest of them.

"It's hidden," Hazel said. "There's magic surrounding it."

"Hazel's right," Duke said with a nod in her direction. "They're very wary of strangers."

"Won't they be upset at the intrusion?" Chanda asked.

"No, I've spent years building a relationship with them. They want to meet interns. Young witches with promise excite them." He was smiling and Hazel knew there was more to it than he was saying. "They're amazing cooks as well."

That got everyone moving. Stomachs had been rumbling for a while. Hazel had been daydreaming about a hearty breakfast, something she'd gotten used to back at home. Their chef always made sure she had a balanced—and big—breakfast to start each day. With the late night out at the village, she'd overslept a bit for her early morning start to her internship. Hazel had only managed to scarf down a few bites before she'd gone to White Willow; her mother had already left and Hazel was worried she'd miss the opening ceremony. So that, and a measly granola bar, had her stomach yowling like she hadn't eaten for days.

The hillside witches were a group of five or so families who'd decided to live off the grid. They'd pooled resources decades back and bought property that extended into a small valley that was impossible to see from the rough path the interns had been on. If it wasn't for Duke pointing it out, Hazel wouldn't have seen it either. The magic they used to cloak themselves was sophisticated and impressive. Hazel wished that Bas had been with them to see for himself what kind of power the humans could wield. She felt it caress her flesh and took in the essence of it to bolster her own magic, giving back as she did, offering her unique signature to bolster them.

"Healer Hart!" An older woman approached, a crooked smile showing missing teeth. Her skin was tanned to a ruddy reddish color, her graying hair looking coarse. She had a limp and was walking with a cane. "Sae guid tae see ye 'ere! We wur praying fur a visit."

"Anne, it's good to see you too." Duke leaned in and gave the woman a hug. "How are the grandkids doing?"

"Ah, weel, intae trauchle as usual." She patted his back as she pulled away. "Ur thae yer students?"

"They are, yes. I thought you folks could use a check-up and these interns need the bedside hours."

"I can't understand a word she's saying," Chanda whispered as she leaned into Hazel.

"Oh, I can fix that." Hazel flicked her finger and muttered a few words.

"I'll let the others know and gather a group for ya. Have you all eaten? First there should be a meal, wouldn't you say?" Anne hurried off before they could respond. Her accent gone.

"What did you do?" Chanda snapped.

"Just a translator spell." Hazel looked at her with surprise. "You said you couldn't understand what she was saying. I figured if we were going to be working, it would make sense to ease the language barrier."

"I liked her accent!" Chanda huffed. "I would have gotten an ear for it. So what? I don't get to hear any accents while we're here now?"

"Sorry, I..." Hazel winced. The spell would last for at least a few hours, but yeah, she'd cast on the whole area. "I can reverse it."

"No," Duke said. "Leave it. It's better for you to preserve your magic for triage."

"Triage?" Mahdyia's eyes grew wide when she looked over Hazel's shoulder. "Oh man!"

Sure enough, a horde of people were making their way to the interns. Some moving slow, some fast. Some carrying cots, and tables as well as stools. Within minutes, they had set up a clinic complete with a small fire and with a cauldron hanging above.

"In case you need to brew poultice or something," an older man said.

"Let's get started," Duke said. "Anne will take care of the food. Eat when you get a chance. We've got two hours to spare here before we've got to get moving. Use your time wisely but make sure you see to everyone."

Orderly lines formed. There was an area set up with a curtain for more private matters. Hazel got herself into a routine. Listen, assess, diagnose, treat. Many of the ailments were purely human in nature. Abscessed teeth, infected cuts, fevers. Other times the illness was a result of magic.

One fellow had been inflicted by a lust spell that had him yearning for a girl who had been exiled from the tribe a few months before. He agreed she was bad news for him but had to be shackled in chains by his parents at night so he wouldn't wander off in search of her. It was a tricky bit of magic that had really dug in deep on him. He'd confessed that some days he didn't eat at all because he was so consumed with thoughts of *her*. It was a horrible thing to do to someone. Luckily, Hazel knew how to unravel those kinds of spells. She'd done it a few times in the field with her mother, and although it took a bit of time and a great deal of energy, she had him cleared and free of it before long.

They were fed. Eating bites of delicious bread, cheese, and cured meats. So fresh and delicious that it had obviously been made on site. There was a lot of laughing and talking going on between the other interns and the locals. Hazel didn't really have time for it though. She ate when she could, shoving bits into her mouth between patients. She was determined to get through the majority of people as quickly as possible. Duke had put them on a timeline and she was nothing if not efficient, so there was no time for chitchat. She didn't mind carrying the weight of the work. When it came down to it, she wasn't there to make friends.

Hazel had cleared her last patient and moved on to Chanda's line. "What's going on here?"

"He's got an old fracture that hasn't healed properly." Chanda ran her fingers up and down her patient's leg. "Right here is the problem. A bone chip."

"Ah, well." Hazel leaned in and dug her fingers close to where Chanda's were. With a concentrated blast of her magic, she had the bone fixed up. Sure, it caused the patient to squeal a bit. Hazel's methods were fast, not necessarily tender, but now the problem was gone and they could move on to the next patient.

"What the hell did you do that for?" Chanda glared at her as she moved to the man's head, soothing him as he moaned away the pain Hazel had caused.

"What? I was helping. Speeding things along. You've got a line up there, I thought I could help you clear it."

"I have a line up because I'm taking my time, getting to know these people. Mr. Burns here has been suffering with chronic pain for years. I promised him that I wouldn't do anything to add to it."

"Oh...I'm well..." Hazel winced. "Sorry, I just thought..."

"You thought you'd swoop in and save the day right? Because that's what you do. Well let me tell you, you're not the only one here with proficiency in spell casting and healing. I happen to be very good at pain management and now you've made me a liar to this man."

"I'm very sorry." Hazel raised her hands and took a step back. The old man wouldn't look at her. "I didn't mean—"

Chanda was fuming, her face blasting rage before she turned her back on Hazel completely.

"Hazel, come over here, I could use your help on this case." Duke's voice was like a lifeline.

She winced, then looked over her shoulder. "Be right there."

Chanda and the old man didn't acknowledge her leaving. Her mind was already shifting to the next patient though so she brushed it off as a lesson learned. She wasn't good at tenderness—she was good at solving problems and healing with urgency. She was definitely a rip the Band-Aid off kind of girl, which, until this Mr. Burns, had worked quite well for her. Perhaps he just had a very low threshold for pain. She'd do better with the next one.

And then she saw who her patient was and knew she was in trouble.

10

Duke had been watching Hazel while she'd been working through the patients. Her bedside manner sucked. Big time. It was what he'd expect from someone who was book smart, spell smart, but otherwise hadn't had a lot of experience working with patients. It was also what he'd expect from the daughter of Mother Knight. The woman had a way about her that was perpetually cold. She was a skilled Healer of course, but she wasn't about the warm and fuzzies. Hazel, it seemed, had adopted that trait.

He knew a different side to her, of course. When her guard was down and she wasn't trying to impress anyone. Ego, it was the biggest battle when it came to new interns. He should know; it was his tragic flaw as well.

"Hazel, this is Lily." Duke motioned to the little girl who sat on the cot, her lips quivering as she looked up at them.

"She was playing with a fire spell about six months ago and as you can see, it went a little haywire."

"I'd rather stick to the adults, if it's all the same to you." Hazel started to turn away.

Lily's body shook, tears welled.

"Hazel, this is your patient now. I'd like you to assess her." Duke motioned for her to move closer.

Hazel sighed, set her jaw. "Fine." She moved closer. "It hurts, right? That's some nasty magic you were playing with."

The scars ran along one side of her face, from forehead to neck and down to her shoulder. They were deep, marring her face in a horrific way. He'd been there the day after she'd done it. The poor girl had been screaming in agony when he arrived and the villagers were at a loss as to what to do for her. Painkillers didn't work; folk magic was useless.

The little girl nodded.

"I can feel the magic burning still."

Hazel leaned closer. Lily flinched.

"I won't touch it, okay?" Her tone was sharp, like her patience was running low already.

"The spell was potent when it first happened. I removed the worst of it when I treated her six months ago. Restored eyesight, closed the wounds but there are areas that are sticky. Threading along her scars that still carry part of the magic."

"Who taught you this spell?" Hazel ran her fingers just over top, not touching, still assessing. Delicate, just as he knew she could be. Those fingers had touched him the same way—or rather, caressed him with tenderness.

Duke tucked back those thoughts and refocused on the little girl.

Lily wouldn't answer.

Hazel cocked an eyebrow, opened her mouth to undoubtedly push when Duke cut her off.

"What can you do for her, Hazel?" Duke looked at her expectantly. What the poor thing felt on a daily basis was something like an elastic snapping repeatedly along her bubbled scars. No relief. He'd done what he could but it would take time. A slow process of undoing what Lily had done. She would never tell him who'd given her the spell but if he had to guess, she probably bartered for it from a Rogue. He hated to think what she'd traded for it though.

"I can leach the magic. It would stop it from spreading and reduce the pain overall." Hazel stepped back from the child.

"Yes, but that treatment would be painful on such a sensitive area."

"It's the quickest method. It would take me five minutes, tops. Like ripping off a Band-Aid."

"No!" Lily screeched. "I don't want it to hurt! It always hurts. Every day. Please, no more!"

Duke gave Hazel a hard look then motioned for her to step away.

She obliged, looking exasperated by the delay. "What's the problem?"

"I've been watching you work your patients. You're fast. You're systematic, but your bedside manner is less than desirable."

She flinched—it was subtle but it was there. Not used to criticism? Probably not.

"You said we were on a timeline. I'm working quickly so we can leave and keep to our schedule. Just following orders."

"Very efficient. Got it. But if you want to keep the trust of these people, and you do or they'll never let you back here again, you have to find a way to treat this little girl without making her cry."

Hazel looked over his shoulder at the girl. Then around at the collection of villagers there. They were watching her. Assessing her. They'd done the same to him when he'd first come years ago. It had taken days to even get them comfortable enough to let him do check-ups. Weeks before they'd let him actually heal them. They were good judges of character though. When he could, he brought new Medics here to break them in. Whenever he found out his team was headed in the general area, he knew there'd be a pit stop at some point. The tribe was the best pass/fail he'd ever encountered.

"Impossible. Her scars are too deep. The magic is rooted there. Any attempt I make to remove it will cause her some pain."

"Not if you work slowly," Duke said. "No one would argue with your skill, Hazel, but a big part of treating patients is in how you interact with them. They are not an assembly line for you to get through. They're humans who need compassion, time, sensitivity."

Hazel glanced back at Chanda, who was still soothing the old man she had fixed. Old Jess. Duke had treated him for headaches in the past. He was a tough guy when it came to everything but illness or injury. He needed a soft touch. Chanda had that compassion. The innate ability to sooth people. She wasn't lacking in bedside manner. She was helping him drink something from a steaming cup, smiling and chatting with him. Duke looked expectedly at Hazel.

She sucked in a deep breath, then let it out slowly, her cheeks a darkening shade of pink. "Okay, I think I know what I can do."

"Good. Now you have to convince her to let you do it." Duke pointed at Lily. "And remember, no crying."

This was going to be interesting to watch.

Hazel looked at the little girl, whose bottom lip was pouting and whose fists were clenched. She didn't look ready to hear what Hazel had to say. And Duke knew the kid could be stubborn as hell.

With another deep breath, Hazel seemed to fortify herself, looked at him one more time, eyebrows raised, then walked to the girl.

She made it about ten minutes, which was five minutes longer than Duke thought she'd last. Lily was a dramatic girl. The sight of blood was enough to have her hyperventilating. Third degree burns to her face and neck...well, *screaming* didn't begin to describe what that little thing could produce.

Hazel wasn't doing anything Duke hadn't done already. Her abilities were superior, sure, her counter spell more direct, and with Duke's help to bolster her, it was working to reduce some of the redness and scarring. They made a good team, for sure. Either way, as hard as Hazel had tried to keep the pain to a minimum, as slowly as she'd worked, Lily wasn't going to give her an inch. The screeching had drawn a crowd, Hazel was doing her best to ignore them.

She was good under pressure, he'd give her that.

Hazel took another pass, her fingers not touching Lily's scars, just hovering above her tattered skin, little sparks of magic jolting and zapping as she drew them down along the bubbled tissue. She had a smile quirking on her lips—just a small one, barely noticeable. Humble to a degree. She knew she had this.

Lily was shifting on her seat, her fists clenching and unclenching as Hazel drew the power of the last of the fire magic out of her. What Hazel was forgetting, and Duke was bracing himself for, was the sudden withdrawal removing such intense magic would cause to Lily.

As she lost the thing that was both a torment and an addiction to her, her screams turned to deep, mournful moans. And then as Hazel got closer to the root of it, Lily started to scream in earnest. Anger, furious rage exploded out of her little body. Losing the magic she'd come to rely on was perhaps more painful than the damage it had caused. True magic was addictive for humans and this little girl had been living with the pain on purpose. She'd refused to let Duke pull the magic away from her in past visits but he'd told her today that it was going to happen. She had no choice —it was that or let it consume her completely.

Duke wasn't strong enough to do it without her cooperation but Hazel was. And it was working.

Hazel was so locked into her spell that the heightened sound of Lily's desperate screams didn't reach her right away. When they did, she was so entrenched in her magic that all she could do was open her eyes wide, a mirrored look of horror locking her in place. Duke could feel her own confusion, rage and fear. It washed over him, gripping him in her whirlwind as she fought to keep the spell going. The girl's screams were horrific. She tried clawing at her own face, at Hazel, punching, kicking out, only to meet a barrier that Duke had invoked, a spell to keep everyone safe.

The villagers were closing in. Looking at him for guidance. Concern written all over their faces, fear amplifying and hitting him from all sides. He'd warned them this day would come. Either with time as he unravelled the spell or if he brought a powerful enough Healer. They knew this is what Lily needed but that didn't stop her mother from running to them, busting through the crowd to get to her only child.

All of the interns were staring at the scene. Everyone no doubt thinking that Hazel was the worst Healer ever. Duke felt a little bad about that.

But this was a lesson she needed to learn.

Lily jumped up from the cot, knocking it over, her expression wild, desperation riding her as she lunged at Hazel. "Stop! Stop! Stop! *Plllease* stop!"

Hazel frowned, looked to him for a second, no more, then shook her head and did what he would have done. She swooped in on the child, busting through the magical barrier that Duke had constructed and wrapped Lily in her arms. She took them both down to the ground. With arms and legs wrapped around Lily, she fought to hang on to her, to keep her from scratching her eyes out, from running away, all the while Lily screamed and cried and threatened to kill everyone there.

Hazel closed her eyes, sucked in a deep breath and then pulled power from the Earth. Duke felt the vibration through his legs, a rush of magic that actually hurt in its intensity. He looked at the other interns—they felt it too. Eyes wide. Mouths gaping. Duke refocused on Hazel, stoking her with his powers. She didn't flinch at the intrusion; she accepted his offering, rolling it into her spell to cocoon herself and Lily.

It took another ten minutes. That's it. She ripped away the

last of the spell and then sent out a soothing balm that stretched far enough to touch him and, by the looks on the villagers' faces, them as well. Lily had stopped struggling. She was quietly sobbing, her little arms wrapped around Hazel. Hazel was whispering to her, cooing endearments and reassurances.

Duke moved to them, motioning for Lily's mother to come as well. "It's okay to take her now," he said.

Hazel locked eyes with him. She looked exhausted. She should have been annihilated but he knew it would pass quickly. Already the Earth was rising up to rejuvenate her. He could feel it like a constant vibration. She was an amazing witch. Truly one of a kind. He could see why her mother thought she was worthy of the Circle.

He held his hand out for Hazel to take. Surprisingly, she did.

"You knew." She was angry, her voice quivering. "It was impossible to keep that kid quiet."

"Yes, quite."

"So you set me up for failure." She dropped his hand the second she was on her feet.

"No." He motioned to the dispersing crowd. "I did what I needed to do to get you to understand."

"Understand what?"

"That showing compassion, caring, bonding with your patient in even a little way goes far with the humans."

Anne was there now, her hand out to Hazel, something glittering there.

Hazel frowned as she turned toward the old woman, accepting the gift and opening her palm to reveal a small amber stone. It was clear—nothing inside, no flaws marring it. It symbolized warmth, compassion, and nurturing. More importantly, it symbolized acceptance.

"It's beautiful," Hazel said. "Thank you."

"You are a good witch," Anne said. "You did good today."

Hazel blushed. "I didn't do—"

But Anne was already walking away.

"You did good today. Remember that when you work on your next patient. You took your time. You didn't rush it. That's the most valuable lesson you could ever learn in the field. Speed is essential all of the time, especially in trauma healing, but you can be fast and soft. Often times, giving that touch of kindness makes everything go quickly and with less struggle."

"I'm still really angry with you." Hazel was clearly fighting a smile as she examined the amber, holding it up to the light so it refracted onto her skin.

"Probably not the last time you will be on this trip." He turned to address the rest of the Healers. "Wrap up your patients. We have to get back on the trail if we're going to make it to the stones by dusk."

11

THE STANDING STONES WERE NOT AS HUGE AS OTHERS IN Scotland but they were still impressive. The magic aura surrounding them ebbed toward Hazel like it was drawn to her. Tendrils of power reached out in colorful bands.

"If you've never experienced centuries old stones, this is the place to be." Duke came up next to her, close enough that she could feel his body heat, smell that unique blend of vanilla and sandalwood. She took a step away, putting more distance between them. As if that would make a difference.

The five stones stood seven feet tall at least, huge slabs that were moss covered, pock-marked and in various stages of decay. Magic would eventually wear them down to nothing. It could take a millennium or more but it would happen. It was corrosive stuff. Overuse could age witches and humans alike rapidly, irreversibly.

Hazel moved closer to the nearest one that stood tall, nestled against another that acted like an altar, flat and long. She could see the remnants of blood there—human witch blood used for spells would forever stain the stones as long as they were there. The layered effect produced an interesting collection of magic signatures. Hazel could feel them all. She hoped it wasn't life blood—that humans hadn't lost their lives there but she couldn't say. She knew that sacrifice had historically been a part of some rituals.

The other interns were scattered around the stone circle, all quietly marvelling at the energy the stones gave off. It was breathtaking. Intoxicating. Hazel ran her fingers along the edge of the stone and felt the jolt of Earth magic there.

She gasped at the purity of it, so raw, available and calling to her. She drew her fingers away only to put them back again a second later. Was this what people felt when she shared her power with them? This vibration that made her want to giggle? She flattened her hand against the stone and closed her eyes, listening to the hum of so many voices, spells cycling through them. She soaked it all in, opening herself up to it more.

"Happy to see you all made it alive." Bridget's voice echoed into her thoughts, pulling Hazel away from the stone's magic like a dousing of cold water. "We scouted the area. All is clear."

Hazel swayed a little when she opened her eyes, dizzy from the surge of power, revitalized too though, like she'd had a few dozen cups of coffee.

Bridget was standing next to Duke, watching Hazel with a look of amusement on her face. "Impressive, right? Bet you've never felt that before." Bridget winked then turned back to Duke. "No trouble on the way?"

Duke shook his head, his eyes only now leaving Hazel. "Made a pit stop to do some work. No problems there. I'll get a fire started."

Bridget nodded as he walked off then turned back to Hazel. "You have any trouble on the way?"

"No." Hazel frowned, shook her head. "Everything is fine."

Well, except for making an ass of herself at the village. Putting her needs ahead of the patients' while she worked efficiently to meet some fucked up quota she'd set for herself. She could hear her mother's voice in her head the whole time. *Faster, Hazel, work faster. People appreciate speed, focus, expertise.* She'd completely neglected the human part of the equation.

"Good. Your mother wants a check in. I'm going to scry her once the moon is up."

Hazel sighed. She wanted to say that she wasn't a child. That she didn't need a check in. Instead, she nodded. "Do you need me to do anything?"

"Set yourself up with the rest of the interns. I'm sure one of them can help you get your tent up. Stay close to the group and be sure to ward your sleeping space. Don't want anything to happen to the Promised One." She winked again. "We'll eat then get some sleep. It's a long day of trekking tomorrow. I know you're probably not used to such physical exertion. It can be demanding on the body."

"I know how to set up a tent," she snapped, then softened her tone at Bridget's hardened expression. "I'm not some... Oh, never mind."

Hazel had been about to say, *I'm not some spoiled princess*. But she decided it was better to keep it to herself. Obviously she had a reputation. Powerful magically speaking, pampered otherwise. If they only knew the drills she'd undergone, the years and years of hard training. She'd told them that she'd travelled on the time lines before. No one had bothered to ask where she'd gone. Her mother had spared nothing in her home schooling. She hadn't gone easy on Hazel either. Hazel had gotten dirty. She'd gotten bloody. This wasn't Hazel's first field trip either. Her mother had prepared her for her one year of intensive testing to fast track her to the Circle. She'd worked hard, so hard. She'd taken hits. She'd been drained again and again and again. She'd had bad experiences, amazing experiences. She'd helped people. She wasn't a spoiled princess. She was quite capable—

"You, Tate, get over here and help Hazel set up her tent. She's never been away from home before." Bridget was barking orders.

Hazel could feel her face heat and anger bubble.

Tate beamed at her, moving before Bridget had finished talking. The others looked at her with pity, disgust, like she was an alien. Like she was exactly what they expected her to be.

"I've been in battle before!" She whispered it at first. No one was listening so she raised her voice. "I've been in battle before!" It came out louder than she'd wanted. Eyes went wide. Bridget stopped barking. Hazel had everyone's attention now. "I told you that I've travelled the time lines. I've been out in the field before. Worked triage, Egypt, Spain, Australia. I did a tour." It was silent all around her. Everyone was staring. "So I know how to set up a tent." She snapped her eyes to Bridget, then to Tate. "I haven't spent all my time at home. I've been working hard. Training hard."

She needed them to understand. She wanted them to accept her.

"How am I not surprised?" Bas said. "Privileged and entitled white witch, with all of the perks of being a Knight. So what? You've gotten your field training already? You want us to bow down to you now? Before you've even stepped into the Circle?"

Hazel's mouth gaped. "No, I—"

"You needed us to know that you're better than all of us, right? It must burn you that you can't use those hours you got triaging already, right? You have to do it with the rest of us for it to count." Bas snorted, then made a big show of bowing to her. "We are unworthy."

"Enough, Bas!" Mahdyia looked at Hazel, frowning.

"That's not what I was saying—"

"Keep it to yourself, sister." Bas righted himself, snatched up his backpack and stalked off. "At least she's only around for a year, right?"

"Just ignore him. Here, let me help—" Tate moved to grab her pack.

"No!" Hazel pulled away. "Thank you! I don't need help."

She stormed off in the other direction. How could she keep

getting this wrong? Every time she opened her mouth, she said something to make things worse. It didn't help that Bas also had a way of twisting her words into something she didn't mean.

"Hazel!" Mahdyia was following her, running to catch up.

"Leave me alone!" Hazel didn't stop, she didn't turn around and when Mahdyia's hand landed on her shoulder, she sent a zap of magic to ward her off.

"Ouch! What the—?"

"Where were you, huh?" Hazel said over her shoulder. "Why didn't you help me back at the village? Tell me I was doing it wrong?"

"Some lessons you have to learn for yourself, Haz." She said it softly, with pity.

Hazel turned to face her. "That's just fucking great. I thought you were my friend but instead you're just like the rest of them, right? Look at me. Poor little entitled Hazel Knight. Too privileged to know what she's doing. Leave me alone, Mahdyia." She turned again and walked away.

"Fine Hazel, suit yourself. Keep to yourself, like you always do. Crawl into that shell and block everyone out."

For all her training, for her years of advanced education, Hazel still had no real idea how to relate to other Healers. Humans, yeah sure, no problem. Talking to them held no expectation, no prejudice. But other Healers knew who she was, what she was destined to be and it made all her interactions feel strained. Weird. Awkward.

Except for Duke. With Duke, she'd never felt that way. Even after he'd found out about her witch status, she hadn't felt weird talking to him.

She stopped walking once she was high on the hill overlooking the stones. She'd thought Duke was human for a year. She'd talked to him, laughed with him, let him get as close as possible. And yet he wasn't a human. So maybe the problem wasn't with everyone else. Maybe the problem was with her.

Being home schooled had it advantages but being unable to connect with other Healers was a definite disadvantage. She was inept at it. Unskilled with small talk. Unable to pick up on the cues that seemed so obvious to everyone else. And that bugged her too. She was good at most things. With training, dedication, time, she could excel at everything she set her mind to. But not this. She sucked at communicating with her fellow witches and she was stuck with them. At least for the next year.

Bas was right. Once she joined the Circle, the only interaction she'd have with other witches would be purely magically speaking. They're be no conversation, no awkward misinterpretations. She'd speak to them through her power and that was it. Probably for the best. Alone, maybe, was better. There was no expectation when you were only dealing with yourself.

Mahdyia always teased her for being sheltered. It had pushed Hazel to seek out other kinds of interactions. Sneaking out of her home when her mother was preoccupied so she could gain experiences that weren't hand-picked for her. She'd thought she was getting life experience but she realized now that it was still manufactured. She'd been hiding behind a mask most of the time. The humans had no idea who she was and denying that part of her identity had not given her true experience with communication.

Bring on the self-pity.

Hazel set her pack down and surveyed the area below. The sun had set quickly, the stars brilliant in the darkening night sky. Heat rose from the stones, making them look hazy. The others were in various stages of setting up camp. They would leave her alone now. Mahdyia would make sure of it. They didn't even glance in her direction.

She wanted to be part of the group, desperately, pathetically. She wanted to go down there and talk and laugh and eat with them. But she didn't want to at the same time. Being alone was easier, less tragic because there was no room for failure.

Hazel sighed, pulled her pack from the ground and unlatched

the tent from the bottom. She knew how to set one of these up. She'd done it at least a hundred times. Her mother had taken her into war. She'd trained with skilled weapons masters. She'd learned the basics of Battle magic. She'd moved from camp to camp, setting up, working triage, helping injured witches, then breaking camp and moving on. She'd always been so proud of her experience. Now she was feeling...what? Hollow? Like she'd cheated somehow?

She unwrapped the tent and rolled it out on the flat patch of ground, a little grassy ledge that would keep her from slipping down the hill. She could do a camp set up in less than three minutes, tent and bed ready to go. She could be inside and asleep in five.

Grab sleep when you can. That was the motto for war. She'd devoted herself to being like all the other Medics but thinking on it now, she'd never really connected with anyone there either. Her mother had always been with her and when people spoke, they'd done so with reverence and respect. Maybe more than she actually deserved. They probably just looked at her like the rest of the interns were looking at her. A spoiled princess playing at Medic. Sheltered from reality because in the end, her mother could whisk her out of there if things got too dangerous.

She paused to finger the amulet in her pocket once again. Her gateway to freedom. Summon her mother, who would bring her home. She slipped it back to the depths of her pocket and swallowed her self-pity. *Suck it up, Haz.* As Mahdyia would say.

"I know you want to be alone but I thought you might like something hot to eat rather than your rations."

Hazel had been so caught up in herself that she hadn't noticed Duke's arrival.

"Just leave me alone," she said, turning away from him and his steaming bowl of something delicious-smelling. She wanted to sulk. To wallow in herself.

He ran his fingers along her arm. "Hazel..."

She melted at his touch. His compassion making her want to weep. Without thinking she turned into his embrace, letting her guard down completely, nestling into his shoulder, arms around his waist.

"Whoa there." He chuckled, holding the bowl of stew or whatever out behind her.

She remembered herself, hardened her heart and let him go, pushing back until she was standing apart from him. "Sorry."

His expression was full of compassion. "Hazel—"

She covered her face with her hands. "No, really, I shouldn't have done that. I meant what I said. We can't be that way with one another anymore."

"Hazel—"

"Just go—"

She gasped as Duke leaned into her, getting close enough to kiss her, his hand on her hip. She didn't move away, instead she angled her mouth up, brushing her lips against his. His lips were so soft, his mouth so welcoming, that buzz he gave her making her feel like nothing else mattered.

He broke the kiss before it became more than a kiss, before it could get carried away as it usually did. "I didn't want to wear the stew, that's all." He chuckled lightly. "I missed you. I've wanted to touch you all day like this."

"I shouldn't have..." Hazel sputtered, words dying on her tongue when his expression went dark.

"I get it. You're used to having all the decisions made for you, right?" He brushed his fingers over her face. "That's what it's been like, hasn't it? Every moment of every day dictated, scheduled? That's why you snuck out to be with the humans, so you could control some aspect of yourself."

Hazel frowned, opened her mouth to speak, couldn't think of what to say.

"That's why you're pushing me away. Why you think you need to."

"My mother—"

"Can we just forget about her for a bit?" He set the bowl down in the grass then took her into his arms and kissed her again. "Can we sit down together? We don't even have to talk. Just sit with me, Hazel. There's nothing inappropriate about that."

"The others..." Hazel glanced toward the stones. No one was there. "Wait...where are the others?"

"Bridget took them into the woods to find some herbs that glow or something." Duke guided her to sit, then handed her the bowl of stew. "Here. I whipped this up."

"How did you?" She was ravished all of a sudden, the smell of meaty stew making her stomach grumble.

"This isn't my first field trip either." He winked then nudged her to eat. "Today was tough."

She nodded, not bothering to speak. Words only complicated things. So instead, she ate. Duke's stew tasted as delicious as it smelled.

"I never told you about the Shaman tribe I worked with a few years ago, right?" He shook his head. "How could I? Before today, we were both human." He winked again, a sly smile on his lips, then continued, "When I first got there, I was so confused. I'd been told that I was sent to heal an elder who had fallen ill from magic overuse, but what I found was not what I expected."

Hazel listened to his voice, her body pressed next to his, food filling her belly and for the first time all day she felt content... happy even. Or perhaps less tormented.

"So the elder I was sent to help was actually a ten year old boy. He was the shaman of the tribe, born with the ability to manipulate shadows. He'd been a protector to his tribe from the time that he was born, cloaking them from danger, giving an advantage. The only way we found them was because his magics were weakened. His skills had been used to the point of exhaustion, his tribe's war chief having realized that not only could his shadow art keep them hidden, but it could also be used as offence, if they took him with them on hunts. What he didn't realize was that doing that warped the boy's nature, turning him into something he was not and placing too many demands on his little body." He sighed. "He had this expectation on himself that he and he alone could keep his tribe alive and safe. That he was destined to be a savior. Even if it cost him his life in the end, it would be a worthy sacrifice. My medical determination was that he suspend his shadows, at least for a few months. Give him time to rest and rejuvenate. But his chief... He had a battle planned and he needed the boy's skill."

"I know what you're doing." Hazel scraped the last of the stew from the bowl and ate it. "Let's get to the moral of the story, shall we?"

Duke shook his head. "Nah, you're right. Lame attempt. Forget it."

"I'm not delusional, Duke, I'm not brainwashed. I know what you all think of me. I know the expectations, what's been promised."

"Hazel, the past year has been one of the happiest times of my life. I live for the field. I crave touring the human world, finding new ways that they use magic, helping them, working with them. But coming home to you, seeing you, touching you, talking to you, was just as intoxicating. Just as important to me. Imagine if you came with me. Imagine if you experienced the humans like I have. The things we'd see. The people we'd help. The tribes we'd discover."

Hazel stayed quiet, thinking about his words. It was unfair of him, really, to put that idea in her head. To give her something else to lust for. "What happened to the little boy?"

Duke frowned.

"Come on, you started the story. Finish it. What happened to him? Did he sacrifice himself in the end? Give himself to his tribe for their betterment?"

Duke cleared his throat. "Yes, he did."

"And what? He died, right? They used him up until he had nothing left?"

Duke shook his head. "No, that's not what happened."

It was Hazel's turn to frown. "So what then?"

Duke took the bowl from her hand and laid it next to his foot. "He went to war with his tribe and his shadows failed. It was his tribe who died. Every single one of them."

"That won't happen to me," Hazel said, even though a niggle of doubt poked at her. "I'll never let my tribe down like that."

"Oh Hazel, don't you see? When you give up your control, when you let your power be used in the Circle—*your* power in particular—you don't get a say in what happens next."

❧ 12 ❧

HER EYES FLASHED WITH ANGER. HE LIKED IT WHEN THEY DID that. It was passion, no matter how you sliced it.

"So what are you saying? I'm going to kill all Healer-kind if I join the Circle?"

"No, I'm saying that your talents might be better used outside of the Circle. That you can't see anything beyond the Circle and that, in the end, giving yourself to the service of all of Healers, while ultimately selfless and honorable, may not actually be what Healers need."

"I get it, okay?" Hazel slumped. Like she was drained of all her fight in that moment. She had to be exhausted after the day she'd had—physically, emotionally. "Whatever lesson you're aiming to teach me right now, I get it. The idea of it anyway. I just don't agree with you."

"Hazel." He reached out to her, pulled her toward him. "This is what training is supposed to be like. Learning. Growing. All I'm asking is that you're open to it. That you're not fixed on what you already know. I've seen you adapt already. When you were treating Lily. When you realized that she was going to scream no matter what you did. You pulled as much power as you could to cocoon her. I felt it. Everyone felt it. It was impressive."

Hazel nuzzled into his chest, pressing her face against him in a way that made him want to sigh with contentment. But he also didn't want to scare her off. Her guard was slipping. The fight leaving her in all areas.

"This is your year, Hazel. To experiment with the limits, if there are any, of your powers. It's your year to explore what kind of witch you want to be. You have the power to choose what that looks like and what you do with it. You have the control here. You can't expect everyone to love you right away, either. The interns, they're competing with you. With each other. They see what you can do and it scares them. That means it's going to be harder for them to connect with you. And you could take the easy way, reject them outright and focus instead on your training but I'm going to tell you something important. These witches you're with right now, they're your team. They'll have your back if you let them. You'll grow together."

"Not Bas," Hazel murmured.

Duke felt a spark of anger at the thought of that one. "No, not Bas. He's got his own demons to slay though and he's already made a decision that will possibly be advantageous for him." Or crippling, depending on how he handled things.

"You mean with Bridget?" Hazel snickered. "I feel like she'll eat him alive."

"Yeah, most likely." He wasn't about to tell her he had intimate experience with that. Very intimate. He wasn't interested in instigating another fight.

Bridget liked to take on the underdog. The one she felt held the most challenge. When Bas's heart had stopped that morning, his fate had been sealed with her. He was her project. She'd strip him down to the bare bones, pull his guts out until he didn't know what went where and then leave him to put himself back together. He'd be a better witch for it, probably, but it would be a hard road to travel. Perhaps it was what that guy deserved though. Maybe not.

"You can't be friends with everyone but you can be a team. Soften yourself with them, Hazel. Offer help. Accept it if they decline. Take a step back and get to know what they're good at, but at the same time, don't let them push you around."

"You're right." She sighed into him, her arms around his waist, body pressed in close.

He felt shock at her easy agreement. "I am?"

She pulled away and looked up at him, smiling. "Yeah, getting to know the other interns will help me when I join the Circle. Mother always said that it's good to know the needs of the Healers before you join the Circle. That way I can direct the power as required."

Duke closed his eyes and tightened his grip, forcing her to relax into him again. Enjoying this moment because it would only be a moment. He knew he'd lose her again before the day was out. Him and his big mouth.

She was so brainwashed it wasn't funny.

"Hazel, I—"

A scream hit them, shrill and loud, breaking the calm of the night. They moved apart, both looking in the direction that it had come from.

"The others." Hazel gasped as she jumped up.

He stood then looked down the hill. They weren't back at the stones.

Hazel started toward the forest. He held her back. "Hang on." He motioned for her to stay quiet while he focused on zoning in on the emotions around them. He closed his eyes, took in a deep breath, then opened himself up completely. Dangerous, sure, but it was the only way to get a true read on things.

Rage, fear hit him first. Then excitement, amped up adrenaline flowing. It was chaos.

Help. Help. Help.

He opened his eyes, clamping down on the emotions before they overwhelmed him and then clasped Hazel's hand. "They aren't far. Let's go."

"What's going on?" Hazel trailed after him, keeping close as they moved swiftly down the hill.

"Rogues."

Duke had felt the burn of their hatred before. Calculated attacks that were usually all about desperation. It was a hard life. Peddling spells and offering magic that was typically untrained, under-practiced and without concern of the recipient. As they had experienced earlier with Lily. She'd never confirmed but her mother had told Duke that Lily had been wandering off into the woods for hours, weeks before she'd attempted that spell. She was old enough to know that Rogues offered more trouble than good, but kids would be kids and the promise of a real witch's spell— one that was usually untouchable for a human witch—was probably too tempting to pass up.

The Rogues would do whatever they needed to do to secure food and material goods. Some resorted to stealing, most to bartering. Some were like travelling magic shows, offering entertainment in exchange for food and shelter. They had been banished by their respective witch clans for some social crime or another. Most were harmless, some were extremely dangerous, like the fugitives who were on the run from the Trappers. Those were the ones that you didn't want to come across. They were ruthless in their desperation and would typically go through a witch or human rather than stop to assess a situation or determine if there was a threat. And they weren't above using dirty spells to get what they needed, even at the cost of death.

"Stay close to me, no matter what happens."

Duke felt a flash of determination from Hazel, strength and power as she pulled her reserves, and then her hand out from his grasp. He wanted to snatch it back but clenched his fist against his leg instead. He knew he didn't have to worry about her. She was a superior witch to him in so many ways, but he worried the whole way down the hill anyway.

Another scream echoed around them as they skirted the stones and moved into the trees.

There were no bursts of magic, not bellows or grunts. Other than that scream, the forest was quiet.

"It's coming from over there," Duke said as he pointed east, where a concentration of emotions swirled loud enough to get past his shields.

"Magic has been cast. I can see it." Hazel pointed in the same direction. "There's been a battle. It always leaves a residue."

Duke winced, hoping like hell that didn't mean they'd lost anyone. If they'd been ambushed... No, he would have felt that, right? He'd been so tuned into Hazel though that he could have missed what was going on in the forest. "Let's go. We'll assess the situation when we can see it."

They moved steadily, stealthily. There were no more screams. No more sounds. He had this sinking feeling that they were going to find everyone dead.

He was surprised though by what they found. Not what he was expecting. The Healers were all fine, looking frazzled but otherwise unharmed. They were hanging back while Bridget argued fervently with a well-armed, fully decked out in camouflage Trapper. They were nose to nose, spit flying, but words hushed. Bridget pointed to the ground. Duke took in what she was motioning to.

There were two witches on the ground just behind them, collared, obviously injured, the reek of magic wafting off them was intense. It must have just happened—the capture. Would explain the screams. Two other Trappers, equally as armed, were standing over the Rogues, both looking like immovable statues.

"Those people need help." Hazel was looking where he was, not at the team of armed Trappers, but at the captives. A man and a woman. The collars that were around their necks were attached to a long pole. The metal was magically reinforced to bind their powers and keep them from casting themselves out of the situation or from harming anyone around them. With faces pressed into the dirt, you could only hear muffed cries, their bodies twisted in uncomfortable and downright painful looking ways.

"Unshackle them so we can treat them. They're obviously in a great deal of pain." Bridget's voice rose, her body shaking. She was losing it.

"Negative," the lead Trapper said, his eyes shielded by black tinted glasses. "These two are set to appear before the judge by tomorrow. We leave now."

"It's inhumane," Bridget continued. "You can't take them without offering some kind of treatment."

"You Healers can only treat them if they're unshackled. We are not unshackling them. No go. These two are tricksters. They've evaded capture once already. Not letting them out of these collars. Besides, there are Healers at the Scrub."

"You'll never make it there," Hazel blurted, stepping past Duke.

The Trapper shifted his gaze in her direction but didn't speak. Bridget was frowning at Duke, looking like she was ready to put a muzzle on Hazel.

"She's dying." Hazel pointed at the woman. "As we speak, her life force is ebbing. If you don't do something in the next ten minutes, she'll be dead, and then what will you do? I'm pretty sure your mandate is to bring them alive, right? The woman especially."

Sexist to be sure, but the maternal line was cherished and protected in all ways. As the bringers of witch life, women could not be penalized with death—too many lost during the Burning Times. Undocumented, but widely known, female witches had been burned, stoned and hanged in the thousands during that time. Any and all means of preventing death to a female witch was the utmost priority to all witch-kind.

"What will your superiors think if you let this one die? Especially when they find out that there were Healers available offering to help?" Bridget turned back to the lead Trapper, clearly accepting Hazel's assessment. "We have a camp just over there with supplies. We can prevent this from getting worse."

"We can't release the prisoners. You saw what they are capable of. If you knew what they'd done—"

"I can create a containment spell," Hazel said. "I can use the stones. It'll keep them from escaping while they're treated. I won't let them go, I promise."

"And there are enough of us here to keep them from doing any damage," Bridget added.

"Once they're healed, they can lash out," the lead Trapper said.

"With you guys here? No way." Chanda moved away from the group, motioning toward the rest of the Trappers. "All those weapons and that magic? Those muscles too? Gosh, I can feel the power ebbing off of you guys. It's amazing." It was like she was batting her eyelashes at them, her words had the same effect. The Trappers all turned to look at her.

But there was something else there too. "You feel that?" Duke whispered to Hazel.

Hazel nodded. "She's using Chaos magic. I can't believe I didn't pick up on that before."

And that was Chanda's secret. The thing she had been trying so desperately to shield. He'd felt it as they were walking. Each time her arm brushed against his. She'd been working so hard to tamp down something. He'd assumed it was her feelings—being around an empath made people wary, like he could reach into their hearts and pull out their deepest desires. They had to be willing, open, even if they were trying not to be. Otherwise, his skill was just sending out a soothing pulse to make people comfortable around him. With Hazel, when she was casting, her power called to him, questing for him to bolster and amplify. She was gasoline to his flame and he craved her magic, her essence like nothing he'd ever experienced before.

"I think she keeps it contained," Duke said. "Locked down very tight."

Chaos magic was volatile in the wrong hands, but if you were born with it, it was a gift of immense magic skill. No wonder she looked so paranoid and jumpy all the time. She had the power within to control aggression, to amplify chaos and create change. A tiny flutter could send ripples out that could alter a battle. The wrong kind of flutter could obliterate a city. It was a heavy responsibility. Chaos magic could change minds. A little nudge in a certain direction. He wondered just how much control she had over it, just how much chaos reigned within.

"If either of these two escape, you'll be held responsible." The lead Trapper nodded at Bridget.

"Understood." Bridget motioned to the prisoners. "Chanda, Mahdyia, get back to the stones and set up a triage station. Duke, you and Hazel get started on the containment spell."

Hazel opened her mouth like she was going to argue.

"You know I can bolster you," Duke said quickly.

"The stones are all I need. You should help the injured."

"Tate, Bas, you're with me. Help these guys lift the injured. Be gentle! You don't want to cause any more damage than what's already been done."

And that was that. Everyone got to work.

Hazel didn't wait for him to reply. She was off toward the stones, leaving him trailing after her, marvelling at how she could still think he had nothing to offer her.

✣ 13 ✣

DUKE HADN'T BEEN WRONG. SHE NEEDED SOME KIND OF working relationship with her peers or the next year would be very long. As much as she would love to focus only on her training, she knew that many of the trials that were headed their way would require a team approach. Like this one. Which was why she'd offered to take herself out of the healing game and focus on protection instead. She didn't have to be at the forefront all the time—he was right about that too. She'd let her ego get the best of her earlier.

"You sure you've got this?" Mahdyia asked. She was laying a sleeping bag onto the altar slab, somewhat of a cushion for the patient. "No offence meant, of course, but you look tired as it is."

Hazel ran her fingers over the stone next to her and felt the pulse of its magic course though her. "I'm sorry, Mads. For snapping at you. And...er...zapping you. I was out of line."

Mahdyia paused for a second then flashed her a smile. "Next time, I zap you back."

Hazel laughed. "Deal." She laid her hand flat on the stone. "And don't worry about me. The power here...it's intense."

"Intense like Duke. I mean, Healer Hart?" Mahdyia winked. "The chemistry between you two...hot."

Hazel felt her whole body flush. "I don't know what you're talking about." She ducked around the back of the stone, looking for the right place to concentrate her attention. Avoidance was her best friend.

Mahdyia scoffed. "I don't think the others notice. At least not on your part. They still think he's a leech, that his attention is unwanted. His eyes on you though... Yeah...smoldering."

Hazel winced. That lie was a hard one to swallow. She didn't like sending the message that Duke was a slime ball. He definitely hadn't been listening to her though. And she was tired of everyone thinking they knew what was best for her. Did she want to wrap herself up in his arms and forget about all the stress of the past day? *Hell yes!* But that wouldn't be good for either of them. The Hazel he'd known for the past year was a simpler version of herself. Unfettered by obligations and destinies. It had been a nice fantasy while it lasted but the reality of the situation couldn't be ignored.

"It is unwanted," Hazel whispered before coming back around the stone. "I just need things to be simple. I just need this year to happen already so I can move on with my life."

Mahdyia gave her one of those looks, the kind of look that made Hazel dart her eyes away, focus on anything but the truth. Mahdyia cleared her throat. "Right. Anyway, that Chanda, she's got some skills." She nodded toward the other witch, who was quietly setting up another bed on the other side of the circle. "Chaos right?"

"Yeah." Hazel studied Chanda as she worked to smooth out the bumps on the sleeping bag. She was powerful—a natural talent with Chaos. Hazel should have noticed it before. Now that she knew, there was an aura of power surrounding Chanda.

"She's a good choice to foist Duke on. She's hot for one but that Chaos, that'll sing to his magic. I'm sure he's extremely intrigued as it is."

Hazel frowned. It would? She looked over at Duke, who was moving toward Chanda, saying something Hazel couldn't hear. Something that made Chanda smile. Their hands brushed as he reached out to help her with the sleeping bag she was setting up and she giggled, which seemed to be her go-to response around him. *Fuck.*

Hazel sucked in a deep breath, fighting the urge to go over there and stick her tongue down Duke's throat. Instead, she moved to the back of the stone again.

Let him be intrigued. I have things to do. Very important things.

Hazel pulled her dagger from its sheath. It glittered against the stone. A gift from her mother when she'd come of age. The blade was silver, perpetually polished and forever sharp; it glinted in what little light the night offered. The handle was carved with intricate filigree, a protection spell as well as one of ownership. The blade held her mark and wouldn't work for anyone else, perhaps an unnecessary precaution because it was taboo to use another witch's blade anyway, but she felt it was too precious to leave unprotected.

She laid the knife against her palm and started to pull the spell she needed from her memory, the words flowing through her mind as she drew the edge across her flesh. One hand, then the other. A spell of this magnitude needed quite a bit of blood sacrifice. She sucked in a deep breath, caught a whisper of Duke's voice and shut him out of her head. No time for that. With hands flat against the stone and magic snaking up her arms, she blocked out all distractions and got to work.

"This witch of yours, building the containment spell... She know what she's doing?"

Hazel heard the voice on the periphery of her consciousness. An intrusion that interrupted her spell casting. She assessed the threads of her magic. Everything was secure and had been for a while. She'd just been strengthening, paranoid perhaps, but she didn't want to take any chances.

"She's one of the best," Tate said. "I mean, out of all of us, she *is* the best."

"Must be powerful if she knew my capture was that sick." It was the lead Trapper speaking, his gruff voice one Hazel wouldn't forget anytime soon.

"We all knew she was that sick. Hazel just has a way of getting to the heart of the matter."

"Yeah, well, I hope you're right because if these two get loose... Well, let's just say there's likely to be a shitload of injuries as a result."

Hazel pulled herself out of her spell and pushed away from the stone. She mourned the loss of being immersed in such power but her head was fuzzy and she wanted to concentrate on what was being said.

"What did they do?" Tate asked. "I mean, what makes them so dangerous?"

"I probably shouldn't be telling you this—it'll give you nightmares." But the way he said it sounded like that's exactly want he wanted to do.

"I can handle it." Tate's voice quivered only a little. He chuckled in an attempt to cover it up.

Hazel was going to reveal herself—she wanted to hear what the Trapper was going to say but she didn't want to do it under cloak and dagger. She started around the stone.

"They're Fire witches." The Trapper's voice stopped Hazel from moving another inch. "Been working their way up and down the woods, peddling fire spells that are too potent for the average witch or human to use."

"No way! We were just at a village where a little girl was burned."

Lily. Hazel sucked in a deep breath.

"Yeah, well, that's probably their handiwork. Anyone else injured there?"

"No, but the girl was pretty badly burned. We helped her... Or, I should say Hazel did. She's amazing, really. She pulled the fire magic from—"

"I'll need to get coordinates so we can check it out. Make sure the danger has been contained," the Trapper interrupted.

"I neutralized the spell myself months ago." Duke's voice joined the conversation. "I can give you directions once we're done here, but the tribe is wary of strangers."

"Good, and don't worry. The humans know we're there to protect them, but we don't actually need to get that close. A mile outside and we can ensure there's nothing residual hanging around that can cause problems." The Trapper paused. "These two, they sell fire spells to whoever they can—typically a low level witch or practicing human who is craving power but has no experience. Then they go off and wait. The spell is designed to consume flesh only. So they wait for it to explode and annihilate the village and then they go in there and salvage what's left."

Savages.

Hazel shuddered. These Fire witches had meant to destroy that whole village? They had used a little girl as their messenger? Lily would be disfigured for life because of them.

Hazel came around the side of the stone, startling the men. "How many times have they done this?"

"I don't—"

"How many times?" she growled.

"At least five that we know of. Six if we count the girl this one just told me about."

"How many lives lost?"

"Countless. The villages don't keep up to date records all the time. Could be hundreds."

Hazel looked over at where the interns were working on the

Fire witches, bedside manner in full effect. "They killed innocents."

"Yeah, heartless bastards," the Trapper agreed. "Now receiving the best care around, from what I can see." His tone was dry, compassionless and full of judgment.

"That's our mandate, Hazel, you know that," Tate said, his voice quiet, like it was meant only for her. "Doesn't matter what they did. If they need care, we are here to serve."

Hazel took in his words. She looked at Duke, who was watching her, arms crossed, face an unreadable shield. Her anger still burned. "You're right." And it sucked. Every witch was entitled to the best care they could offer, no matter the circumstances.

She moved to the first slab, fury still riding just beneath the surface.

Mahdyia glanced up as Hazel approached. She looked worn out, her hair pulled out of her ponytail in wisps around her face. There was dirt smudged under her eye and a scratch on her cheek. Bridget was on the other side of the slab working on the unconscious woman. Hazel could feel the magic swirling around them as Mahdyia moved her hands over the Fire witch's torso.

"What's the prognosis?"

"She'll live." Mahdyia swiped her hair back with her forearm. "Looks like she was hit a few times with a powerful surge of something." She motioned toward the Trappers and their weapons, indicating where the *something* likely came from. "She has four broken ribs and some internal bruising."

The collar had been removed and the witch was unconscious. She looked harmless lying there, her face relaxed, a spray of freckles across her nose. Not exactly the picture of a killer.

"She has death clinging to her still." Hazel ran her hands along the witch's body, not touching, just waiting for a telltale jolt to direct her.

"Her head." Tate was there now, his hands hovering at the witch's temples. "Feels like a brain bleed."

Hazel nodded. The humans had highly skilled surgeons to do these kinds of operations, ways of opening the skull and fixing problems. Witches had to use other means since they were dealing with magic injuries and a not-so-human anatomy. Made a little differently, witches required specialized care of their own.

"How will you proceed?" Bridget stepped back, crossing her arms.

"I can pull the magic out," Hazel offered. "Slowly." She glanced toward where Duke was busy working with Chanda and Bas on the other patient. "If someone else can manage the pain, keep her under?"

"I can do that," Tate said. "I'll monitor her heart as well. Make sure we don't lose her."

"I've never done a brain repair before." Mahdyia looked hesitantly at Bridget.

"You know the procedure. Follow the damage path and as Hazel pulls the magic out, you be there to repair. You should aim to stop the bleeding and reverse the trauma. I'll be here if you have questions." Bridget took up a spot on a nearby boulder, obviously intent on supervising only. "What are you waiting for?"

Mahdyia looked at Hazel, resignation there. She lacked confidence and Hazel didn't understand why.

"You've got this," Hazel said then moved into position. "You ready?"

Tate nodded, his hands still hovering over the witch's head.

Hazel nodded one more time at Mahdyia then closed her eyes. This was going to be tricky. As soon as she entered the woman's magical sphere, she was hit with her thoughts. A by-product of Hazel's gift. On the one hand, it was very useful to be able to assess the strength and scope of a witch's magic, especially when undoing the damage it caused when used as a weapon. On the other hand, it gave her direct access to the inner workings of a witch's mind and that was not always very appealing. When she'd been in Bas's head, his thoughts had been mostly clear, distinct, perhaps cloudy in parts, the effects of normal levels of self-delusion and perception. She hadn't probed too deeply, but he was a good person—a good witch underneath it all.

Things were different when she entered this witch's thought stream though. Very different. Dark and dirty. A grit that made it difficult for Hazel to see the edges of the damage and retract the magic that was there. She didn't like the taste of it in her head; it was worse than chaos, it was incomprehensible madness.

The flashes of rage, fire burning, echoes of laughter, glee at the destruction. They watched, *oh goddess*, they watched the fires consume. Took pleasure in the screams. Hazel wanted to pull out. She wanted to block the voices in her head, the laughter, the horror of it all. But then she felt the margin of the damage—devastating damage. If she didn't pull the magic out, it would continue to destroy everything in its path and the witch would die. She deserved to be punished for what she'd done. She and her partner were monsters. But it wasn't for Hazel to pass judgment or to mete out punishments. This woman would go to the Scrub. She'd suffer immeasurably for her crimes. All Hazel had to do was make sure she got there healthy and ready to face the consequences.

Hazel gulped back the hard lump in her throat, reached out for Mahdyia's magic and pulled her closer, giving her a path to follow as Hazel did her work.

Mahdyia didn't resist. Once she saw the source, she zoned in. Hazel followed her example and Tate kept everyone alive.

❧ 14 ❧

"SHE'S DEAD! SHE'S DEAD! YOU KILLED DELILAH!"

The screams shredded through Hazel's foggy brain. She felt the sharp edge of a blade against her throat, the rough press of fingers digging into her waist, holding her back against a hard body.

"She's not dead!" Mahdyia was trying to speak calmly, but Hazel could see the desperation in her eyes. "She's breathing, look!"

The grip on Hazel tightened, the blade dug in, stinging as it drew blood. "Why isn't she moving?" The rough voice behind her was dangerous and deadly, like there was nothing to lose.

"She was badly injured. We've been working on her, trying to heal her."

"You're killing her!"

"No," Hazel croaked, wincing as the movement caused the blade to cut into her skin.

"No? Why won't she open her fucking eyes then!" The rough voice growled into her ear. "Wake her up!"

"Drop your weapon!" The Trappers were surrounding them,

lethal looking guns drawn, all pointing at Hazel and the witch who held her. "Drop the blade or we'll shoot."

"You can't, you'll hit Hazel!" Mahdyia said.

"You can't!" The witch laughed, mockingly, raising his hand to brandish a flame. "You can't get close enough to save her. It's too late for all of you!"

Hazel felt the heat of it, smelled the singeing of her hair. She could hear and feel the magic building in the Trapper's weapons as well. They'd take the shot, kill her to spare the rest. She wondered if her destiny really was up to interpretation.

"Drop your weapon, dissolve that spell!" the lead Trapper bellowed, trigger finger twitching.

"Don't shoot!" Bas stepped in front of the Trappers, blocking Hazel from their line of sight. He had his hands up. "I can help." He turned before getting a reply, only glancing at Hazel for a second before focusing on the witch who held her.

"Fredrick, right?" Bas still held his hands up. "I worked on you, over there." He pointed toward the ground where a sleeping bag was still laid out, where Chanda stood clutching her arm. She'd been hurt somehow, probably when Fredrick woke to find himself free of his collar. "I healed you. Me and the other Healers here, we aren't out to hurt you. We're here to help you."

"Wake her up!" Fredrick screamed. His movement brought the fire closer, making Hazel feel like her face was burning.

Where was Duke? She shifted her eyes, trying to find him.

"We can't, not yet," Bas said.

"You lie!" With another roar, Fredrick launched his ball of fire.

Bas maneuvered out of the way. The Trappers ducked. The fireball exploded against one of the stones. Magic splattering like it was filled with gel, flames sticking. To get that on your skin would be devastating. Everyone seemed to realize it at the same time.

"Get down, now!" The Trappers screamed, weapons raised.

Bas jumped forward, his lips moving, his eyes set on Fredrick.

Hazel felt his spell launch, she felt it strike her like a sticky web, enveloping her, dosing her magic until it was only a muted flame and then nothing.

Fredrick screeched then let her go in a frenzy of movement, trying to pull the webbing off of himself.

Hazel stumbled to her knees, hands in the dirt, the Trappers moving in. And then Duke was there, practically covering her with his body, his arms wrapped tightly around her.

Fredrick was screaming, whether from Bas's spell or the reality that he was being collared again. Either way, he was incensed.

"You okay, Hazel?" Duke panted into her ear, his voice quivering slightly.

She pushed herself up to her knees, flexing her arms to get him to let her go. "I'm not hurt," she said.

He sat back too, letting her go so he could stand.

Mahdyia was standing above, worry etched on her face. "You sure, Hazel?"

Hazel looked around. Bas was watching her, gauging her reaction no doubt. "I can't feel anything." It was disorienting. "I think...I think I've been bound."

She'd never felt anything like it. No pulse of magic beating at her or humming through her.

"It won't last forever," Bas said. "You'll be fine by morning."

"It's so...so...sticky!" Not in the literal sense, but magically speaking, it was like super glue.

"I drew on your magic and his, Fredrick, to wield it. Custom made. Works better that way."

Hazel was impressed and also kind of disturbed. It was so quiet all of a sudden in her head.

"You cast a binding spell? On Hazel?" Mahdyia looked ready to explode as she turned on him. "Are you some kind of idiot? Do you know what you've done?"

"No, Mads, it's okay." Hazel looked from Mahdyia to Duke.

"I'm okay, really." She tried to stand but her legs were wobbly. After a failed attempt, she let Duke help her up, leaning on him once she was on her feet. "He did what he had to do. No harm done."

"Your powers though!" Mahdyia was at her other side now, propping her up, checking her out. "He had no right! It was reckless."

"It's okay, Mads." Hazel touched heads with her cousin. "I'm okay. It feels..." She looked at Bas again. "Peaceful once you get used to it." She laughed at the idea of that. No pressure. No expectation. "Thank you for that." She nodded at Bas and didn't exactly know if she was thanking him for saving her life or thanking him for giving her freedom, if only for a few hours.

He wasn't sure about her, she could tell from his narrowed stare. She smiled and tried to convey gratitude. He nodded then turned away, walking over to Chanda and Tate.

"We've got this," the lead Trapper said as he hauled Fredrick up by the collar. "She's had enough healing time. Wake her up and get her on her feet." He pointed to the other witch, Delilah, who was only now starting to rouse. They collared her immediately while she was still disoriented and pliable, not wanting to have another explosive situation, Hazel was sure. Delilah wasn't totally healed but no one argued with the Trappers. Delilah was well enough to make the journey. The Healers at the Scrub would tend to her there.

Hazel rubbed the side of her face. Dizziness struck her suddenly, her head spinning. "I think I need to lie down," Hazel said. She meant for Mahdyia to hear her and do something about it, but it was Duke who responded.

"I'll get you to your tent."

And there was no argument. Not from Hazel or from Mahdyia. Just Duke leading her away from the stones that she couldn't feel, and away from the witches that she couldn't sense.

Bliss. Silence. And yes, peace.

Duke had to practically carry her up the hill. She was giggling by the time he got her to her tent.

"You okay?" His frown was deep, making him look intensely concerned.

"I'm...I'm great!" Hazel giggled again. "I can't feel anything! For the first time in my life. I mean, it's weird, sure, to not have any power but it's so...so...quiet."

He was looking down at her, she was looking up, their bodies close, his arms around her suddenly, hand splayed on her back, the other in her hair. She tilted her head, locked eyes with him.

His eyes *were* smoldering. Burning her up with the heat of his lust.

"Kiss me," she said, lifting herself on her tip toes. "Kiss me, now!"

"Hazel," he groaned and then pressed his lips to hers. Gentle at first, tender, soft.

Her body zinged and when he started to pull back, she flung her arms around his neck and pulled him down. Fierce passion exploded through her, her lips devouring his, tongue entangled with his. Swirling, tasting, sucking, moaning as they tumbled into her tent.

She couldn't get his clothes off fast enough, getting tangled in her own in the process. Naked was good. Her skin was so sensitive, responding to his hands, his lips. She licked her way up his chest, circling his nipples, nipping then soothing. She slid her body against Duke's, feeling his muscles tense, his hands moving to her hips, his cock jerked up to greet her as she rolled herself back up to sit on top of him, then sheathed herself to the hilt.

She liked riding him. Loved how he felt under her. How his hands moulded to her breasts, tweaking her nipples, cupping her flesh. She pumped him fast, abrading her clit with each stroke, a delicious sensation, the pulse of her rising orgasm making her moan long and low, her eyes closed, head tilted back.

He rolled her, so her legs were over his shoulders, ankles to ears, his hands on her hips as he drove into her harder, faster, going as deep as her body would allow, his balls smacking her ass, his expression fierce. Claiming her. Marking her. She shivered and closed her eyes against it.

Too much...too much.

She couldn't stop the wave of her climax from cresting, not when he was driving so deep, stroking so relentlessly. She couldn't stop the flashes of ecstasy as he erupted into her, plunging until every last spasm was wrung from her body and his.

He stared down at her, letting her legs slide from his shoulders, his hands guiding her feet to the floor, his semi-hard cock still buried deep, still pulsing.

His eyes sparkled like they always did, looking stunning. "You are—"

She flexed her hips, rolling her pussy along his cock, interrupting whatever he was about to say.

His eyes flashed wide, then hooded immediately, his train of thought no doubt lost.

She fingered her nipples, flicking as he had done, watching as lust fell on his face, his eyes hungry for her.

His hands were on her hips again and he flipped her around, barely breaking contact as he did. Plunging back into her from behind, deep thrusts that had her moaning all over again, lost in the sensation of being fucked good and hard.

How could she have ever thought she'd had enough of this man? How could she survive a lifetime without him?

He reached forward to cup her breasts, holding them tight in his palms while he drove into her, his body covering hers so that all she could feel, all she could smell, all she could hear, was him.

With one hand bracing her weight, she ran her other hand down to her pussy, forking her fingers around his cock as he thrust, giving him more friction so that he groaned louder with each stroke. Squeezing her tits harder until he finally released her, pinching down to her nipples, flicking the hard points until she was crying out the same way.

She moved her hand up, fingers pressed into her clit, rubbing until her climax rose again—wisps at first, a slow delicious rise that made her want to squirm away from its intensity.

His cock stiffened more, his thrusts became urgent, his need palpable, matching hers. She cried out as her orgasm rammed her, his following close behind. Pumping her full of his cum until all she could do was collapse to the floor, wrung out, spent and giggling once again.

"What's so funny?" He pulled out of her then laid down, taking her in his arms as he did, breathing heavy as he pressed his lips to her forehead

"You and your empathness." She giggled again. "I just realized that's why it always feels so damn good. So damn impossibly good. It's your magic." Of course he could make her feel that way—his powers were all about stoking those emotions, feeding into them. Just like Mahdyia had said, he was honey to her bee.

He kissed her again, then pulled back so she could see his eyes. "You feel your own magic back?"

Hazel frowned, confused. She tested her powers. Nothing. "Nope." She giggled again before nestling into his chest with a sigh. "Blissfully silent."

There was a pause. Just his breathing and his heart thundering. Lulling her to sleep.

"Then it's impossible for you to be influenced by my magic. The binding would prevent that from happening. My magic only works on you if it's got a source to connect with."

Her eyes flew open wide. *What?*

He gripped her harder so she couldn't rise, capturing her in his embrace.

"So you can't say it's not real," he whispered into her hair.

§

Okay, that threw her. Big time.

She tried to poke holes in it. Tried to will her magic back so she could prove that she had a spark of something that he could stoke. But there was nothing. No way to prove him wrong. Her thoughts swirled for hours and all the while she couldn't bear to rise from his embrace. She kept her head on his chest and listened to his heart thunder away.

Exhaustion won though and somehow she managed to fall asleep. But while she was sleeping, she was dreaming about her mother and the Circle and chasing something...something that was just out of her reach.

She'd woke in a panic, surprised that Duke didn't stir. She took it as a sign to get out of there.

Her powers were back. She felt the zing of the magic around her, including Duke's. The peace she had felt the night before had vanished and rather than sit there staring at his gorgeous body, mulling over his words and how they made her feel, she slipped out, washed up and put her clothes on.

She fingered her mother's amulet, the stone smooth under her thumb. She'd put it back on to remind herself of obligation, of duty. She slipped it under her tank top, hated the cold feel of it against her skin.

It was early enough that the others hadn't stirred, the sun just cresting the horizon, the night's chill still frosting the grass.

She sucked in a deep lungful of crisp air and sat quietly on the stone slab altar. It had been nice to be without powers for a bit but to go permanently without them was not something she craved. Her powers were threaded through her being, part of her personality. Without them, she'd acted impulsively, irresponsibly.

What Duke had said was also problematic for her. So the passion was real. Fine. Her feelings not influenced by his magic. Fine.

No, it *wasn't* fine. She sighed. What she felt for him was not fine. It was distracting. It was powerful. It conflicted with everything she thought she understood. And yet, it felt so right. So damn good.

She didn't believe in soul mates. That was always just fairy tale and fantasy. She didn't love him.

But she sure did like him a lot. Like a lot a lot.

"I won't put that in my report." Bridget came up from behind, two steaming cups in her hands.

She startled Hazel out of her thoughts. "Um, what?"

Bridget offered her a cup then sat down next to her on the stone. "What happened last night. I won't put that in my report to your mother."

Hazel took a sip of the tea, peppermint with honey. It slid down her throat, giving her a pleasant burn all the way to her stomach. "Oh yeah, with the Fire witches? Right, better to keep Mother in the dark on that."

Bridget snorted into her cup. "Well, that and Healer Hart, right?" She nudged Hazel.

Hazel sputtered her next sip.

"Oh don't get me wrong, I totally get it. Did get it, in fact, back in the day." She winked at Hazel, grinning. "So I know he's too fine a male specimen to pass up." She patted Hazel's knee before standing. "Don't worry about your mother finding out. What happens in the field, stays in the field. This is your time to enjoy yourself and I won't be the one to roadblock that."

Hazel's heart was thundering. She struggled to keep her face neutral. "You and Duke..."

"Oh yeah, years ago." Bridget chuckled, waving her hand in dismissal. "We had a thing when he was an intern. No worries, I get it." She winked again. "So have fun!"

Hazel had a frozen smile on her face. Frozen like frosty and firmly held as she watched Bridget walk away.

She'd had a thing with Duke? *A thing with Duke?*

Hazel tossed her tea out of the cup to splatter to the ground.

Funny that Duke had never said a word to Hazel about that.

Not *haha* funny either.

Hazel stood from the stone. She put her cup down where she'd been sitting. Brushed her clothing for twigs or dirt or whatever, squared her shoulders, and then headed to her tent. Where Duke was.

She didn't like that he'd been with Bridget. And she didn't like that she didn't like that.

❧ 15 ❧

SHE DIDN'T LIKE THE TASTE OF JEALOUSY IN HER MOUTH, OR the feel of it in her heart.

Vulnerability was a weakness she didn't have time for.

So she stopped her trek to the tent. Stopped herself cold.

"Morning, Hazel," Tate said. He was starting to dismantle his tent. "You sleep okay?"

Hazel nodded. "Yes, I did." She frowned as her brain circled around a sudden plan. "Hey, Tate, can I ask you something?"

Tate stopped what he was doing. "Sure thing. Shoot."

Duke had asked her once if she was so secretive because she had another lover. If there was someone else keeping her from him. That was before he'd known who she was, who her mother was, but that didn't mean it couldn't apply now.

Hazel moved closer to Tate. "You know what's been going on with Du-Healer Hart?"

"The unwanted attention?" Tate gave a knowing look. "Oh yeah, I can see it. I've been trying to keep him from getting to you. Sorry that I haven't been on it as much. Things got crazy last night."

Hazel rested her hand on his forearm and leaned into him. "I appreciate your help. I was wondering if you'd be interested in helping me a bit longer? I mean, while we're on the field trip."

Tate's eyes were wide, his cheeks growing red. "Of course, anything you need."

"Well," Hazel said. "If you and I pretended...uh...you know..."

"To be interested in each other?"

"Well, yeah, I mean, just so that Healer Hart gets the message. I think if he thought I was interested in someone else..."

Tate was nodding with her words. "Brilliant idea! I'm totally on board."

"You don't mind?" Hazel winced. "It's just pretend."

He smiled and patted her hand. "I know you have an important destiny, Hazel. I'm honored to be your friend and happy to help."

Hazel beamed, problem solved. "Thanks, Tate!" She stretched up on her tiptoes and kissed his cheek, or meant to anyway. Tate turned his head so that their lips brushed. "Oh!"

Tate's face went scarlet. "Hehe, sorry." He shrugged. "Better for the show though, right?"

Hazel's face was hot too. She nodded. "Better for the show."

"Hazel!" Duke's voice echoed from across the stones. "Can I speak with you over here?"

Tate smirked down at her. "Uh oh!" He winked. "You need me to step in?"

Hazel smiled back, shook her head. "I'll handle it."

She met Duke halfway, ready for battle. Far enough away from the group that they wouldn't hear the argument, not far enough that they wouldn't see it though.

"So you leave my bed and immediately go off and flirt with another guy?" Duke was fuming, his nostrils actually flaring.

"It's my bed and no, that's not what I do."

"So what was that?" He waved toward Tate.

Hazel shrugged. "He's a sweet guy. With no history of sleeping with a Master Healer. And he has no interest in Bridget." She hadn't meant to say that—it just slipped out.

Duke opened his mouth, closed it, narrowed his eyes at her. "What does Bridget have to do with this?"

It was Hazel's turn to narrow her eyes at him. "Why don't you tell me?"

"We have a history."

Hazel crossed her arms. "So I've heard."

"And what, you thought I was a virgin when we met?"

What would be wrong with being a virgin?

"I asked you how you knew her. You had an opportunity to tell me about your past," she said instead.

"I didn't think it was important." He mirrored her stance, arms crossed, shoulders squared, eyes locked on hers.

"So you get to decide what I need to know? Just like you get to decide what my destiny really is? What I'm really meant to do with my life?"

"No...I—"

"That's all you've been doing here. Mocking my beliefs, questioning my life. You want me to believe you care about me? Well, then, you should accept that I can make decisions about my life for myself. If you really cared about me, you'd do that." She uncrossed her arms and took a step back. "And you'd leave me the hell alone because I can't give you what you want me to give you."

A beat of silence had her heart ramming hard against her chest.

He lifted his finger, pointing at her and stabbing the air. "You don't fool me, Hazel Knight. You want me to believe that you don't love me. You want to push me away, to piss me off so that I turn my back on you. But I won't. I can't. I'm going to see this through until the end. Until you step into that Circle and shut me out for real. Until then, until that moment, it's fair game. That's life, Hazel. Things don't always go as planned. I may not have been part of your plans, you maybe didn't factor me in, but I'm here, and I love you and I'm not going anywhere. No matter what you do to push me away. So go ahead. Tell me you hate me. Tell me you want nothing to do with me. Flirt with another guy. Lie about your feelings. Until I hear it from your heart, I won't believe it."

Hazel balked. How dare he! "You presumptuous ass—"

He leaned forward and brushed his hand over her cheek. "I won't rest until you understand what we could do together if you stay with me. If you choose me. Deny it all you want. Flirt with Tate all you want. I know, deep down, what your heart craves."

"And there you go again, trying to tell me what I'm feeling."

"I'm an empath, Hazel, and you're wide open to me. I've always known your heart even when I didn't know your identity. I feel your uncertainty, your fear, your dedication. You're blinded by that dedication. If you choose to join the Circle, I'll accept it, I will, but not until I know you've been honest with yourself. Honest about your feelings."

"I won't sleep with you again." Hazel couldn't think of what to say other than that. A small thing she could control. Fine, he could see into her heart, or whatever—she'd never been good about concealing her feelings. Her mother could read her like a book as well. Which was why her usual tactic with her mother was to evade and deflect. Evade and deflect would have to work with Duke as well.

"Everything okay here, Hazel?" Tate asked, his looming figure coming up next to her.

Duke didn't bother to look at the other man. Instead, he cocked an eyebrow at her then turned and walked away.

"Healer Hart!" Chanda bounded toward him. "Can you take a look at my arm? I heard you have some skill with deep bruises."

"I enlisted Chanda's help," Tate leaned into her to say. "They seemed to be getting along yesterday."

Hazel watched Duke put his hands on Chanda and felt jealousy lick up her spine once again. "Yeah, good idea, I'm going to go dismantle my tent."

"I'll help you," Tate said cheerfully.

With another look in Duke's direction, Hazel sighed, then started up the hill. "That would be great, Tate, thanks."

Why was it that Hazel was surrounded by people who seemed to always know what was best for her? Like her destiny was locked in place.

Hazel stutter-stepped on that thought.

Like her destiny was etched in stone.

For the first time in her life, she had a niggling of something that was so foreign she wanted to reject it outright—vile, toxic doubt.

What if her destiny wasn't so clear after all? What if she *did* have a choice?

"Hey, Hazel, you okay?" Tate was at her side, helping her to come the rest of the way up to her tent. "Thought you might slide down the hill there."

Hazel frowned, rubbing her hand over her heart. She looked down the hill at Duke, who was still touching Chanda. Her heart ached more. He glanced up at her then, eyes fierce, frown firmly in place. He knew. Oh goddess, he knew.

Her uncertainty was shining back at her, reflected in his gaze. But there was something else too. He'd said he loved her and she hadn't even flinched. Why? Because of all the things she couldn't get a handle on, that wasn't one of them. Duke wore his heart on his sleeve and whether he said the words or not, she knew his heart was hers. What she didn't know was how he expected her to give him hers when it belonged to the Circle.

So she did what she did best. She avoided him. Not

completely hard to do once they got back on the trail that was not a trail. The forest was thicker on the other side of the stones, the magic headier. The general noises were different too. Animal sounds odd, otherworldly.

"I've heard folk tales about feral familiars living in these woods," Tate said. He'd taken up as her walking partner again, letting her move ahead when the trail narrowed, lifting away branches that threatened to knock her out or tangle in her hair. At one point, he'd even lifted her over a fallen log. That had been over the top; she'd frozen like a rod. He'd easily put her back down and whispered an apology. Quick learner.

"It's not a folk tale," Bridget said over her shoulder. "There are ferals roaming around here. Some of those noises you're hearing are familiars."

"They're drawn to this place. The magic is so potent," Duke confirmed. Chanda was next to him again, walking side by side when she could.

Although Duke wasn't as attentive to Chanda as Tate was with her, Hazel did note when he pointed out a tripping hazard or chuckled at something she said or let her hand linger a tad too long on his arm.

It wasn't fair. These feelings of jealousy. The fact that he knew she had those feelings. She wanted her mind to be quieted and was half-tempted to ask Bas to bind her again.

"I've heard they're dangerous when they've gone wild," Tate said. "Untamed familiars only cause trouble."

"My mother had a familiar," Bas said, startling everyone enough that no one seemed to know what to say. He cleared his throat. "A cat, of course. She loved that thing to death."

Familiars typically attached themselves to human witches. A magical companion that bolstered a human's powers and offered some element of protection. It was rare to see a witch from any clan with one. It suggested weakness. Wrongly suggested, but as with most prejudices, it didn't have to be based on fact, only belief.

"She was an apothecary, pretty old school. Trained under her father in the old country." Bas wasn't talking at any of them in particular, that was clear. He kept his eyes on the trail, his tone even but his shoulders were tense, like a coil that was ready to spring. "Her familiar, Echo, came to her when she was..." He paused, cleared his throat. "In need. A stray, already a cranky old fucker of a tomcat. He was wild, untrained, would spit and hiss if you looked at it the wrong way. Hated men." He chuckled awkwardly. "But that cat stayed with her right up until... Well, until the end. Damn cat threw himself into the fire."

"Your mother was burned?" He'd said as much the day before but Hazel prodded anyway. If he was talking, she wanted to know what happened.

"Her shop was targeted, yeah. A kid died, one she'd been treating. The humans, they turned on her. Got themselves into a frenzy. Even the sheriff turned his back on her. It was a mob. I was away—" He coughed. "I wasn't there when it happened. I saw the aftermath, heard about the cat. I believe he was trying to get her out but she was trapped in the back. The door had been deliberately barred. He didn't leave her. He stayed until the end."

"Oh fuck." Chanda covered her mouth.

Hazel understood now, why he hated humans so much. Why he was so resistant to work with them.

"Anyway, that's not why I'm telling you this. I didn't mean to tell you that actually." He mumbled the last part, like he was silently chiding himself for the spill. "My point is, familiars are loyal as fuck, so saying that the wild ones are dangerous is bullshit. When they find their witch, when they choose you, they'll fight alongside until the bitter end."

Everyone got quiet, lost in their own thoughts. Hazel was lost to hers, cycling around Bas and what she'd seen in his head. Puzzle pieces clicking together. When she'd been in there, she'd felt so much shame, so much pain and so much hatred. She hadn't understood at the time. Hadn't made the connection because she hadn't known about his mother but it made sense now. He'd said he'd been gone when she was killed and for some reason, in some way, Bas felt responsible for her death.

"So, since we're all about the sharing," Chanda said with a glance toward Duke. "I guess you guys figured out that I'm endowed with Chaos." She looked over her shoulder. "I mean, I know Hazel has it figured out, what with her ability to pick up on that kind of thing."

Duke shrugged. "You have nothing to be ashamed of. Your gift is impressive."

"It's dirty magic." She raised her hand. "I know, I know, that's not politically correct or whatever but it's true. Slime ball magic. I've heard it all before. I can corrupt, I can persuade. I can make a situation very, very bad."

"Were you born with it?" Duke asked. He was curious. It was a rare skill, especially for a Healer.

"Yep. Had it all my life. Had to learn the hard way that controlling it, keeping it contained, was the only way to deal with it."

"I'd imagine that you've faced quite a bit of adversity because of it," Hazel said, sympathy clear in her tone. "It's strong. It must take so much energy to contain."

"Yeah, it does. It's exhausting actually." Chanda sighed. "My parents didn't know what to do with me. A Chaos witch, what a disaster for the Healers of my family. Such an embarrassment." She chuckled bitterly. "I'm not whining. My parents are good people. There's a tradition of Healers in my family though and a Chaos witch just didn't fit. Much too flashy, too dangerous for them. I learned how to control it. For a while I just worked very hard to suppress it, so I wouldn't embarrass them, or hurt anyone. But they didn't ask me to snuff it completely, or to deny its existence. That was on me. They hired some of the best Battle witches around to help me with controlling it once I realized that I couldn't contain it forever."

"You're Battle trained?" Bridget asked, her curiosity obviously piqued. She gave Chanda a once over, an appraisal that could mean many things for Bridget. Her lust wasn't restricted to any gender. She was an equal opportunity kind of lover. Or so Duke had heard.

"Yeah, I am. Had to learn Battle magic to better control my Chaos." Chanda didn't notice Bridget's hungry gaze.

Duke wondered just how many of the interns Bridget was set to corrupt or, as she put it, educate off the books.

"And they didn't want you? I'm surprised they didn't recruit you right then and there," Bridget said as she sidled closer to Chanda.

"Oh, they tried. But like I said, my parents wouldn't have it. I was going to be a Healer, no negotiation. Follow in my parents' footsteps. I do have a lifetime offer to join the Battle witches if I want though." Chanda shrugged. "It took a lot, like trying to fit a square peg in a round hole, ya know? I learned how to use it incrementally with healing. It helps with the patients. Gives me a way to sooth them."

"I've seen that," Duke acknowledged. "You are very good with your bedside manner."

"Thank you." Chanda blushed.

Duke felt Hazel, her energy spiking. Was she jealous? He

didn't probe. She'd made it clear that he needed to keep his distance. The last thing he wanted was to push her away more. She'd found out about Bridget, fine. He wasn't exactly keeping it a secret. Okay, he was totally keeping it a secret. His past with Bridget was complicated and tied up in a lot of emotion. She'd used him, then stolen from him and finally discarded him. At the time it had been devastating, and that was embarrassing in and of itself. Now he saw it for what it was, despite his reluctance to prove her right. It had been a learning experience. A hard one. He'd learned to protect what he valued and to be limited in his trust. Not a bad idea when you were dealing with magic wielding folks.

Hazel finding out about it the way she had, mainly not from him, was not the way he wanted things to go. She deserved to know about his history. Even the less appealing parts. For that to happen though, he needed time alone with her to talk. Something she had proven to be very resistant to.

"I've got a question." Bas's voice was gruff and sharp. "Doesn't it bother you, Tate, to have such a feminine skill? Elemental right? That's women's magic."

"Why would that bother me?" Tate stood taller, whether subconscious or not, his spine straightened, chest pumped up. He was a big boy with big magic. "I'm not the only male with Elemental skills."

"Yeah, but you are rare. Come on, admit it. You got teased a lot as a kid right?" Bas was smirking over his shoulder. Deflecting, no doubt, the discomfort he felt for unloading his personal history on everyone. That over-share had been surprising.

"Hey, listen man, I get that you had a shitty, traumatizing experience with life. Your mom dying, that sucks, but I'm not rising to the bait. My mother is a white witch, endowed with Earth magic and so am I. I think having some sense of femininity within helps me better understand my patients. Gives me more compassion. And it certainly helps with the ladies."

Bas snorted.

Duke had to admit, that last bit wasn't very convincing. Tate screamed *nice guy*. Too nice. Too safe. It was more likely Tate had seen the bad side of the friend zone way too many times. Hazel might be taking some comfort in her newfound closeness to Tate but Duke didn't feel threatened. Much. Duke would much rather it be him who was at her side at the moment but he could wait.

"What, like Hazel? You're sweet on her, we can all see it. Flirting with the Promised One, as if you had a chance."

"Enough, Worm," Bridget cautioned, then lowered her voice. "We discussed the attitude, remember?"

Bas snapped his gaze to her, then disregarded her words. "Hazel the closet case. I bet she's still a virg—"

"Enough!" Duke had him in a headlock and choking before he could finish that thought. "Show some respect."

He wrestled Bas to the ground, only letting go when his face was so red it looked like it would burst.

Everyone had stopped walking and were staring at him. Duke challenged anyone to say anything, meeting their eyes one at a time. No one did.

He stepped over Bas. "Time for lunch. The Wilting Trees are over that ridge. We'll stop there." Duke turned to Bridget, ignoring Bas as he grunted and groaned his way to his feet. "You better put a muzzle on your dog before I do."

Bridget had her arms crossed and was eyeing him, mouth open like she was going to argue. Instead she gave a tight nod.

He turned back to face the other interns. "Follow me, and keep your eyes open. Weird shit sometimes happens at the Wilting Trees."

"So why are we going to stop there then?" Chanda asked, fear edging her words.

"Because it's cool weird shit."

Duke loved this place. The trees were huge and gnarled, with limbs that stretched out like octopus tentacles. Thick, twisted, offering curves to sit in and plenty of shade to rest under. It was covered in places with soft moss that made a rather comfortable bed in a pinch. The air was fresher there, it seemed. Earthy, mossy, sure, but not in an unpleasant way. The trees gave off this sweet aroma that made you want to inhale deeply with each breath. Duke had always found it relaxing. He didn't get to visit as often as he liked but when he was in Scotland, this was one of his must-go-to places. He found peace there and a place to collect his thoughts.

It was also enchanted.

"Hazel, come here." Duke motioned to her, ignoring the glare that followed. "Here, stand next to me."

She came, obviously reluctantly.

"Hold out your hand." He didn't give her a chance to protest and grabbed her hand, flipping it palm up before letting go. "Blade?"

"What are you doing?" She pulled out her blade despite the question.

"I assume you know the basics of shadow casting?" He had his own blade out and quickly made a cut to his palm, motioning her to do the same.

"Of course." She drew the blade across her hand. "I know the basic spell."

"Recite it." He folded their hands together and felt the jolt of united magic. It was heady and made him dizzy. "Trust me." He winked.

Hazel narrowed her eyes for a second longer, then did as he asked, reciting a simple spell that would summon the shadows. While she spoke, he dosed her with his power, amplifying her magic by stoking it deeper so that it cascaded like a wave in every direction.

The leaves on the trees rustled, like a strong wind had suddenly taken up.

"Keep going," Duke encouraged, loving the vibration of her power as it shivered over his fingers, down his arm, along his spine, to his feet and straight into the ground.

She said the spell again. And again. The trees were swaying up high, sending beams of sunlight through the dense foliage.

There was a hush. A sudden silence. He could feel the expectation of the interns around them and then, like a rush sweeping them one by one, he felt their awe.

"Hazel, look," he whispered. "Shadow Banshees."

Floating through the trees, around the trunks, twirling along the branches were bright wisps of color: blues, reds, pinks, yellows. Like rainbow clouds were moving through the forest toward them. Unlike their screamy counterparts, these banshees were mostly quiet, peaceful, and curious. They were born of magic residue. Spell castoff that interacted with the trees in some way to create the beautiful creatures. They were lithe with human-like features. Not dangerous, exuding innocence most of the time. Their eyes sparkled and changed color and their touch was feather soft.

They explored the area around the interns, sensing newness probably. Inexperience, definitely. Three zoned in on Hazel, trilling excitedly when they brushed up against her magic. They circled her, stroking her tentatively. First her hair, ghostly fingers along her nose, her throat, lifting her hands, marvelling at her power no doubt. They were drawn to her like she was nectar, and soon so were all the other banshees.

"What's going on?" Hazel was giggling. A huge smile on her face. The attention of the Shadow Banshees was pleasant, he remembered. Like a gentle massage everywhere they touched. They gave of themselves as well, sharing their power with witches who were open to it, infusing what they had to empower the witch.

Hazel seemed to be soaking it up, her eyes alight, her cheeks glowing.

"Your power intrigues them. They won't come for just anyone," Duke said, unable to contain his own smile. She was so beautiful. His little village girl. His heart ached for her in so many different ways.

She giggled again.

"Is that why you needed Hazel's blood?" Mahdyia asked, a smile on her face as well.

You couldn't be in a bad mood around the Shadow Banshees.

"Yes, I knew they'd be drawn to her. She's like nothing they've experienced before, I'm sure."

"I feel so…strange," Hazel said. "Like plugged in."

The Shadow Banshees swirled around her one more time and then started cycling through to the other interns, looking, no doubt, for unique signatures. Duke knew they'd find Chanda's Chaos and Tate's Elemental natures almost as fascinating.

"They offer us all a power top-up in their presence. Soak it up. It's completely natural."

The Circle, where Hazel was determined to go, gave Healers much power. Power that could be directed for different purposes. But it was manufactured to some degree. Taking from five core witches for decades made the power stale—reliable, sure, but not natural. Duke understood why Hazel's power would be so damn appealing to her Mother and to the Circle. Her power was a pure source as well, with an intensity that he'd only ever experienced in small bursts out and about in the wild.

The Shadow Banshees circled around him now, making him forget his frustration instantly, stroking his hair, tugging at the tips in a way that was almost orgasmic, tingling his scalp, down his spine. Their fingers trailed along his jaw, soft lips caressed his lightly, chastely. They fluttered their eyelashes at him, gave charming smiles, entwined their fingers with his and whispered things in his ears. Things in a language he would never understand but that made his muscles lose all tension and his brain melt into nothing but peace.

They were mesmerizing. Their power infused into him like a jolt. Giving him a boost he hadn't realized he needed. He felt recharged. Grateful.

"Thank you," he whispered.

The Shadow Banshees trilled again in their sing-song way. Then they began to drift away. Circling the trees, the branches, and then up to the canopy, disappearing into the shadows once again.

"That was incredible!" Chanda said. Her cheeks were flushed, her eyes bright, breathing rapid.

All the interns looked refreshed and in awe.

"Thank you." Hazel touched his hand. "That was amazing."

"Only because you're amazing." He smiled at her deepening blush, turned his hand so that their fingers entwined. "There are so many things like this that I could show you. So many wonderful creatures, experiences that I want to introduce to you, if you'll come with me."

Her smile dissolved, her eyes darkened. She dropped his hand and stepped away.

And off to the side was her cousin, watching with a frown that mirrored his. She locked eyes with him, something meaningful there, nodded once and then moved off to join Hazel as she turned her back and walked away from him.

❧ 17 ❧

"Come with me," Mahdyia said to Hazel, not waiting for an answer. She nodded toward Bridget, who waved her off, then beelined into the woods.

"Where are we going?" Hazel couldn't help her voice from catching. She felt dizzy after experiencing such a high from the Shadow Banshees only to crash to such a low at the reality that Duke was off limits to her despite what her heart sang. The Banshees had whispered things to her. They'd stroked her inner thoughts, bringing the ones about Duke, her feelings for him, to the forefront, and it had made her so happy at the time. So peaceful. But then reality took hold. Her destiny hung heavy once again around her neck, the necklace from her mother the reminder as she'd meant it to be.

"There's a Hag who lives in these woods. Bridget told me about her last night. Told me how to find her."

"So? Why do we want to see a Hag now? Aren't we headed to their village?" Hazel stopped following. "Honestly, Mads, I'd rather go sit down with the others and eat some lunch." *I'm not feeling good. My heart hurts,* she wanted to say, but she couldn't get those words out. They were too close to the truth, too powerful to deal with.

Mahdyia came back for her, grabbed her hand and pulled her onward. "No, you don't. We need to see this woman."

"Why?" Hazel suddenly felt anxious, like her life was spiralling out of control. Too much conflict in her head. "What are you up to?"

"If I tell you, you won't come." Mahdyia tugged harder. "And you need to come, so trust me."

Trust me. That's what everyone wanted from her. Blind trust. Like they all knew what was best for her. Her mother, Duke, Mahdyia.

"Mads...I don't—"

Mahdyia stopped abruptly and Hazel crashed into her. She turned, righted Hazel, hands on her upper arms and looked her dead in the eyes. "You need this, Hazel. I know you don't think you do and I know you're getting damn sick of everyone telling you what you need but I'm asking you to please indulge me. We need to see this woman. It's a once in a lifetime experience and since our time is running out for those..."

"Ouch." Hazel frowned.

Mahdyia rolled her eyes but not in a harsh way. She took Hazel's hands into hers and began to stroke her skin like she had when they were little. "Remember that time we rigged up all those water balloons in the ballroom?"

The memory of that day flashed into Hazel's mind like it was yesterday. "Oh yeah, how could I forget?" Her mother had a big gala that night. The Board and all of the hospital's benefactors had been set to arrive any minute and Mahdyia and Hazel had decided the place needed some color. "Mother's black and white affair."

Mahdyia was beaming, her eyes sparkling. "All those women and men dressed in expensive gowns and tuxes, looking like a million bucks with their hairstyles and makeup."

"And wigs!" Hazel snorted.

"Remember how angry your mother was? How furiously she scolded?"

The balloons had been tethered by the magic of ten year-olds, hundreds of colorful globes floating up high enough that no one noticed until it was too late. It had looked so pretty, for the minutes they were suspended.

"Oh yes, it was so scary."

"Terrifying."

"She was soaking wet!"

"You'd think some of those old crones would have melted or something with the way she acted." Mahdyia continued to stroke her hand. "You remember you didn't want to do it?"

Hazel chuckled. "You were the idea girl. I was just a soldier."

Mahdyia hugged her, then pulled away again. "I didn't regret it. Even when Mother grounded me from magic for a whole month."

"Neither did I," Hazel whispered. "It was worth the punishment. I giggled over that memory for months."

"So did I."

"Once in a lifetime. You can't get that look of shock more than once." Hazel chuckled softly.

"No regrets." Mahdyia nodded. "I missed you though, Hazel. She wouldn't let me see you for that whole month too. You remember that?"

Hazel frowned. There had been so many months where Hazel had been immersed in studies that she couldn't recall a punishment involving not being able to see Mahdyia. "No, I don't."

"She used to do that a lot. Keep me from seeing you. She knew it was a true punishment for me. To be separated from you."

Were there tears in her eyes?

"Mads?"

"I would never do anything to hurt you, Hazel, and I would

never put you in danger. I think I've proven that to you over the years. Trust me on this. I need you to come with me to see this Hag. Please." Mahdyia let her go, turned and continued walking.

Hazel watched her for a minute, sighed, then followed. Whatever she was up to wouldn't kill Hazel, of that she was certain. So what if they had a little adventure together? Like Mahdyia had said, those would be coming to an end soon enough—better to soak them up while she could and give herself some happy memories to take with her in the Circle.

And that thought, not for the first time on this trip, made her heart heavy. It wasn't just Duke she'd be losing. Her cousin, who had been her only friend for much of her life, would be off limits to her too.

It bothered her that she hadn't known about the punishments Mahdyia had endured. She knew that her mother didn't approve of the trouble they'd gotten into when together and that trouble had usually been at Mahdyia's prompting, but Hazel had been a willing participant, eager for a little fun after so much work. She hadn't known her mother blamed Mahdyia solely for it. Keeping them apart because she was a bad influence, no doubt. Hazel wasn't surprised. Her mother had disapproved of anything and everything that distracted Hazel from the serious business of preparing for the Circle.

But her mother couldn't be around all the time. She was an important woman with many things and people demanding her attention. When she was away or preoccupied, Hazel always took advantage, seeking Mahdyia out for a little adventure. Goddess, she would miss that.

If only things didn't have to be the way they were destined to be.

And that was the first time she'd ever given thought to something like that. *If only...* She shook her head, trying to clear the negativity away. She couldn't let her thoughts get tangled up. She didn't want to travel down a dark path and mire herself in depression. Destiny was destiny and hers was set, right?

She rubbed the heel of her palm against her chest, trying to ease the ache there. If that was true, if she had no other choice but follow the destiny she knew, then why did it hurt so much all of a sudden? Why was it feeling like a loss?

She got herself moving, catching up with her cousin after a few minutes of hard trekking.

Mahdyia was quiet the whole way. No bantering or chatting, not even a snide comment here or there. She was lost in thought and so was Hazel. The noises from the forest soothed her. The birds had a unique chatter that sounded like tinkling bells and whoops of joy. The breeze rustled leaves like a shiver down the spine. The earthy smell filled her head with warmth and calm. Even without the Shadow Banshees, she found this place to be so peaceful. One by one, step by step, she was able to let some of her angst and sorrow go, getting lost in what the forest had to offer. She clasped Mahdyia's hand and entwined her fingers. Neither of them said a word, they just kept walking.

"What's that?" Hazel felt the brush of magic, old magic, on a gust of wind. The trees were thicker, not as huge and imposing but more densely packed. Hanging from the branches were talismans. Hundreds of them.

Mahdyia reached up to stroke the feather of a lower hanging one. "It's a ward."

It was a bird skull, bleached, on a twine rope that was coated in spots with what looked like blood. There were beautiful long feathers attached, black, gray, striking white, vibrant red, green, even some that looked like peacock feathers. There were smaller bones that acted like chimes, clanking together in the breeze.

Hazel shivered. There was an ominous feel about the place.

"We're almost there," Mahdyia said. "Over this way. Bridget said that the wards would lead the way."

"What are the wards trying to keep out, I wonder?" Hazel

reached up to touch one as she passed under it. She felt a jolt of magic. Powerful human witch. "What kind of Hag is this woman?"

Mahdyia didn't answer.

"Mads?"

She disappeared around a tree and when Hazel caught up, she almost ran right into her. There was a cottage, straight out of a fairy tale...the horror kind, not the princess kind.

"Is it made out of gingerbread?" Hazel asked, eyes wide as she took everything in.

The house had to be one room, an oddly shaped stone bricked rectangle with a thatched roof and a stone chimney that was smoking. The door was arched, made of wood panels with a stained glass window shaped like a star at the top. There were two other windows, one on either side of the door that were too grimy or sooty to see through.

The talismans were everywhere, rattling constantly as they stood there staring.

"Mads, why are we here?"

Before she could answer, the door creaked open. Very ominous. A shiver ran through Hazel's body. Mahdyia reached out and grabbed her hand again. As silly as it was, she didn't resist the gesture.

"Do we go in?" Hazel whispered.

Mahdyia looked at her, gulped, then nodded. "We came this far."

"Girls, in or out, make your choice." In a blink a woman appeared and then disappeared at the door. It stood widely open now.

"Did you—"

"Yeah." Mahdyia squeezed her hand. "Love you, Haz. Don't kill me."

"What?" Hazel was too shocked to register that Mahdyia was leading her in, moving too fast for her to object.

Once inside, Hazel was blinded by the darkness. She had to blink away the spots that floated in front of her. Only candles appeared to be lit along with a fire in the fireplace. The air was stifling. Heavy with incense. Mahdyia sneezed twice, then a third time.

"Make a wish," a croaky voice said. "Make a wish, make a wish, make a wish." A crow stood on a tall T-shaped perch moving from side to side, flapping its wings in agitation. Another talisman dangled from the wooden arm, rattling as the crow moved. "Make a wish, make a wish, make a wish."

"Oh hush, Gilbert. Honestly, you are a nuisance." A woman came out of the shadows, bent over with a huge hump on her back, her long white hair dangling almost to the floor. She moved slowly, aided by a cane that also had a talisman, sparkling crystals dancing in the firelight and swaying with each of her moments. "Girls, welcome. Take a seat."

Hazel looked around and noted two stools off to the side. She grabbed both and positioned them across from where the old lady was now lowering herself into an easy chair, which totally did not suit the rest of the cabin. White leather with plush looking cushions, it took up almost half the small space even without the recliner portion out.

"Pretty girls," Gilbert croaked, clicking back and forth on his perch. "Pretty witches."

The old woman chuckled. "Observant, ain't he?"

"You're American," Mads said. "No accent."

"Aye," the old woman winked. "I'm a transplant. Came out here for the trees. I just couldn't leave them. Or maybe it was for a man. Can't remember."

"You're a Storm Hag?" Hazel was still trying to piece together what they were doing there.

The old woman looked at her, studying with a critical eye. "You're carrying a heavy burden, child." She leaned forward as much as she could. "You're weighed down by it."

"A burden?"

"Her destiny," Mahdyia said matter-of-factly.

"Ah, destiny. Yes, yes, quite the burden."

"Destiny is what you make it," Gilbert squawked.

Hazel snapped her gaze to the bird. "What did he just say?" She could swear she'd heard that before...somewhere.

The old woman was out of the chair then, snatching Hazel's hand. She pulled Hazel forward, startling her almost off the stool as she pressed her forehead to Hazel's and clasped both of her hands. Her skin was so soft, hands wrinkled and also very strong, gripping her like an iron fist. "Hush, child."

Hazel froze. The old woman smelled like campfire and cigar smoke, musky in a way that wasn't totally unpleasant. Her breath was sweet though and it washed over Hazel as she spoke. "You're here for a reason. A very important reason."

"I am?"

The woman squeezed her hands harder. "You're meant to learn sacrifice. Devotion. To commit yourself to the Healers. Born of the Great Mother..."

"Great Mother"—squawk—"Great Mother," the bird chimed.

Oh goddess, Hazel shivered, familiar words coming out of the old woman's mouth. Her prophecy, the one etched in stone. "You're a Mystic." Soothsayer, mystic, fortune teller. A human possessing the magic of portent and prophecy. Hazel could wring her cousin's neck.

"Hush, child," the bird said.

"Be silent," the old woman hissed.

Hazel wasn't sure if she was talking to the bird or to her.

"You've muddled it, child," the soothsayer said. "You have such power to create change. You have such love surrounding you. True love. Undeniable love. Oh child, why are you muddling it?"

"I—I—my destiny...my mother expects it...I have to do what's right. To sacrifice for the Healers." The words felt hollow. When had she lost her conviction?

"Destiny, destiny, destiny, destiny!" The bird was so riled up, flapping its wings, tapping on something in between words.

The Hag pulled away and in a quick flash pricked Hazel's thumb. A drop of blood welled and the old woman lifted Hazel's thumb to her lips and ran her tongue over the wound. Hazel stifled a tremor of revulsion. It was so intimate. Too intimate.

"What you believe is corrupted by the desires of others." She reached into Hazel's shirt, ignoring any concept of personal space and withdrew the amulet her mother had given her. She spat on it, a mixture of saliva and Hazel's blood, then rubbed her finger over it. "Child," the old woman said as she stared down at the amulet. "Do not be led by the desires of others. To be selfless, sometimes you need to be selfish. Destiny is what you make it. It's never set in stone."

She dropped the amulet. It thudded almost painfully against Hazel's chest. The old woman moved back, shuffling slowly until she was once again in her chair.

"A drop of blood from you," the old woman said to Mahdyia as she waved her closer.

Mahdyia nodded, shifted from her stool to her knees in front of the woman. Her thumb was pricked in the same way Hazel's had been. Sucked on in the same way too. But instead of talking, the old woman beckoned her closer, so close that Hazel couldn't hear what was being said, despite straining to do so.

"Pet the bird," Gilbert squawked. "Pet the bird."

Hazel startled when the bird landed in her lap, wings fluttering. It pecked at her hand then looked up at her expectedly.

"Oh hush," Hazel whispered, but complied, running her finger over the bird's silky head and down its body.

It shivered under her attention, nudging for another round as soon as she reached its tail.

"He likes you," the old woman said. "That's a good sign."

"Promised One," the bird squeaked. "Pretty witch."

"Aye, Gilbert, that there is the Promised One." The Hag

winked at Hazel. "But promises are only wishes. It's in the action that we set our course."

"Thank you." Mahdyia was on her feet again, looking a little ashen. With a trembling hand, she pulled a purple feather from inside her shirt and handed it to the Hag.

Where had she gotten that?

"Oh, thank you, dear. This will work wonderfully." The Hag stroked the feather lovingly, earning a squawk of protest from Gilbert.

The bird flew back to its perch, huffing and cackling as he did.

"Jealous, ain't he?" The Hag waved toward the bird with her feather. "Hush you. I'll be getting you some tasty meat in a minute."

Mahdyia motioned to Hazel. "Let's get back to the others."

Hazel stood, then remembered the piece of amber she had from Anne. A stone was better used as a gift than a keepsake, her mother had always said. She fished it from her pocket then held it out to the Hag. "For you."

The bird fluttered, then swooped toward her, snatching the amber out of Hazel's hand.

"Hey!"

It flew off before she could stop it and landed on the old woman's hunched back, the stone in its beak, the bird somehow squawking the whole time.

The Hag chuckled. "Gilbert says thank you." She waved her hand. "Be on your way girls. There's an angry wind blowing this direction." She pushed herself to her feet, Gilbert still on her back and started toward the other side of the cabin

"That sounds ominous," Hazel whispered as they moved to the door.

Once outside, the wind was indeed blowing. Not as hard as Hazel would expect given the Hag's words but enough that it sent a chill of foreboding through her body.

"Let's go, the others are waiting on us." Mahdyia started down the path, not waiting for Hazel as she marched along.

"Thanks for that, by the way," Hazel snapped, practically running to catch up with her cousin. "Would have been nice to have a say in the Mystic deal."

"If I'd told you, you wouldn't have come," Mahdyia said over her shoulder, not slowing.

She was right about that. With the exception of the one her mother had sought out at the time of her pregnancy, Hazel had always believed Mystic magic to be one of the more unreliable and easily warped kinds of magic. It was impossible for her to feel it for some reason, one of the few kinds of magic that didn't sing to her. She had no sense for it and it therefore made her nervous.

"Hey." Hazel had to jog but she finally managed to tap Mahdyia's shoulder and stop her from continuing. "Why was it so important that you couldn't tell me?"

"Because you're so damn blind, Hazel!" Mahdyia snapped, flashing anger as she turned. "You're so brainwashed by what your mother has told you that you can't see what's right in front of you."

Hazel felt like she'd been slapped. She let her hand drop and took a step back. "That's not fair."

"What's not fair? That I'm showing you the truth? That life isn't all laid out for you like you believed it would be? That there's uncertainty and choice? That you could make mistakes? Mistakes, Hazel, like walking away from a man who loves you in the name of a destiny you've only ever been *told* is truth."

"Not this again, Mads—"

"You heard that Hag. You felt her power. I know you did. She knew your prophecy. She had a different take." Mahdyia crossed her arms. "Tell me you didn't feel it. Go ahead. Tell me."

But Hazel couldn't deny what Mahdyia was saying. She had felt it. Like a rock dropping in the pit of her stomach. She'd heard the truth in the Hag's words—she just didn't want to think about what it meant.

"Mystic magic—"

"Oh please!" Mahdyia threw her hands up. "You'll make any excuse, won't you? Unbelievable, even when the truth is right in front of you..." She shook her head. "What's most amazing to me is that you'll question this Mystic, but not the one your mother sought. Why is that, do you think?"

"Mads...I..." She brushed her hand over her face and through her hair, her mind whirling, making her dizzy. "I just—"

"You want to know what she said to me?" It sounded like a dare, her tone bold, challenging.

Hazel felt that sinking feeling in her stomach again. She was about to say no...that's what she wanted to say.

"She said—"

The most awful screeching echoed around them, bouncing off the trees, carried on the wind. It whipped and slashed at them, the noise drilling inside Hazel's head. She covered her ears, darting her eyes all around to find the source.

"What—"

Swooping down from the canopy were the Shadow Banshees, screeching like their evil counterparts. They shot through the forest, intertwining with one another, pulling each other's hair, yowling and bellowing the most horrid noise.

They ignored Hazel and Mahdyia, seemingly set on wreaking havoc with their voices as they traveled the forest, heading toward where the rest of the Healers were.

"We better get back and find out what the hell is going on." Mahdyia grabbed her hand.

Hazel nodded. "It's not good, whatever it is."

❧ 18 ❧

THE SHADOW BANSHEES WERE SCREECHING AN EAR-PIERCING wail that made Duke's ears throb. He didn't have to see them to know that something was very wrong.

"What direction?" Bridget was quickly repacking her bag, motioning for the others to do the same. Whatever they'd managed to wolf down was lunch, no time for anything else.

"North." Duke had his eyes set on the direction Hazel and Mahdyia had left. "I'm going to find Hazel. Get the others back on the trail and we'll meet up."

Just as he said that, the Shadow Banshees swooped from the canopy, swirling around them as they had before, but this time it was with terror in their voices and anguish on their faces. The shrill sound, the intensity of their emotions sent Duke to his knees, his hands clamping over his ears, as if that could block the noise out. Pain, like a thousand blades stabbing into his brain, distracted him from whatever it was they were trying to tell him.

"Duke!" Hazel was at his side, her hands on his hands, her voice muffled, like he was underwater and she was diving to save him from drowning. "What's happening?"

The Shadow Banshees circled a few more times, sidewiping

him, clearly growing frustrated with his inaction, before they flew back up to the trees and continued their screaming farther into the forest.

The relief at their departure had him almost weeping. He closed his eyes tighter, sucked in a few deep breaths as the pain slowly began to ebb. He lowered his hands and then hugged Hazel. "You're back."

"Of course I am." Hazel didn't resist. In fact she wrapped her arms around him too. "Why wouldn't I come back?"

"The Shadow Banshees..." He sucked in a few deep breaths. "Oh goddess." He pulled away and looked to the others. "We have to go, now!"

"What did you hear? Did the Shadow Banshees tell you something?" Hazel looked confused, much like the rest of the Healers.

"The Storm Hags are in serious trouble. I couldn't make out exactly what is going on but the Shadow Banshees conveyed their distress. We need to get to that village now."

"It's still a half a day's trek at least," Bridget said, but she was already moving toward the path.

"That distress call they sent you, Bridget, it wasn't specific was it? They didn't indicate what the problem was?" Duke managed to shake off the rest of the trauma from the Shadow Banshees' wails, hooked his pack over his shoulder and grabbed Hazel's hand.

Again, she didn't protest. He looked at her, looked down at their hands and when she didn't say a word, smiled. He didn't know what had changed, but he wasn't going to squander it.

"The distress call came via scrying. It was garbled but clear that they needed assistance," Bridget said. "There was urgency but not like this—nothing suggesting something so dire."

"Well, whatever is going on there is bad. Really bad." Duke felt it like it was woven into his soul. The Shadow Banshees couldn't use words with him, or a language that made sense, not in the state they were in, and he'd never have understood with the amount of pain they were causing. Instead, they'd conveyed with mirrored emotions. Fear—no, *terror*. Pain—scratch that—*agony*, and anger, so much red-hot anger. "This is magic gone bad for sure. We need to be ready for a lot of carnage."

"What does that mean? Like battle? Active carnage?" Chanda asked, panic clearly lacing her question. "Is it a good idea for me to even be there?"

She was worried about her Chaos and whatever they were going to find. Her emotions whipped at Duke. He couldn't blame her—chaos begot chaos. She could do more damage if things were out of control there.

"I thought you said you were battle trained?" Bridget asked, disappointment clearly edging her question.

"I am!" Chanda snapped. "But battle training and healing don't go hand and hand, you know? I'm either battling or I'm healing, not both. I can't divide my attention like that. It takes all of my concentration to keep my own Chaos under control."

"You're going to have to lock it down, Chanda," Duke said sternly. "Your fear feeds the Chaos, you know that. You're not a child, you're a trained Healer. Intern or not, you have spent years honing skills that you will have to call on now. We go into this with eyes wide and magic ready. All of you need to be prepared for whatever may come." He met the stares of each of the interns, Hazel last, squeezing her hand as he did. "Human witches and their relationship with magic is unpredictable. They don't always abide by the same laws and rules as we do."

"No respect for it," Bas blurted.

"No knowledge of it," Duke corrected. "Their training comes at the knees of their grandparents and parents, raised on folklore and centuries of trial and error. Grimoires so old that the pages are worn, spells sometimes get lost or mutated because of that. Sometimes they stumble on power that they can't control. We need to assess the situation, come up with a plan and then work with the humans to make sure we effectively tackle whatever is going on in the safest way possible."

"I can null them all," Bas suggested, his words not carrying the venom they had a moment before. "Like what I did with the Fire witch. I could bind them. I've never done it on a large group, but I could try."

"We'll keep that in our back pocket for now. It's too unpredictable of a strategy to just throw out there. We don't want to bind all the magic, including ours and leave everyone vulnerable."

Bas nodded.

Duke turned back to Chanda. "You got your shit under control? We need you there but if you're too scared, you're more of a liability than a help." He knew his words sounded harsh but when it came to Medic care, mindset was more important than anything else. If they were walking into a battle, he couldn't have anyone going rogue with wild emotions that would throw him off.

Bridget moved in next to Chanda and whispered something that made her blush.

"Yeah, okay." Chanda met Duke's eyes and nodded. "You can count on me."

"Good, now we're going to head north, follow the trail until we clear the forest. If I remember correctly, the Storm Hags live in a valley where there's a deep lake. We won't be able to see what's going on as we descend because there's a layer of fog that conceals it. Am I right, Bridget?"

"Yes, so far so good. I was last here about three years ago. While there's one main path to the gates of the village, I do know of another route in that is more in line with our current travelling direction. It'll mean going off path for a bit of hard trekking but I think it's wise we approach this cautiously. Chanda and I will scout. Duke, can you keep tabs on the emotional side of things?"

"I'm on it." He turned to Hazel. "Which means I'll be pretty preoccupied with sussing out the voices in my head." He winked. "Can you keep the troops in line?"

Hazel widened her eyes, but the surprise passed quickly. "Sure, okay. I can do that."

"Hear that, suckers?" Mahdyia said. "Hazel is in charge and seeing as I'm her cousin, I'm second in command." She moved around Bas and Tate, nudging them with her shoulder.

Tate took it good-naturedly.

Bas scoffed then walked toward Bridget. "What the hell, you're leaving me here with these losers?"

Bridget gave him one of her scathing looks, no words needed.

"Whatever," Bas scoffed again, mumbling something under his breath as he moved back to join the group.

While everyone else was busy adjusting pack straps and whatnot, Duke took the opportunity to kiss Hazel's hand, earning a startled gasp from her, her eyes darting to make sure no one saw.

"You sense anything amiss, you call to me, okay? I'll be within eyeshot and I'm tuned into you as it is, so any spike of concern should rattle me enough to pull me out of my head. But all the same, yell loud, okay?"

Hazel nodded. "Be careful."

"Always." He smiled, wanting so badly to lean in and kiss her but instead squeezed her hand one more time before letting go. "Let's get a move on, witches."

Half a days' trek away meant that he really had to work to home in on the village that lay ahead. The fog that concealed it also acted to muffle his intruding magic, but if he concentrated hard enough he should be able to get a read on what was going on, and it would only get stronger the closer they came. The goal was to have a good idea of what they were walking into. Every witch knew the basics of self-defense—when it came to spell casting anyway. With Chanda and Bridget both battle trained, they had an advantage if there was something more than just illness causing the problems.

The descent was gradual. The trees sloped slightly, leaning more and more in the direction of the sun as they moved closer to the village. The path they were on became less of a path, splintering off in multiple directions until there was nothing left to follow visually. Duke could see how easy it would be to get completely turned around in a forest so dense.

He was zoned in on the emotions. Being an empath meant different things to different witches. For him, he'd always been attuned to feelings. With the way people projected emotions, it was enough to overwhelm him completely if he didn't have some control over it. He'd learned that as a child, the sensation of being bombarded with people's shit had him near crazy for the first few years of his life. Inconsolable crying, fits of rage, temper tantrums the likes of which shook the walls and caught the neighbors' attention. Luckily his mother understood, as an empath herself, what was going on and instead of throwing him in an institution for insane witches as was the norm, she'd patiently worked with him to hone his skill. That's what made him so rare in the world of Healers and witches alike. Most empaths did go crazy from the intensity of the emotions they absorbed—too much sensation making them lose their minds completely. He was lucky he'd been born into a family of them, Healers all, and some of the most powerful empaths in the country.

Duke had first learned how to block it out completely. His mother helped him, so that when he experienced his first moments of complete silence as an infant, he recalled the sense of peace and hope it gave him. Like a comfort blanket covering him in quiet, giving his mind a chance to heal. It was an unlikely memory for such a young child to remember, but he did because he'd known even as a baby that his mother had saved his life. From then on, as his awareness grew and his maturity progressed, his mother helped him develop techniques for controlling the floodgates of his powers. He rarely left himself wide open. Even with Hazel, when he'd thought she was human, he hadn't ever been so vulnerable. It was too risky. But opening it just a little usually gave him enough of a sense of the situation. His default setting allowed for a trickle, opened enough to get the drift of what was going on, not open enough to cripple him.

The Shadow Banshees had forced him open wider, which was why it had caused him so much pain. Their emotional noise had been too powerful and had caught him off guard. He'd been too focused on Hazel, worried about where she was and why she was taking so long. Rookie mistake. But when it came to Hazel the witch, he was discovering that his usual defenses were all off. He craved her emotion, and the chance to bolster her powers. He'd never wanted to be close to someone like he did with her—physically, emotionally, magically. Even if it made him so vulnerable that it distracted him, cost him. She was just that tempting.

She was within eyesight of him now. Not straying too far, looking like she was completely focused on moving forward, which was wise considering how treacherous the non-existent pathway was. Trees sprouted branches that hung low and were hidden among leaves. Moss made the rocks and roots slippery and shadows played with dark crevices, making holes and divots appear to be solid. He glanced over the group of interns, each lost in their own thoughts and staggered in a kind of line, moving just as tentatively, but with a steady pace of urgency that Hazel encouraged. The interns were a motley crew and had probably all faced adversity in some form or another, based on what he'd learned about them. They were probably all thinking they were independent and alone before this field trip, each carrying the burden of their unique powers and experiences.

Hazel would make a good leader for them. With all of her innate power and years of training, she had a regal air about her that demanded obedience, or at least it would once she figured out how to use it without pissing everyone off. She had been raised to embrace and celebrate her uniqueness, something the others would need to learn as well. If Duke knew anything, it was that White Willow only recruited the best Healers from witch families, the ones with the most potential. They were at the start of their journeys but he had no doubt each of them would rise.

He scanned the group, checking their emotional peaks and

rested on Hazel, of course. For now she was pouring out a mixture of trepidation and a bubbling of excitement. It was childlike in a way, the curiosity to discover what lay ahead. Something he had always loved about her, even when she had been just a village girl. For all her many talents, she was just a baby in the witch world. Being in the field would give her a crash course in what magic could really do and would hopefully show her a life outside of the Circle that was worth fighting for.

"What is that?" Hazel asked, her words echoing in his head.

He flinched, snapped out of his thoughts and turned to look at where she was pointing.

A small clearing appeared out of the fog. The ground levelled unnaturally against the slope of the hill. Grave stones poked up, roughened markers ranging in size, some beaten and broken down by the elements and years while others looked brand new.

"We're getting closer." Duke waved for them to slow as they entered. The ground was soft, some mounds looking too fresh for his liking. "Skirt the cemetery. We'll meet on the other side."

"Some of these are kids." Bas had ignored the command and was standing in front a newer grouping of stones, crouched to read the inscriptions. "All six of these are children." He waved his hand to indicate which ones.

Duke frowned as he moved closer, being careful not to tread on the graves. There was lingering sadness in the fog, which wasn't unusual for a cemetery. But it was fresh, so fresh that Duke wasn't surprised to see the dates on the gravestones. "Whatever is happening here caused this."

The children ranged in age from a year old to five years old. Each had died within a few days of one another. Not all were from the same family but in a village like this, family by blood was just a technicality.

"Hazel, do you get a sense of magic here? Anything lingering that we need to know about?" Duke looked over his shoulder at her.

She had her arms wrapped around her body, her face pale, tears welling. "The fog, it's muffling things."

Duke nodded. He'd had to work harder to penetrate the fog as well. "Push past it. Focus on the graves. Here, come here, touch the ground."

Hazel looked about ready to shake her head and step back, but in a flash resolve came over her. She flexed her hands and moved forward, coming to crouch next to Bas. With a determined look at Duke, she lay her hands on the fresh mound, letting her fingers sink just a bit into the freshly turned earth.

Her eyes were closed for seconds before she jolted up, jumping back from the grave, dusting her hands off like she'd touched fire.

"What is it?" Duke moved to her side, holding her arm, feeling the vibration of her power, tempted as usual to open himself up to it and let it consume him completely. "What did you sense?"

She stopped brushing her fingers and looked at him. "It's bad magic, Duke. What killed these kids, it's really bad."

"Dark magic?" Bas asked, still crouching by the grave, his hand on one of the stones.

"Black magic?" Tate asked, his voice quivering a little.

She looked from Duke to each of the others, slowly shaking her head. "I've never felt anything like this. It's darker than dark, blacker than black. It's like an abyss."

"Ah, shit." Duke cursed, turning away from the group. "We need to get to the village."

"What is it, Duke?" Hazel asked, fear riding her question.

"Succubi, exceptionally deadly ones."

❦ 19 ❧

"MORE SPECIFICALLY, SUCCUBI MAGIKA, AND LIKELY THEIR counterpart Incubi Magika too," Duke said.

"Magic seducers?" Bas stood slowly from his crouch. "Like instead of sex, they want power?"

"Yeah, that's right. Someone in the village must have invoked them. They can only come if called. They're sneaky though, and entice in devious ways. They travel in packs, sending out scouts to find pockets of magic then target the outliers, those witches who have been outcast from a tribe or who are sick and vulnerable already. Could be why we're seeing children here. They'd go for vulnerability over power hub. The child invokes, encourages a bond. Once the Magika latch on to their host, they suck them dry of all magic. Slowly at first, while they put the call out to their kind, like an infection. Once one breaks the defenses of the tribe, the others can get in quickly. The child encourages others to invoke, and it spreads faster like that. We need to warn Bridget and Chanda." Duke looked stricken with worry. "They target humans—"

"Because they're weak?" Bas suggested.

"Because their magic is diluted and they're easier to manipulate. Ignorance, even in the Pagan tribes, is deadly. Another reason why outreach is so important." Duke sounded perpetually annoyed with Bas. "In any case, Chanda and her Chaos would be a magnet for these beasties. We need to make sure they're aware of what we're walking into."

"We can use this, can't we?" Hazel reached into her shirt and pulled out the summoning amulet. Her mother had meant for it to be a means of connection with Hazel but she knew it could be repurposed if necessary.

Duke narrowed his eyes at the stone in her hand, then widened them just as suddenly. "Where did you get that?"

"My mother..."

He stormed to her before snatching it out of her hand, almost yanking it clear off of her neck in the process.

"Ouch, hang on, it's attached."

He loosened his grip with a flick of his eyes that maybe was an apology, then resumed staring at the stone, rubbing his thumb over it repeatedly. "Ten years..." he mumbled.

"It's a summoning stone right? My mother gave it to me when I was a child in case I needed to connect to her."

Duke looked up at her then, his lips pulled into a grimace. "It's not just for summoning. Son of a bitch!" He growled. "Take it off!"

"What? No!" Hazel tried to get the stone back, wrapping her fingers around Duke's and forcefully trying to break his grip. He wouldn't let go though. She didn't like the stone under normal circumstances but now that he was making such a big deal, she didn't want to give it up. "Hey, let go. My mother gave this to me."

"Do you know what this does?" he spat, his eyes blasting fury.

She flinched, realizing that there was something she was missing. "It summons?" She pulled her hand away.

"Yeah, it summons, on a basic level, but that's not what it's meant to do. That's not the primary use." He raised it up, shaking it a bit as he did. "I found this stone ten years ago. It was mine and it was taken from me."

"You think I stole it? That my mother stole it?"

"No, I think it was given to her, but that's not the point." He yanked on the chain, muttering a spell as he did so that it snapped from her neck.

"Hey!"

"This stone doesn't just summon, Hazel, it siphons. Your mother gave this to you, right? When you were a child?"

Hazel nodded.

"And she told you to wear it, to not take it off?"

Wear it always, Hazel, so I know you're safe. Hazel recalled her mother's words, repeated so many times when she was growing up, and nodded again.

"She's taking power from you, feeding off of you with it." He covered the amulet with his fist, out of sight and slipped it into his pocket. "She's siphoning power from you. Stealing it from you. You didn't give her permission, right?"

"She wouldn't do that—"

"Of course she would! She'd do just about anything to use what you have." Duke raised his voice. The others were crowding now, watching the show.

"Duke, I don't—"

"Why are you so blind to this, Hazel? Why the undying loyalty? That amulet—when I found it, I knew it was priceless. All you have to do is place it on or near a magical target and you can take however much of their magic without them knowing. Your mother can do that with just a touch, I'm sure, but why rely on that when you have a gem that will do it for you? Like she's plugged in to you always, even if you're not in the same location."

"My mother would never—"

"Yes she would, Haz," Mahdyia stepped forward, looking like she was swallowing something awful, a look of pity on her face.

"She would do that. She'd suck you dry if she could. I've seen it, the hunger on her face when she looks at you. When she touches you. I believe what Duke is saying. What the Hag said. Your mother is a selfish woman only looking out for her best interests. That's why she wants you to join the Circle on her behalf. Not because you're special, not because of your power, but because she's too selfish to do it herself." Mahdyia touched her arm. "She did it to me, when she punished me for getting us into trouble. She didn't just forbid me to use magic, or block me from seeing you—she took my powers from me. Scrubbed me. That's why I'd disappear for a month or so when I was punished. If you saw me, you'd know and she couldn't have that. It's what she does, Hazel. She takes what she wants. That she'd skim off the top of your power without your knowledge or permission doesn't surprise me at all."

"Mads." Hazel gulped past the lump in her throat. Her head was spinning. She wanted that stone back. She wanted to ask her mother what was going on. But in her heart she knew. The words of the Hag rolled through her head.

Destiny is what you make it. Nothing is set in stone.

Mother, what have you done?

"You feel it, don't you?" Duke said. "Now that the stone is gone? You feel the void, right?" He pulled the amulet out again and swung it toward her.

She felt a distinct jolt then, small, easily missed but it was there. She felt it and nodded. "Am I really that naive?" she whispered.

"To trust?" Duke asked.

"Yes," Mahdyia said bluntly.

Hazel flinched. "Take it away."

"Where'd you get that?" Bridget was there, anger spewing as she marched toward the group.

Duke curled his fingers around the amulet.

"My mother gave it to me," Hazel answered for him.

"Why does he have it?" Bridget pointed at Duke.

"I gave it to him. We were going to use it to summon you." Hazel held her hand out for the amulet. She motioned for Duke to lay it on her palm. "I wasn't sure how to use it."

"Well, I'm here now, so put it back on."

Hazel gulped, shook her head at Duke's open mouth. Silencing him as she took the amulet. "I'll put it in my pocket for now, I'd rather not have something hanging around my neck." Which was what she did, slipping into the pocket in her pants.

Bridget nodded with apparent satisfaction then turned back to Duke. "We've got a problem."

"Magika?" Duke said casually. "Yeah, no shit. Where's Chanda?"

"I'm right here." She came out of the trees, ambling slowly, looking like she'd been run over by a train, her hair dishevelled, clumps pulled from her ponytail, face streaked with dirt.

"A swarm of them attacked as we neared the village. We managed to beat them down but I can't say that'll be the last of them." Bridget motioned to the opposite side of the graveyard. "The village is infested."

Hazel moved over to Chanda, assessing for visible injury as she did. The girl was barely standing on her feet, her body swaying with each breath. "You okay?"

Chanda closed her eyes, using a tree to brace herself. "I've had better days."

"Anything get inside you?" Hazel whispered. She reached out with her power, trying to detect anything amiss laced within Chanda's signature.

"No, they tried though. Came at me hard and fast. But that was part of my training, an inoculation for little beasties like that. I'm immune...or as immune as possible. It just took the wind out of me, that's all." Her eyes were wet, a stray tear tumbling. "Scary as hell."

Hazel glanced over her shoulder to see Bridget and Duke

engaged in a heated discussion. Duke was pointing toward Hazel so she was sure she knew what the argument was about.

"Can you show us how to do that? The inoculation? It's like a shield, right?" Hazel asked as she turned back to Chanda.

Chanda nodded. "Yeah, good idea."

Hazel motioned for the others to join them and quickly, as the spell was a simple one, they built shields of protection against the Magika.

"Join hands," Hazel said. "I'm going to make the shield connect so that we'll be stronger."

"I can help with that," Bas added, taking Hazel's hand as he spoke.

She nodded to him, a silent agreement to work together. "Repeat the spell one more time. Don't worry about what Bas and I are doing—just be open to it, okay?"

Each of them nodded. Hazel squeezed Bas's hand and then they started once again. The interns were vulnerable. Even Hazel was vulnerable for all her book smarts. Untrained for this kind of thing. She understood that's what the field trip was all about, exposure to experiences so that the interns could develop not only a repertoire but also immunity to more wild forms of magic. Without this experience, she would have never even known that the Magika existed.

There were so many entities and creatures out in the real world that it would take centuries of reading and studying to learn about them all. The shield they were building together would work to protect them as a group, allowing for each of them to draw on one another if needed, like a moving force-field that strengthened the weakest in a time of need. It would work as long as they were in the vicinity of one another, whether holding hands or not.

All of this she would miss once she joined the Circle. Experience that would make her a better Healer, a better witch.

She gulped, shoved that thought aside. No time for wallowing.

Hazel infused her magic, feeling Bas's touch weave it all together and attach to each of the interns. It was a strong bond, one that was almost indestructible thanks to their combined efforts.

Once they were done, Hazel could feel the buzz of renewed energy. Like she was connected, if only for a moment, to each of them. That was the other thing she would never experience again, the connection to other Healers. Not like she was right now. The loneliness she'd always felt had abated the more she got to know these interns. And in a year she'd have to willingly walk back into that kind of loneliness again.

With a sigh, she let her hand slip from Mahdyia's but kept a hold of Bas's. "I'm sorry for intruding on your thoughts yesterday." She squeezed his hand before letting it go. "Sometimes it's hard to control."

He eyed her suspiciously. "Okay. Tell me, what did you see?"

Hazel shrugged, heat rising to her cheeks. "Nothing clear, really. I mean, a lot of anger, sadness." Images had flashed for her: fire, screaming, a cat. Now that she knew part of his story, it made sense. "You were there, when they burned her. I know you said you weren't but you have memories of it." She touched his arm. "You know you're not responsible, right? I mean, I felt that the clearest—the guilt you carry but it's not your fault. You didn't set that fire."

His expression darkened, any openness that had been there momentarily closed now. "You don't know shit, Hazel. Really. You think you do but you don't. Stay out of my head, lady." His hostility slammed her hard as he stormed away.

And then there was Bas, who maybe she wouldn't miss so much once she joined the Circle. She closed her eyes against his anger, sucked in a breath, then blew it out and opened her eyes.

"Hey, you okay?" Duke was there, a comforting hand on her back.

She turned to him, confusion clouding everything as she looked into his eyes. "I don't understand what's going on."

"That stone, as long as it's on you, your mother can access your powers with it." Duke ran his finger along her pocket. "I can take it out right now and no one will see."

Hazel felt a flash of panic, and guilt. Such conflicting emotions. It was hard to reconcile them with everything else. "It's better I keep it." She clenched her hand around his to stop him from digging it out. "So she doesn't suspect."

Duke frowned, then nodded slowly.

"It's not like it's draining me. I mean, I haven't even noticed."

"Probably because she'd been doing it your whole life. Hazel." Duke took her hand. "Just consider it, okay? I hate the idea of her taking from you, even now that you know, for your whole life it was done without your knowledge. That's wrong. Even if it's your mother. *The Mother*. It's still wrong. Criminal, in fact."

Hazel closed her eyes. She understood what he was saying. She did. But they were talking about her mother, a woman she would have given anything at the asking. But that was the thing that was bugging her in that moment, the thing Duke was saying out loud, clearly and without mincing words. Her mother, the Mother of all Healers, revered leader and worshipped for her power in and of itself, had taken, without permission, what Hazel had. She'd been likely doing it from birth, with or without the stone. She probably felt that she had a right to Hazel's gift. But that wasn't true. Taking without permission was stealing and stealing from another witch was punishable by law. That's why the amulet was so valued. Duke had found something that was capable of stealing another witch's powers without him or her knowing and it could be used across great distances. Her own mother had been using the stone on Hazel since she was a teenager.

Hazel let that sink in fully.

She'd insisted that Hazel wear the amulet everywhere, at all times. Such treachery. To prey on the unconditional trust of a daughter. But something that Hazel's mother would do, had done in other ways. To Mahdyia, to others. Hazel had witnessed examples of her mother's ruthlessness in the name of punishment or self-preservation over the years and it was always disguised as effective leadership. Why wouldn't she do it to her own daughter as well?

It would be easy for Hazel to push it away. To bury the feelings of betrayal and disappointment. To ignore the truth. But Hazel realized that easy had been her go-to most of the time her mother was concerned. Cowing to her dominance and commands over and over again. Was it possible that the woman didn't have Hazel's best interests at heart? Was it possible that the Mystic was right and that destiny was fluid? Changeable? Had her mother been lying to her for her whole life?

It seemed more and more probable.

Hazel opened her eyes. "If you found the stone, why did you give it up? I mean, how did my mother get it to begin with?" She suspected it had something to do with Bridget. The fact that Bridget even knew Hazel had it was telling.

"It was stolen from me when I was an intern."

"By Bridget?" Realization dawned. "You were one of her boy toys, weren't you? Not just a one-time thing, right? She'd used you for sex." She flicked a glance in Bridget's direction. "And then she snatched the gem out from under you, right?"

He had sense enough to blush at least. "And then gave it to your mother, I guess." He shrugged. "Hey, I was young and naive. We all make mistakes, right?"

Hazel felt lighter than she should in that moment. So the love affair between Duke and Bridget had been nothing but that—an affair that ended when she'd gotten what she wanted from him.

"It's in the past anyway. I found the stone, wanted to present it to Mother Knight myself, earn a place in her esteem. But now that I know what she was going to use it for, I'm kinda glad I didn't." He checked to make sure everyone was busy doing something else, which they all seemed to be, then brushed his fingers down the side of her face to touch her bottom lip. "I'd never do anything to hurt you, Hazel. Not on purpose anyway."

She kissed his fingers and smiled. "I think I know that."

20

"CHANDA AND I TOOK CARE OF THE IMMEDIATE THREAT," Bridget began. "But you all need to be wary of new attacks from the Magika. They don't like to lose a plentiful source and may act vengefully when you start triaging."

Duke stayed close to Hazel. He wasn't going to coddle her or try to keep her from danger, that wasn't his job, but he didn't want her to get hurt either. He'd been happy to see the interns take the initiative to dose themselves with protection. He had a long-standing immunity from years of exposure to different kinds of succubus—one experience in particular that had given him lots of protection. It had made for a funny story after the fact, probably, but maybe not one that Hazel would find too amusing.

The most common succubus feed off of sex, and years ago, when Duke was first learning to work the field, he'd stumbled on a group of them. They'd nearly consumed him with lust—near death for sure, if his Commander hadn't pulled him out of there in time. Yeah, okay, so maybe not funny at all. He shoved that memory back where it belonged.

"What's our plan going in?" Tate asked.

"Stick to your training. Assess the injuries, tackle the most severe first, sweep the village. Population here is around seventy-five." Bridget cringed. "Fewer, I guess, now. Make sure you go into every home and structure. Villagers could have been stricken while working in barns and the forest. We'll set up by the main fire and Duke will organize the healthy villagers to help locate those who are sick. I'll speak with the Storm Hags. Hopefully none of them have fallen ill."

The Storm Hags were usually the oldest witches in the village. Years of training and honing skills led them to the honor. Despite being old, they weren't frail, and like the interns, they would have taken precautions against the Magika immediately. It really just depended on how quickly the attack came and what other defenses they were able to erect in that time.

"We didn't see much through the fog when we were attacked," Chanda said, wrapping her arms around her torso. "The village seemed quiet and I didn't feel Chaos other than from the Magika that were attacking us."

That was unusual. Magika thrived on chaos and disorder; it was the most effective method of invading a village. They incited fear, wreaked havoc, then latched on like leeches, to suck the host dry.

"Be cautious going in. The Magika are known for being sneaky," Duke addressed the group.

"Blades out, make a cut, get some blood flowing and arm your-selves with a deflection spell. Nothing fancy, just something that will stun if required. We don't know how the Magika infection will impact the villagers. It's possible they may attack us when we step out of the fog, thinking we're coming to hurt them. It's not uncommon for hallucinations to come with this kind of infection as well. Be prepared for anything. Bas"—Bridget nodded to him —"can you work the fire and whip up a brew that will help the purge?"

Bas nodded. "Yeah, I have a recipe. I'll get on it and meet you inside." He didn't wait for a reply and instead moved to the trees, using his knife to pry a part of the bark away.

His mother was an apothecary—it stood to reason he had been trained as well. Duke was impressed that he had stepped up. Brewing a concoction would take him out of the trauma game. Duke had to give him credit for setting aside his ego for once.

"Chanda, I need you to work triage, but if there's a whiff of trouble, you're in battle mode. Got it?" Bridget said.

Chanda looked hesitant until she glanced at Duke, seemed to recall his words and straightened her back, her eyes taking on a determined look. "Got it."

"Mahdyia, you diagnose. We know there's infection—what we don't know is what side injuries that has caused. Any weakness to the humans will prevent us from purging the Magika. Mark your patients on a scale. One is infection only; two is broken bones; three is internal bleeding; four is dire complications."

Mahdyia nodded.

"Tate, I need you working with Mahdyia. Watch her back, use your Elemental skill to read the environment. Bring whatever energy you need to in order to help comfort the patients and treat the wounded."

"You got it, boss."

"Hazel." Bridget turned to her. "I need you to do the purge. Start small, work your way up to the deeper infections. Duke will join you after he's organized the healthy villagers. Between the two of you, we should get a handle on this quickly."

Hazel glanced Duke's way and gave him a small smile. A team, again.

"I'll supply the others as well," Hazel said. "Draw from me if you need it. I've got enough power to go around."

Everyone stopped what they were doing and all eyes moved to Hazel.

Aaaand she still didn't quite have a handle on social inter-actions.

"What? That's what I'm here for, right? I'm a power hub. Use me." Hazel shrugged.

Bas snorted then turned back to his work, mumbling some-thing as he did.

"You're more than that and you know it," Mahdyia snapped.

"Enough," Bridget barked. "Use Hazel like you would the Circle. She's offering, so take it." She nodded at Hazel who squared her shoulders, spine straight and nodded back. "Blades up, get cutting, and then let's move."

Duke patted Hazel's back with a little shake of his head.

"What?" Hazel looked genuinely confused, her shoulders bunched, palms turned up.

She came by it innocently at least.

He started walking, his blade in hand, ready to get bloody and deal out some magic.

The village was eerie as hell, just like Chanda had suggested. Quiet. Strikingly so. Not a sound of anything. No animals—even the birds were silent. They made it through the fog and to the centre of the village without running into anyone. Not a soul to be seen. The thatched roof cottages were closed, shutters latched, doors shut. No one peering from the windows. It was like a ghost town and Duke feared that they might be too late.

He couldn't feel a sign of life, not on the surface of things anyway and the crushing reality of that almost sent him to his knees. Hazel slipped her hand into his. He didn't need to look at her to see her concern. She was as attuned to him as he was to her. *A team.* He squeezed her hand, then drew from her power as a layer of protection and opened himself up a little wider, probing out tentatively, snaking his awareness past the doors and windows.

He found the beat of life, barely there, such little energy that it was hardly detectable. There was no fear, no agony, just resignation and quiet pleas for death.

"Go find the Storm Hags," Duke said to Bridget. "The villagers are in their cottages, weak and dying. I don't think we're going to be facing a battle here." He looked toward Tate and Mahdyia. "We'll make a sweep, clockwise."

Bridget was already moving, Chanda in tow. The Storm Hags, once elevated to the distinction, lived by the lake, outside of the village and high up in tree houses where they were closer to the clouds and better able to manipulate the fog.

The rest of the team got to work doing their assigned tasks. A basic spell to unlock and open the doors, a call out to warn the villagers and then in they went. Hazel let Duke's hand drop and moved to a more central location to summon her power. He could see that her palms still bled from where she'd opened them already. There was blood dripping to the earth as she lowered her hands toward the dirt. The magic began to rise up, stirring the dirt at her feet. Like a mini tornado, her power swirled around her, whiffs of color rotating, stinging Duke's eyes with its beauty.

She was amazing.

She brought her hands up, hovering just at her waist, the magic billowing, her hair swishing all around in a frenzy, and then with fingers splayed she send it out like a wave. He felt it wash over him as it moved to the others, bolstering them while they worked, giving them a charge so that their power was precise and flawless. He buzzed with it, the tingling feel of her power touching each nerve in his body, making his body zing.

With a mental push he redirected the flow, sending a boost back to her, using his connection to Hazel to bolster her even more. It had a cascading effect—his power working to bind them all so that each of the witches were connected, tied in, and working as a team with a circuit of magic.

Bas was concocting the brew in a giant cauldron that had

already been in the central fire. The fire itself had died at some point, just smouldering ashes left, but he had stoked it alive within seconds. Duke could tell he had done this many times before.

"First batch will be ready in five minutes, Hazel," Bas called out as he stirred the giant pot with hand movements only, his power acting like a spoon. "You purge them, this will help restore their strength and keep them safe. I've layered a protection spell as well as some fortifying ingredients. Foolproof."

Hazel brushed her hair back from her face then nodded.

"You ready?" Duke said.

"Ready."

He took Hazel's hand—he'd never get enough of that—and they walked together to the first cabin that Tate and Mahdyia had cleared.

It was a family of four. Two adults, mother and father and two children. Mahdyia had written numbers on them all. Chanda was currently at work mending the father's broken leg. The rest were marked with ones. Infection only.

The cottage was stifling, days of being holed up with no circulation it seemed. Even with the door open, there was little air movement. Duke swept his hand out and blasted the shutters wide. He caught sight of Tate out the window, who picked up on the cue. Within seconds a breeze swept through, the gift of wind from the Elemental. Duke turned back to Hazel and the patient she was crouching next to.

The mother, with sallow skin drawn close to her bones, the contour of her skull visible, looked like a corpse, her breathing so shallow it was barely there.

"There's only one feeding." Duke pointed to the child, a girl with long brown hair who was curled into a tight ball, a low moan escaping her chapped lips. "One Magika to purge here. Focus on the child, I'll handle the rest."

Hazel shifted over to the little girl and didn't hesitate. With blade in hand, she opened her palm and then did the same to the little girl, lancing the child's chest just enough to establish a link before she laid her hands over her small body, fingers splayed as she chanted the words that would begin to tear the beastie from the child's core.

Duke felt the battle, which wasn't much of one from this Magika. It was drunk on the magic it had siphoned, having gorged itself on all four witches for days. Hazel stripped it away with little resistance, her witch blood working to poison the beastie with so much power that it couldn't fight, it was too over-whelmed. The greedy things just didn't know when enough was enough. With a screech, the Magika exploded, splattering its stolen power out, some of it landing on the owners it had been stolen from, useless to them in this form.

"What a waste," Hazel said with a sigh. The little girl roused, cracking her eyes a little bit. "Hey sweetie, it's okay. You're okay."

The little girl's eyelids fluttered. She moaned something unin-telligible.

"Thank ye," the mother croaked from her bed. "We couldn't ficht thaim. They came sae fast."

She was trying to rise from the bed but Duke encouraged her to ease back down. "You're too weak still."

"I've got some brew." Bas appeared at the door, a large steaming cup in his hand.

Duke rose and moved out of the way, encouraging Hazel to do the same. "We've got more villagers to deal with."

Hazel brushed her fingers through the little girl's hair and nodded to the mother. "You'll be okay."

The woman nodded back, eyes switching to Bas, who approached with the cup.

"Small sips. It'll protect you from secondary infection," Bas said.

"Please help!" A teenager came running toward them as they

stepped out of the cottage. His hair was long, matted and dirty, his face and clothing in the same state.

Duke stopped him from getting too close. "Tell me what's wrong." He nudged Hazel to assess, which she was already doing.

The boy sucked in deep lungful's of breath. "Ma cousin, there's somethin' wrong wi' him."

"Where is he?"

Hazel shook her head. "No infection."

"How is it you've escaped infection?" Duke asked.

The boy's face reddened and his eyes dropped to the ground. "A, um, A ran. Whan the beasties came. I telt thaim no tae play wi' thae nasty things, I telt thaim. But they didn't listen. I got scared an' I ran. Far. The woods, they got quiet. Sae quiet. An' whan I came back it wis too late."

"You send the distress call?" Duke asked. "Where are the Storm Hags?"

"I did. A remember hou' Mistress Rose showit us. She knows me. I'm Peter. Mistress Rose always picks me tae help her 'cause I'm a quick learner." His blush deepened. "I don't know where the Hags are. Couldn't find thaim." The boy took Hazel's hand, tugging her forward. "Will ye come, please? Ma cousin, he's really sick."

They let him lead, moving to the other side of the village that was partially hidden in the woods where a mid-sized barn stood. One of the swinging doors was wide open, dirty hay spilling down a ramp and darkness within. Duke could hear rustling inside; he probed and felt the ebb of terror, confusion, pain flow back to him.

"It attackit him. He tried tae ficht but the beastie wis too strong. There's other kids in thare, an Healers, like ye."

Hazel gave a startled look to Duke.

"The Hags have apprentices, wise women and some men who show strong magic potential. They aren't powerful enough to be risen to Storm Hag status yet but they have more magic than the average human. They often act as Healers in tribes like this. It's part of our outreach, to help train them."

"Is this where they were treating the sick?" Hazel asked.

Peter nodded.

"Tate, Mahdyia, we need you here," Duke called over his shoulder.

"The Hags aren't in the trees." Bridget was out of breath as she ran back into the village. She caught sight of Peter and immediately moved to him, wrapping him in her arms as she did. "What happened here? Where are the Hags?"

Peter was shaking harder now, tears streaming down his cheeks. "Oh mistress, I don't know! The Hags are gone! Ma cousin, he's sick, they're aw sick."

"Shhhh," she cooed, running her fingers over his head, somehow avoiding getting snagged in the knots. She looked up at Duke. "The Hags wouldn't have left willingly."

"I know."

"The Magika are strong in the barn," Hazel said. She had her blade to her palm, ready to draw blood. "But they're too busy feeding to notice us yet."

"They're doing a good job hiding the scope of their power," Duke said. "I didn't feel anything until we came close enough."

"Sneaky, I told you." Bridget nodded, then moved Peter away from her body. "Go to the lake, boy. Do that spell I taught you, remember the one? For protection?"

Peter nodded. "I did it. I remember it."

"Good. Do it again and stay put. I'll come and get you when it's safe."

"Yes, ma'am. I will." He wiped his tears with the back of his dirty hand then ran off into the trees.

"We work the same way. Chanda and I will corral, keep those fuckers inside the barn. Hazel and Duke, you purge. Tate, Mahdyia and Bas, distribute the brew. Keep the Magika from reinfecting. Our magic build should be enough to obliterate them once they're free of the hosts."

"I can make sure of that," Tate said. "I'll pull electromagnetic pulses. Once they're free of the bodies, I can zap them."

"Good idea." Bridget looked at each of them. "Ready?"

"Ready," they all said in unison.

21

THE MAGIC WAS DENSE IN THE BARN, FLOWING ALL AROUND THE open space. The targets in here, a cluster of humans with strong magic, made it a feeding frenzy for the Magika.

Hazel felt it like a whip against her skin. Splashes of power hitting her from all sides as the Magika ripped and tore strength away from the humans, greedy and apparently oblivious to their arrival. It made her gag, the brutality of it. The magic floating around wanted to collect inside her, drawn to her power, but she rejected what was there. Stolen magic, taken without permission, would have to find another place to rest.

She shook it off, scanned the layout of the room.

It was obvious to Hazel what the human healers had tried to do. They'd corralled the sick in one location, a hospice of sorts, with cots and mattresses, the hay cleared away as best they could. There were no animals to contaminate the large space. It was clean, or at least it had been. In the dank area where daylight only penetrated so far, Hazel could see the bodies strewn haphazardly. Healers had fallen next to patients, suddenly overcome by the infection, having had no protection to ward themselves, knocking down tables that had held bowls with various liquids, towels and bandages. All were too weak to do much more than writhe or twitch where they'd fallen. Their voices appeared to have been stolen along with their magic, reduced to quiet moans of distress emanating on a breath, like a whisper.

"They're strong," Hazel reported to no one in particular. "Stronger than the ones in the cottage."

"How many can you feel?" Duke was next to her, his fingers almost touching hers, his body so close she could smell his delicious scent despite the pungent aroma of the barn.

She wanted to breathe him in deeply, to take comfort in that. She liked him there. Had come to expect him at her side. And for once, the thought of that didn't terrify her. "A dozen, maybe more." She couldn't see the beasties, but the feel of them, the repulsive essence they gave off was like a vibration of negativity. To take a witch's magic...

"What are you waiting for?" Bridget barked as she bullied her way past them, separating Hazel from Duke, a spell sparking on her fingertips.

Hazel adjusted her footing. *Showtime.* She stretched her awareness out once again, seeking even though she didn't want to, finding the thread of one of the Magika like a tail. Bile rose to the back of her throat and she pushed it down then grabbed the Magika between her fingers, pulling gently, testing the strength of its latch to its host. Strong sucker, feeding hungrily from the more powerful of the human witches—the healers who'd only been trying to help. She could feel the healer's magic, a flame that flared at Hazel's touch. Awareness, recognition, hope. Hazel's magic would feel like a lifeline to the woman.

"Hang tight." Hazel projected the thought, stoking that flame, distracting the Magika as she intertwined her fingers in its essence, slimy like worms, with stinging spikes that tried to grip her back. *"This is gonna hurt like hell but I promise you, I'll win."*

She felt the healer's hope surge, a promising sign. *"Fight back. Help me."* She also felt Duke there, his magic coming up under her, strengthening the foundation of her power. He'd been there every time she'd cast, giving her a boost like a buttress, his magic melding with hers so seamlessly that she couldn't distinguish hers from his. It felt right to be so connected, bonded in a way that she'd never felt with another witch or human before.

He wrapped his hand over hers, his voice in her head. *"Ready?"*

She didn't have to answer. Three beats of her heart and she pulled the Magika's tail, Duke's strength enhancing hers. The beastie resisted, dug in deeper, latching out with spikes that did little to penetrate Hazel's shield. The creature was screeching in panic, anger, loud and obnoxious in her head, but she didn't relent. She pulled harder, yanking with everything she had, even though the healer was wailing too, her cries of agony matching the Magika's cries of outrage. It was like a tug of war, a battle over this poor human's magic and the Magika did not want to let such a rich source go, but Hazel wasn't about to give up.

After pulling from the depth of her power while gathering what Duke offered, she sent it out, like a tether to hook to the beastie, anchoring securely so when she yanked back, she felt the first tear, like a seam ripping. Pouring all her power at that weak spot, she wrapped the tail around her wrist and dug in her heels, then tore the damn beastie out.

"It's out, it's out!" She heard the shouting around her. "Hazel, let go!"

Against all instinct to grip tight, she flung herself free.

"Stand clear!" Tate yelled. "Clear!" Fingers splayed, homed in on the beastie, Tate let loose his power.

A shock wave thundered through the barn, followed by a dosing of something soothing, calming, Chanda controlling the Chaos as best she could, the struggle evident on her face. She was keeping it together though. Chaos wanted to win—it would spread through the room, heightening anxiety, fear, action, but Chanda was tamping it down. Hazel could feel it like a blanket on her skin. Comforting in a way and it helped her focus on what lay ahead.

The Magika were aware now, attack ready and unwilling to leave their hosts without a fight. Hazel sucked in a deep breath, pulling from the airborne magic around her despite its nasty origins. There was no time to be picky, no time for niceties—she realized that now. She needed the power that was floating there and she'd give back with every life she saved. She fortified her stance, nodded to Duke, then joined in on the next one.

And so they worked. Systematically, diligently. Each witch had his or her job and as a team they culled the pack of Magkia down to just two stubborn fuckers.

"Stop, Hazel, stop," Duke's voice echoed in her head. She was so engrossed that it wasn't until he shook her that she became aware of the urgency.

"What? I can't stop now. I've got this one." It was a slippery one, evading her grasp, jolting her with some kind of residual magic. Nothing that she couldn't handle but annoying and distracting, penetrating her shields in a way that didn't make sense.

"Hazel, you need to stop and look." He had her in his arms, trapping her hands between them to stop her from casting any more.

She snapped out of her spell and looked where he was directing, where all the Healers were now looking.

"Ohhhh, shit," Mahdyia said.

Someone had been moving the patients away from the mayhem. Bas was administering the brew to keep the ill from getting re-infected. That left one remaining victim on one side of the barn and she was in worse shape than Hazel had realized.

"Assess," Bridget barked.

The human witch was a middle-aged female, probably about five-eight and underweight to the point of emaciation. Hazel guessed she'd probably been thin to begin with and the Magika were feasting on whatever was left, taking her essence along with her remaining body fat. Her body was ravaged, long dark hair was ragged looking, clumps missing, strewn all around, blood all over her body, her clothing torn to shreds. She was flopping on the ground like a fish out of water, her mouth gaping, struggling for breath, foaming at the corners of her lips, eyes bloodshot, cheeks hollowed out.

"Broken bones," Mahdyia said. "Multiple deep contusions, internal bleeding." She sucked in a deep breath, wiping her hand over her brow. "Might be a brain bleed."

Gouges ran down her arms and legs. Hazel took a step closer, thinking her eyes were betraying her. "What the..." What looked like bubbles or ripples seemed to run under her skin, undulating from her neck down to her torso, arms, legs.

The healer jolted up, her back arching, her mouth open wide, a silent scream there. She tore at her flesh, scratching, ripping, obviously in agony.

"We have to do something," Hazel said, moving closer. "Restrain her!"

Duke stopped her with a firm hold on her arm. "The Magkia are consuming her, their latch is too deep."

"So what? We just let them have her?" She wanted to tear free, to push away that feeling of resignation and defeat.

"She's bleeding from all of her organs," Mahdyia said. "I can't see how we'll save her even if you can break her free of them."

Hazel gulped. She looked at the poor woman, then over at the other witches and humans scattered around. They were just coming to full awareness, eyes darting, the appearance of conscious thought taking hold, like a spark of awareness. They looked scared, exhausted, but there was hope too.

"I can do this," Hazel said. "We can do this." She shook free of Duke, quieting him with a hard stare. "Get your blades out. Bas, I need you here too."

She was going with instinct, trusting her gut. They needed to pool their power, unify.

"What are you planning, Haz?" Mahdyia was all in, her blade at her palm already.

"A circle." Hazel's mind was spinning with the possibility. "We can create our own circle here."

"Impossible," Bas snorted even though he'd left his patient and was walking toward her. "Oh wait, I guess not for the Promised One."

Hazel ignored his sarcasm. "I need you to weave the spell."

Bas's eyes widened. "Me?"

"Yes, that's what you do, isn't it? You unify spells? So I need you to do that. Just follow my lead, okay?" She didn't wait for him to respond. "Cut your palms, join hands."

"Hazel," Bridget started, sounding uncertain.

"This I can do." She slammed Bridget with a determined look. "This is what I was born to do. So let me do it!"

Silence. Eyes locked. A storm waging. Bridget had been given Hazel as a ward in some way. Her mother would have stressed the importance to keep her safe, to not let her be reckless, impulsive.

"I can do this," Hazel repeated firmly.

Bridget nodded, stepped back to her place and pulled her knife.

No one else argued. Hazel slid her blade across her palm, one then the other, then resheathed it.

"Ready?" She looked at Duke, who was by her side once again. He nodded, clasping hands with her and Bas was on the other side.

The magic rose quickly, suddenly, almost without her control. The moment the circle was closed, when Bridget and Chanda joined hands, Hazel felt the surge of power envelop her. Blood mingled with blood. It was intoxicating. She nudged Bas, not invading his mind like she had before, just a gentle push to get him going. He started to weave their magic together, pulling from each of them to manufacture a rope of power that united them all.

Swept up in the swirl of magic, she began her chant, focusing on a spell that would dislodge the remaining Magika and hopefully restore the human healer's life force to what it once was.

No, not hopefully. It *would*. Because Hazel was the Promised One and this was her destiny.

❧ 22 ❧

WHAT HAZEL HAD DONE WAS NOTHING SHORT OF A MIRACLE. Duke was now on the opposite side of the village, helping clear away some damage that had been caused by the wayward magic, blowback from Hazel's spectacular spell.

She'd vanquished the last of the Magika. In her spell, and with the unity of the impromptu circle, she'd created a vortex that was ultimately both cleansing and healing. Most of the infected had been completely restored. Wounds had healed, magic had been re-infused. With a few exceptions—the last healer who'd been so ravaged and a couple of others with internal injuries needed more care—everyone had come out almost as good as new.

She was working with some of the villagers, helping restore order. She and a village woman were laughing as she taught Hazel how to knead some dough on a long wooden table.

"The Hags are still nowhere to be found." Bridget came out of the tree line, looking frazzled. "There's no trace of them."

"It's strange." Duke shifted the last of the wood over to the pile and dusted his hands. "They wouldn't just abandon the tribe." From what Duke knew, there were three Storm Hags. Humans who'd reached a level of magic skill that elevated them to the honored status. They not only manipulated weather—wind, rain, sleet and snow—but they could also influence other aspects of nature. Their magical abilities and affinity with the Earth gave them a mastery of most of the white arts. Spells that all human healers had basic knowledge of, the Hags had perfected. In many ways, their dedicated practice and devoted worship of magic had gifted them with the ability to create unique spells that even the white witches couldn't begin to wield effectively. A lot of that had to do with the fact that they didn't shun the darker side of their power. No human did.

That's what he'd noticed in his years as a Medic. They didn't discriminate and although cautious of dark magic, they used it when they needed to. White Witches, Healers from White Willow, would never use anything that even hinted at the nasty stuff. It was taboo in thought and forbidden in action. It was also something that Duke envied in his human counterparts. They weren't bound by the same laws and therefore could experiment to create stronger magic and unique spells. There was danger in that, of course, but the possibilities were endless in all directions.

"No, they wouldn't leave without a good reason to." Bridget rubbed her hand over her face, looking exhausted. "Peter said that the last he'd heard from them was an order to put a call out for help. He said that they were besieged by something."

"The Magika?"

"He didn't know, just that they were in distress and that their order to him came on the wind and was barely a whisper."

"So maybe they fled in an attempt to keep something worse away. The fog remains so they didn't leave the village completely unprotected. Perhaps in their leaving, they unintentionally provided an opportunity for the Magika to grab hold."

"I can't make sense of the time line. It seems like it was chaos here, the healers recall some of what happened before they became infected. Gathering the sick villagers in the barn, administering aid, but then they were struck down without warning, no onset of symptoms." Bridget started walking toward the central fire. "I'm going to investigate some more. I don't feel right leaving until we have a clearer picture of what happened."

"Definitely not before we find out where the Hags have gone," Duke agreed. "Why don't you take Chanda with you? Backup just in case." Although it could extend their field trip, he had an uneasy feeling about the Hags' absence and agreed that they couldn't just abandon the humans without some idea of where their magical foundation had gone.

Bridget waved agreement over her shoulder and headed toward the Chaos witch.

The other interns had been hovering around Hazel, Duke noticed, checking in with her, seeking approval. Probably understanding more now what lay within her. Why she was the Promised One. Like she'd earned the celebrity status her mother had worked so hard to build for her.

For all the sudden attention, Hazel was gracious about it. Smiling, joking, even enduring a few soft jabs from Bas. Duke saw a change in her though. Her shoulders weren't as tense, her smiles easier to come. She was like she'd been when he'd known her as a village girl. Not carefree necessarily but her guard was down to some extent.

He watched her walk toward the well with a bucket under her arm and a trail of little girls following her wake, all chattering excitedly about something or another.

"Hazel," he called, catching up with her just as she put the bucket under the spigot.

Her smile didn't waver when she looked over at him. "Oh, just in time!" She motioned to the handle. "I think I pulled a muscle or something in my shoulder. It would help if you did the heavy lifting."

"Of course." Duke bypassed her and the group of girls. They could have modern conveniences. That wasn't an impossibility. But the tribe had been living off the grid since before there was a grid. While some of the villagers had left over time, seeking out the big cities and the technology that came with it, many had stayed behind, choosing this kind of life—a simpler way where the magic was more accessible and nature provided what they needed. Duke could appreciate it. It had its place. But he also enjoyed plumbing and taps and five star hotels with room service.

"Girls," Hazel said, calling the group of kids around her. "Why don't you show Healer Hart what you can do?"

Duke was poised with his hands on the lever, ready to start pumping. Hazel motioned for him to get going. He pulled the lever up, flexed his muscles and began to bring it down. The girls joined hands, all intently staring at the spout where the water was beginning to trickle.

As the first gush came pouring, one of the girls flicked her fingers, while another one waved her palm. Instead of the gushing into the bucket, the water flung up on a magic induced wind and whacked him in the face.

He stumbled back, stunned at the trick, soaking wet. "What the...?" he sputtered.

The girls all ran off shrieking and giggling.

Hazel was holding her sides, laughing as well. "I'm sorry, I couldn't resist." She pulled a towel from behind her back and handed it to him.

"A little warning," he said as he blotted his face.

"Where would the fun be in that?" She moved closer to help him. "They tried to do it to me a while ago and I spoiled their trick."

"So you thought I'd be a better victim?"

"Yes." She smirked. "Better you than me."

He chuckled as he tossed the wet cloth at her head. She ducked, catching it in her hand. "The little devils are good, aren't they?" she said as she glanced toward the group of girls who were still cackling.

"Promising witches for sure." He motioned toward the tree line. "Hey, can we talk? Walk and talk?"

Hazel's smile wavered for a second. She glanced back at the central fire where her cousin was chatting with some of the villagers. "Um, sure."

They caught each other's eye, a silent look passing between them. Duke couldn't tell if this was going to be a good or bad conversation.

But it was a conversation that needed to happen.

It was dusk, the sun had set already and the last of its dying rays were blanketing the trees in warmth. Duke knew of a place. Quiet, peaceful. Not too far a trek.

"Like old times," he said as they moved into the trees, his thoughts drifting to the nights they'd made love under the stars, with no earthly idea about what was to come.

The feel of her skin under his fingers, his lips having no boundaries, tasting every part of her, making her moan, covering her with his body. Her limbs moving, hands running down his back to squeeze his ass, digging her nails in as she cried out—

"I know what you're going to say," Hazel started, her face turning a lovely shade of pink, snapping him from his lusty thoughts.

He cleared his throat, wanting to adjust his pants, his cock rock hard and aching. "You do?"

"I told you so?" She ducked her head, letting her hair cover her face a bit. "I mean, I felt it—what you were talking about. When we formed the circle together, I felt like we were all connected. That I could make a difference."

He stopped her, his hand on her arm, then swept her hair from her face. "You saved their lives. Without you, we wouldn't have been able to use that spell. That human witch would have died."

"Well, it wasn't just me..."

"No, it wasn't. But if you hadn't have suggested it, stood up to

Bridget and demanded your role, it wouldn't have happened. You believed in yourself and in your friends and you made it happen."

"My friends?" Her voice was a whisper of disbelief.

"Yes, the beginning of friendships. That's what happens when you train alongside one another. You learn to rely on each other's strengths. You may not always agree. You might not always get along, but I believe you've formed the basis of a few friendships here."

She was quiet, contemplating his words, maybe. He got her moving again. He had a destination in mind. One he thought she'd love.

He let the silence hang for a bit. Putting distance between them and the village. The sounds were changing, birds chatter becoming muffled, the air turning mistier. They were almost there. He put the call out, using his empathic magic to part the veil that separated the secret place from the forest.

"We can be friends too," Duke said, his voice cracking a bit. It had to be said. He had to stop pushing or else he knew he was going to lose her completely. How could he compete with her mother and a lifetime of beliefs—a lifetime of identity building? They had a year together. He'd take that year, even if it was only a year. "I mean, if that's what you want."

"Duke...oh my... Where are we?"

As they passed through a curtain of mist, Hazel reacted just as he'd expected she would. Her smile was bright, all stress from the day disappearing. He'd found versions of these places all over the world, typically close by a human Wiccan or Pagan tribe where magic ebbed and flowed, waiting for someone to soak it up.

"It's beautiful!" Hazel's eyes were wide, taking it all in.

Waterfalls cascaded from a rock cliff in steps and jutting stones. Like a staircase that went up about twenty feet, moss covered and sparking with crystallized stones, it reflected a strange magical light that Duke had never been able to figure out. And the water was always warm.

"It's like a fairy world or something." Hazel brushed her hand along the colorful flowers that grew by the pool of water that the falls dropped into. Splashes bounced onto the leaves and petals, shimmering there before sliding off to the soft grass below. "How did you find this place?"

"They call to me but sometimes it's hard to pinpoint location right away." He shrugged. "I just found one back home, after we parted that last night. I was going to take you there on the solstice."

Hazel looked up at him through her lashes. "Oh!"

He pulled her close, unable to resist her, his arms around her waist, hands clasped at the small of her back, body pressed close to his, almost every part touching. Special friends, for a year. At least so she could know a time in her life where she was loved by one man with all of his heart and devotion.

"Oh!" she gasped again.

He looked down at her, fighting to keep his senses closed. He didn't want the disappointment of her rejection to come through his magic. If she didn't want this...

"I love it," she whispered.

And he could swear that she meant something else.

With a sweet smile, she stretched up and pressed her lips to his.

The feel of her soft kiss, her body moving into his, pressing her breasts against his chest, made him pull her closer. She threw her arms over his shoulders, hands draped around his neck, fingers tangling in his hair so that the tug sent a tingle down to his toes. He opened his mouth to her, tongue probing, tasting her sweet mouth like he'd been starved for decades.

She pulled away on a breath. "Are we alone?"

"Completely."

"And no one will be able to find us?" Her eyes were dancing.

"Nope. Not unless we want them to."

Her lips curled into the cunning little smirk he loved so much.

She pushed him backward, startling him into sliding down the embankment, and then all out flat on his back into the pool. The water encased him, sucking him down with the weight of his clothes.

He sputtered his shock as he resurfaced. The water was warm as usual, but for the briefest of moments, he thought maybe she'd tricked him, maybe he'd misread... But then his gaze fell on her. She was dancing as she kicked her pants off, flinging her tank top next. She twirled in her black panties and bra, nothing fancy about them, but showing just the right amount of skin to make his cock pulse all the harder.

"You'd better get in here," he growled, splashing water her way.

She gasped when it hit her. "Oh, that's so warm!"

He nodded as he popped the button on his pants, struggling to get them off his hips, the water making everything heavy and clingy.

She reached around her back, unclasped her bra and let it fall forward as she leaned down. He dived under so he could free his legs from the pants, swimming to the edge at the same time. When he came up, she was leaning closer, obviously looking out for him. He jumped up and grasped her ankle, toppling her into the water. She had barely enough time to utter a startled shriek.

Her naked body was slick against his, nipples hard little pearls that he sucked deep into his mouth, taking most of her breast as well. Twirling his tongue, nipping with his teeth. She had her hands on his cock, stroking him, squeezing him, just the right amount of pressure, cupping his balls gently, reverently. He loved her touch. He loved everything about her.

You've got her for a year.

He wanted her for more.

With a moan, she took her hands away and replaced them with her pussy, using the water to glide, her hands on his hips, sheathing him deeply inside her. He trailed his mouth to her collarbone, her throat and then her lips, kissing as he shifted his cock, pumping her slowly. Making sure he was grinding deliciously against her clit. Making sure she gasped each time he withdrew and then slammed back inside. Deeper, as deep as he could go. He wanted her. He needed her. And if he dwelled too long, he would crumble on the knowledge that he'd never have her. Not really.

"You are so beautiful," he whispered against her ear, then sucked her lobe, earning another groan of passion.

"So are you," she gasped, her hands encouraging him to go faster, harder, to take her until she couldn't breathe.

His balls tightened, his climax rose swiftly. She flung her head back, moaning in a rush as he filled her full of his cum, her pussy squeezing until he had nothing left inside of him. Until he'd given her everything he had.

They floated together, his arms wrapped around her, just under her breasts, her head resting against his shoulder. A blissful existence that he could enjoy forever, if only he could keep his mind off of those nagging things...the hammering of his heart, the thudding of emotions wanting to crash in on him.

"Hazel—"

"I know what you're going to say," she whispered, then sighed.

He braced himself.

She turned, using a jolt of her magic to keep them afloat as she rested her arm across his chest and her chin on her hand. "We only have a year."

She'd said it. What he'd been thinking. His heart was crushed. This is what he'd offered her. Friendship.

"How could I think..." she started, gulped, her eyes sparkled, wet. "How could I think that anything at all could compare to you?"

He frowned. Blinked. "Uh...what?"

She giggled, then sobered just as suddenly. "I was so sure, everything I've ever known, my whole life until I came on this trip. Until I felt and saw and experienced things on my own, without my mother here to guide and caution." She broke the spell so that they both had to stand, neck deep in the water, hands clasped to arms to keep from floating apart. "Even though I've been fighting it, not wanting to face the truth, I realize that everything my mother had ever told me was meant for one purpose."

He dared not speak.

"To serve her." She stated it as fact. "To serve Healer-kind. To serve the Circle. But..." She shook her head, her hands moving to his chest, fingers splayed. "But how could I think that those things would mean the same thing to me after you?"

Duke couldn't trust what he was hearing. "Hazel, I know—"

"You were right. My mother slanted everything so that all that mattered was my destiny, the destiny that she controlled. And maybe she was doing it for selfish reasons. Maybe she was using me. And if that's true, if she can be so selfish and still be a great Healer, a great witch, then why can't I?" She looked up at him, open, wide open. "Why can't I be selfish too?"

"It's not selfish to choose love, Hazel." He kissed her forehead. "What you've done here, for the village, how you united your team, that is not selfish. You gave, you healed. And you can do that and still serve Healer-kind. And one day, when we've lived a long life and helped so many, we can join the Circle together and give the last of our power, if you want." A compromise—better than a year of special friendship. "I'm the one being selfish, Hazel, because I just can't imagine my life without you in it. Right here, with me, not part of a Circle where I'd never be able to touch you again." He lifted his hand to her face, brushing back a stray bit of hair. "It's selfish of me to want you all to myself, but I do because I love you. I fell in love with you when you were just a village girl and now I love you just the same. My heart is yours."

"I feel blissful, like when we would meet in Salem Village, and I don't want to deny myself that kind of happiness." Hazel smiled, then curled into him, laying her head to his chest, arms wrapped tightly around him. "I do love you, Duke and I will do anything to keep you in my world, so I'm selfish too. I don't want to live a life-time without you in my arms."

In that moment, without giving it too much thought, he opened himself to Hazel, to all that she was, taking in the emotion of her words, trusting what his gut had been screaming all night. She did love him. With everything she had, and he felt it slam into him like a tsunami of purity that would consume his very soul.

SHE'D HAD A CURRENT OF PANIC RIDING HER SINCE SHE'D declared her feelings for Duke. Not because she regretted it. No, she'd spoken truly. Honestly. For once, she'd let her guard down and ignored expectation and obligation and instead focused on her wants and needs. She'd fallen in love with Duke over the past year. It had been foolish to think she could detach herself without it doing major damage to her psyche. And what kind of witch would she be then? How could she help others if she was crumbling in on herself because she'd denied true love? It sounded like a fairy tale, she knew, but maybe that's what she deserved right now. Maybe it was time to put herself first.

So the panicked flutter in her stomach wasn't that. This was something else. Maybe the thought of having to tell her mother all that she'd discovered on the trip? To stand up to her for once and confess that Hazel had decided she was not going to the Circle. She had a year to do that. Plenty of time to ease her mother into the decision. And she had Duke and Mahdyia's support, maybe even her new friends.

No, that wasn't it.

Something else.

"We should get back to the village," she said as she pulled her panties on, her body still wet, making it tricky to get the cloth over her hips.

"You feel that too, huh?" He was using a spell to dry his clothes, which he'd just rescued from the bottom of the pond. "Thought I was the only one picking up on it."

"Yeah, something isn't right." Hazel snapped her bra on and quickly got into her pants and tank top.

"Let's go." Duke held his hand out to her, the drying spell still crackling along the seams of his shirt.

She smiled, pushing aside her anxiety for a moment so she could enjoy him for one second more. Bypassing his hand, she wrapped her arms over his shoulders and kissed his lips. "If we must," she giggled.

"It feels good to hold you." He hugged her tight, squeezing her for a second longer before letting her go.

It did. Just being with Duke felt good. Right.

They held hands as they moved through the veil, and Hazel felt the change in everything as her body broke free. The air was different, thicker, more heavily scented with dirt and musk. The sounds seemed loud, harsh, and something was crashing through the trees toward them.

"Hazel! Duke!" It was Mahdyia, her hands cupping her mouth, shouting so loudly that she didn't hear them respond.

"Mads, what's wrong?" Hazel grabbed her cousin's arm, swinging her around.

"Where have you two been?" Mahdyia looked frantic, incensed. "I've been looking... Oh, never mind." She turned to Duke. "There's something wrong with Bridget. She found the Hags." Mahdyia gulped, wincing as she did. "It's not pretty."

"Let's go." Duke still clasped Hazel's hand as they moved quickly back to the village.

"There, over there." Mahdyia pointed to the central fire where a group of villagers were gathered.

They pushed their way through the throng.

"What happened?" Hazel couldn't keep the shock from her voice, the horror at what was lying there.

Bridget was on the ground, gouges, deep ones, marring her cheeks, her arms, her hands raw and ragged, fingernails torn down to the nubs. Convulsions raging. Everyone was clear of her, waiting for the seizure to pass. She was foaming at the mouth, her body covered in sweat.

And next to her lay another body—old and withered, blood covered, sunken cheeks, but somehow still conscious.

"I tried to stop it..." the Hag sputtered, pointing to Bridget.

"Shh." Bas was kneeling next to her. "I've done what I can but there's something infecting both of them. It's too strong to fight."

Hazel closed her eyes, shutting out the horror as she reached out with her senses, homing in on the thing that was ravaging Bridget.

But there was nothing there.

"I don't understand." Hazel opened her eyes again. "It's not a Magika. It's not anything."

"What?" Duke knelt down next to Bridget, trying to take her hand, to check her pulse. "I don't sense anything either."

"So what the hell is going on?" Mahdyia waved her hands toward the Hag and Bridget. "They have catastrophic injuries, internal bleeding, broken bones, and it isn't stopping. It's happening right now."

"But there's nothing causing it!" Hazel said. There was no magic infection, nothing for Hazel to grab a hold of.

"I can't find Bridget's pulse," Duke said, his expression grim. "Tate, you may have to zap her."

"She's dying," Chanda was off to the side, biting at her nails as she stared at the bodies. "We were searching for the Hags. She was talking one minute, just a normal conversation, pointing out a plant or something and then *wham*! She went down. Like hard. She couldn't breathe, she couldn't see."

"This is out of our league," Tate said.

"We need my mother," Hazel croaked, her mind swirling, panic grabbing her by the throat.

"Do not...do not..." the old woman mumbled, trying to push herself up on shaky arms, only to crumble back down with a weak scream.

"Her arm is broken," Bas said as he picked her up gently, the frail little thing nothing in his arms. "It snapped, just now."

"Something is causing this," Hazel said. "We need to remove them from the source."

"Where are the other Hags?" Duke asked.

"Dead. They're dead!" Peter was on his knees wailing, his hands covering his face. "I saw thaim. Heads torn richt aff! They're dead!"

"Peter came just as Bridget went down, carrying this Hag. We got them back here somehow. We didn't know what else to do!" Chanda's eyes were darting all around. "It's some kind of infection, right? We brought it here now, didn't we?"

"Lock it down, Chanda." Duke was trying to get Bridget into his arms but she was convulsing too badly to secure her. "There's no infection. There's no magic here. Hazel would feel it—I would feel something. We don't know what this is but we do know that it'll kill them if we don't do something."

"We need to get back to White Willow," Hazel said. "We need to bring them to my mother."

"How do we get back? Bridget was the only one who could time shift!" Chanda's voice was still high, panic edging every word.

"We can't bring them back to White Willow," Duke huffed as he wrapped his arms around Bridget. "They'll never make the journey."

Hazel's brain was spinning, the feeling of panic rising higher until it was thudding painfully in her head. She needed Chanda to tamp the Chaos down. "Slow down...wait...we need to—"

"Hazel can do it," Chanda yelled, snapping her out of her thoughts. "She knows how to time shift."

"They'll never make it," Duke yelled. "Tate, I need you here, now."

"It won't work," Hazel said. Tate's magic would kill Bridget. "Duke, think about it. Her body is too frail. If Tate zaps her—"

"It has to work. We're out of options! I will not have her die out here. Not on my watch." He was so fierce, with his strong arms wrapped around Bridget.

And she felt, what? Jealous? She gulped, shaking it off. Bridget was going to die if they didn't figure something out.

"Everyone needs to calm the fuck down," Bas said, still holding the Hag. "Chanda, lock your shit down, now! The Chaos is building."

It was an order, spoken without the heat that everyone else seemed to convey. It snapped like an elastic band and everyone looked to Chanda, who stood there blinking like she'd been slapped. She nodded, closed her eyes and within a few moments, calm had settled.

Hazel felt her mind clear of the panic that had been thundering. She reached into her pocket and pulled out her mother's amulet. "We don't need to shift time lines." She pulled her blade with the other hand.

Chanda opened her eyes again, swaying a little as she did. "What?" She sounded drowsy, her eyelids fluttering as she struggled to focus. "We can get home?"

Mahdyia nodded knowingly, reading Hazel's thoughts as only a cousin could. "Of course." She pulled her blade too. "I'll encase us —you do the rest."

Hazel nodded back. "Move closer together. Bas, I need your blood for this too."

Bas didn't argue. He turned to Tate and passed off the Hag gently before pulling his own blade and making the cut. "Ready."

Mahdyia was already forming a bubble around them, encasing

them in a spell that would keep them bound to one another for the journey. Hazel's mother had given her the summoning stone—a stone that kept them connected always. Perhaps it allowed her mother to siphon from her, Duke was right about that, but more importantly, it gave her an open door to wherever her mother was. A one way ticket.

"Hang on, folks," Hazel mumbled. She cut her palm, clasped the amulet then lifted her hands up. "Mother, I need passage."

The spell swept her up, pulling the rest of the group along for the ride. A portal opened, shimmering above, a gaping maw of darkness that looked ominous. Hazel felt her mother's power pulse and reached toward it. In a heartbeat, they were all sucked in.

They landed to the shocked expression of her mother, who was sitting behind her desk in her huge office. The second Hazel's feet touched the floor, the amulet shattered, splintering into a dozen pieces in her palm.

"Mother..." Hazel tossed the pieces aside. The men were lowering Bridget and the Hag to the carpeted floor. "There's something wrong with Healer Rose and this Storm Hag. We can't figure out what it is."

Her mother was on her feet, eyes wide with dawning realiza-tion. "You brought a human Hag here?" A dark blush of scarlet started rising from her chest, to her neck, her fists clenched at her sides. She was clearly ready to blow. "What were you thinking?"

Her mother's rage had never been the bellowing kind, but it brought the thunder in its quiet delivery.

Hazel flinched.

"This. Ground. Is. Sacred...It's—"

Before she could utter another word, Hazel felt the rumble of magic, rolling through the floor, up her legs, into her body. She stared down at Bridget and the Hag, who were lifted from the ground, like puppets. Unconscious on invisible strings.

Bridget's eyes had rolled to the back of her head, the whites visible as her body shuddered with another seizure. The Hag's head lolled on her neck, her body limp, hanging in a grotesque pose.

Their mouths popped open, closed, then open again and a faint cackling began. "Foolish, foolish witches. How easily you are tricked." And then the cackling grew louder as magic swelled out from the bodies.

Oh, shit!

Hazel looked to her mother, who had come around her desk to face the new threat, her expression set in battle mode. "You are not welcome here."

More wild cackling. "I was invited. Brought by a Promised One. An offering was made and now I'm here. And I will take my fill." A gruesome smile on the Hag's face, teeth stained with blood. "I will *always* take my fill."

"What is it?" Mahdyia whispered.

But Hazel couldn't speak. She couldn't voice the unbearable mistake she had brought upon herself. To invite such a thing into White Willow. How could she be so stupid?

"Bacchus Demonius." Duke cringed, his gaze on Hazel as he raised his hand to his heart. "Like the granddaddy to the Magika."

Hazel watched like it was happening in slow motion. Duke, Tate, Chanda, Mahdyia, all falling, hands to their chests, pain on their faces, gasping for breath. The magic was swelling like a wave, sucking into a vortex that was this demon. It was feeding and it would take and take.

"Mother!" Hazel clasped hands with her Mother, the two of them bound, a shield of protection raised by the Great Mother, spreading out to cover her friends.

"You must cast with me, Hazel. You must follow my words." Her mother's voice was sucked away, taken as the demon fed.

It would suck them all dry—every witch in the hospital, every magical artefact. It would obliterate the Circle. The shield would only hold for so long.

What had she done?

The shield shimmered around as the demon tried to invade. Hazel watched as Duke and the others slowly started to rouse, shaking off the effects of the demon. Bridget and the Hag were still being used as puppets, conduits for the beast to channel the magic. Eventually, the power would overwhelm their corporal bodies and they would be obliterated just as the Hags back at the village had been.

It was so clear to Hazel now. Years of theory, education that had been stuffed into her brain was playing out in front of her. But that was the problem with book learning. It was words on a page. It wasn't real until it was real.

"Hazel." Her mother's voice was strained, veins popping in her neck. "You must go to the Circle. I will give you a passageway. You must go."

"I must join the Circle?"

"It's the only way. I need the power. I need *your* power. Unite the Circle or we will all die."

"No!" Duke shouted, wild eyes darting from Hazel to her mother. "No Hazel! Don't join the Circle. If you do, you'll never be able to leave."

He was right. Once she joined, it was a lifetime commitment.

She locked eyes with him. Her mother's voice battering against her at the same time.

"Hazel, go now, I don't know how much longer I can keep this going. The passage is open. Go, girl, go now!"

Duke shook his head. Eyes pleading silently. *"Use this circle."* His voice was in her head. *"Claim your destiny, Hazel. Harness the power around you."*

He wanted her to go to the Circle?

And he opened his palms, deep strikes from his blade already there, then turned his back to her, arms splayed, the full depth and breadth of his empathic magic exploded in the room as he left the shield.

Hazel and her mother flew backward. Everyone else fell to the floor, covering themselves from the debris flying around the room.

"Duke!" Hazel screamed. "No!"

The demon dropped Bridget and the Hag, bodies falling in lumps to the ground and picked up Duke instead. Its feeding was noisy, grotesque, and obviously consuming the demon's attention.

"Healer Hart has made the ultimate sacrifice," Mother said. "It's time for you to join the Circle and make sure it was not done in vain."

Hazel's heart was shattering right there in her chest. She tore her eyes away from Duke to her mother.

"Make his sacrifice worthy. Claim your role, child, so that I can save the Healers."

Hazel blinked, her brain so fuzzy. Duke didn't want her to join the Circle. He didn't want her to commit herself there.

She felt something tug at her hand, and looked down to see Mahdyia there, on her knees, rising, grasping Hazel's fingers, then her hand as she pulled herself to her feet.

"Use the circle, Hazel," she yelled. "*Our circle*." She motioned to the others, who were slowly rising also, stumbling into a circle.

The circle. Like what she'd done at the village.

That's what he'd meant.

"Mother, I need you to hold that shield." She didn't wait for a reply. Instead, she moved in closer to her circle of friends, her supporters. "Open your palms, witches, we've got a demon to destroy."

❦ 24 ❦

DUKE ONLY HAD ONE THOUGHT, AND IT STARTED AND ENDED with pain.

The demon feeding from his magic was excruciating. It tore and ripped through him, shredding the magic from his very core.

He had to hang on. He had to keep it distracted so that Hazel could do her thing.

Please make her do her thing.

But he thought that would never come, the pain was so bad, so intense that he couldn't see anything past it. He couldn't feel Hazel even.

That is until he did feel her.

Like a swell of water, he felt her rise beneath him, the foundation of her power bolstering him as she built up her spell, layer by layer, brick by brick. The demon was gorging, unaffected by her presence, not realizing what she was doing, what any of them were doing.

Duke would have smiled if he wasn't in such agony, an agony he knew was about to get worse when they ripped the beast from him.

He clenched his eyes shut, bracing for what was to come and wasn't remotely prepared when it did.

"*You ready?*" Hazel's voice was in his head. "*Cause this is gonna hurt like hell.*"

And it did. Like the burning fires of hell were scorching him from the inside out, his brain short-circuiting, his thoughts zoning in on only one thing.

Hazel. Please. Make it stop.

&.

HE WASN'T AWAKE. HE KNEW THAT. IT WAS TOO FOGGY, TOO languid. He was lying on the forest floor, staring up through the trees with his arms behind his head and Hazel draped over his chest.

"I wish we could stay like this forever," she said, her words muffled.

"We can." He lowered one arm, tightening it around her waist, before kissing the top of her head. "We can stay like this forever."

She giggled, her head popping up so she could look at him. "You wouldn't rather me be like this forever?" She pushed herself up, straddling him so that her slick pussy was hovering just over his aching cock. Her naked breasts swaying slightly as she wiggled her hips. "Or like this?" She nestled herself lower, sliding her wet lips over the shaft of his dick.

He half chuckled, half groaned, bringing his hands up to cup her breasts, to flick his thumbs against the hard peaks of her nipples. She threw her head back, her hips still moving, still teasing him with her wet folds.

"I'd rather you like this," he said as he wrapped an arm around her back and brought her closer, higher so that he could taste the sweet pebble that jutted so prettily. Rolling his tongue against her nipple, sucking and then stroking until she was the one moaning, the movement of her hips more urgent, slower.

"Like this," she gasped as she lowered her hand and moved his cock so that the tip was sheathed. "Or like this." And then took him all in, right down to the base, her cream slicking to his balls.

He released her tit from his mouth, so he could palm her breast once again. She rocked her hips, sliding her pussy up and down, grinding her clit against his shaft.

Her eyes were locked on his. Intensity there, burning to his very soul.

"You are mine," he growled.

She nodded, didn't speak, then closed her eyes and pulled herself up, knocking his hands away so that she could play with her own tits. Flicking and pinching, writhing on his dick, her pretty lips parting with gasps and moans.

He could die right here. This had to be paradise.

"I am yours," she echoed his words, her voice husky.

She lifted her hands away from her breasts; he wanted to reach up and play again. To fondle and cup. She was bouncing on him now, working into a frenzy, his climax rising, building with each pump. Her ass sliding down so low that it kissed his balls, her pussy gripping so tight that he thought he was going to scream.

He lifted his hands to her hips, helping her ride, rolling his groin up to meet hers.

And just as his climax was there, within reach, cresting and ready to blow, she stopped. She stopped and looked down at him like she was confused.

"I can't be here right now." Her eyes were glassy, unfocused. She pushed herself off of him, leaving his dick to jut and throb, the cool air bringing pain.

"Hazel...what..."

But she was walking away, her naked back to him.

"Hazel!" He tried to get up, to rise and chase after her but he couldn't move, not a finger, not a twitch. It was like he was bound, strapped down. He couldn't see anything holding him though.

"I am yours, Duke. Yours for eternity." Hazel was standing just in the distance, facing him now.

A cloaked figure approached her from behind, a glinting blade in a covered hand.

"Hazel! Look behind you!" He struggled to release himself. Strained with everything he had. "Hazel!"

The blade rose high, Hazel turned toward it, not at all surprised. "It's my destiny."

And then the cloaked figure slashed Hazel across the neck, somehow sending a splatter of blood to land on Duke's chest. The drops burned into his flesh, making him scream. "Hazel!"

But the cloaked figure didn't stop, opening her wide, trailing the knife down her middle, blood soaking, muscle and sinew popping, veins bulging and all the while she just stared, her lips moving silently.

"Hazel, no!" he screamed and thrashed, but he could do nothing to stop the torrent.

❧ 25 ❧

His dreams were obviously awful. Hazel tried to sooth Duke the best she could, pressing a wet cloth to his head as she murmured to him, cooing sweet words, hoping he could hear her.

"Duke, I'm here. Please wake up. Come back to me."

He'd been like this since they had vanquished the Bacchus Demon. As she'd ripped that nasty beast away, it had taken part of Duke with it.

It's my fault you're like this. Please wake up. Please, Duke.

That had been two days ago.

And he'd been cycling through horrid dreams that made him sweat and scream and lash out.

Nothing calmed him. Nothing she did, anyway. He would settle, would even get a smile on his lips at times and then it would start all over again.

His screams were so disturbing, so tortured, that they'd moved him to a private room of the hospital. Deep in the basement where a wing was reserved for the most gravely ill. Death row, the orderlies whispered, thinking she couldn't hear. *Death row.*

They'd spared no expense in this section of White Willow though. The room was decorated luxuriously, more like an upscale hotel room than a hospital room. Walnut furniture, wide screen TV, ensuite bathroom, a recliner and sofa for guests to rest and wait for their loved one to die.

Duke, wake up! You're strong. You can beat this. Please.

What had she done wrong? How could she have done it differently? She replayed the battle. It was the same spell she'd used on the Magika back at the village, only magnified because she had the White Willow Circle there bolstering her and the others, her friends forming their own circle, a super charge of power that sent her spell out almost beyond her control. But she *had* controlled it, directed it with Bas's and the rest of the interns' help. She'd obliterated that demon. Bridget and the Storm Hag had recovered almost immediately. But Duke—he just lay there, a crumpled heap, no visible wounds, but unconscious and unresponsive.

"I've been hearing rumors." Her mother was standing at the doorway and startled Hazel from her thoughts. "About you and him."

Hazel closed her eyes, her shoulders bunching under the heavy weight of her mother's judgment.

"It's not what you think." Hazel couldn't imagine what her mother had heard. She couldn't imagine who would have ratted her out. Mahdyia? No. Never. Bas? Tate? Chanda? She didn't think they would. Or was her mother just surmising based on the fact that Hazel hadn't left Duke's side since he'd fallen, since he'd been moved to the dungeon of a suite?

"Oh, Hazel, it *is* what I think." Her mother came to the end of the bed, her hands curling on the footboard, jewelled rings on several fingers that helped her target specific spells, sparkling with crystals that amplified her magic when required. "I realize now that he was sacrificing himself for you. Right? When he opened himself up, an empath of his ability and years of training would know what that would do to a Bacchus Demon. Like offering drugs to an addict. He drew that demon away from us so that you could join the Circle."

Um...what?

"Not *the Circle*, Mother." Hazel tried to keep the anger out of her voice. He didn't want her to join *that* circle.

"That's what he said, isn't it? Claim your destiny. You know what your destiny is. It's etched in stone. He was so selfless, protecting the Promised One. That's what everyone is saying—all of your companions on the trip, that Healer Hart took special care of you. Acted as an appropriate mentor, took you under his wing, and helped to guide you to new understandings of your powers. I will forever be indebted to him for that."

Hazel choked on a surprised laugh and disguised it with a cough. Oh yes, he'd taken special care of her all right.

"He came so highly recommended. Years of dedicated service." She reached out to stroke Hazel's cheek. "He's a strong Healer. Deserving of special care. We could save him."

"What?" Hazel sobered immediately.

Her mother moved around the bed to her side, an arm over her shoulder. "If you join the Circle now, I can use the power to heal him. Wake him from this coma."

Hazel looked up with surprise. "You need my power?"

"Oh Hazel, it was foolish of me to send you out on that field trip. To expose you to such danger. I realize that now. And you must feel such responsibility. Too much. You always cared too much." She squeezed Hazel's shoulder. "That's what makes you such a good Healer. But, child, I was wrong to send you out. I hope you can forgive me."

"Mother, no, I—"

"And now you feel responsible. But I'm telling you, Healer Hart can be restored and you can be safe and sound, if you join the Circle now."

"But my training..."

"It was just to appease the Board. I have petitioned them for leeway here and, after they heard what happened, they have agreed. It is better for you, and for everyone, if you forgo your training and unite with the Circle now. Claim your role, Promised One, and help me save Healer Hart."

"Duke," Hazel croaked.

"Indeed." Her mother bent down to kiss the top of her head. "*Duke* has made quite an impression on you."

"Mother, I—" She looked up, wanting so badly to just spill it all out, to tell her mother what had actually happened. How she felt about Duke, everything.

"You want to save his life, don't you?" Her mother was looking at her with one of her signature half smiles, the kind that said there was something she wasn't saying. "Because, of course, he will die if left in this coma for too long."

"What?" She'd looked it up, Bacchus feedings could result in comas, yes, but they didn't last forever, a strong witch could—

"Those dreams he's having. They're killing him. The Bacchus left a nasty toxin behind. It must have been infected with something. If we don't get it out, well, I'm afraid that he'll probably only make it another day, maybe two before he succumbs."

"A toxin?"

"Yes, a terrible one. His breathing will get more and more shallow, his heart slowing until it can't sustain the vigour of his nightmares." She spread her hand along the edge of the bed, smoothing the sheet as she walked down the length of it. "There is only one way to reverse it. A spell that takes years to master."

Hazel felt her throat seize.

"I can do it, though. But only if you join the Circle."

Hazel couldn't form words.

"I know you will do the right thing. The worthy thing, for the most deserving Healer Hart...Duke... You are after all, the Promised One."

She watched her mother leave. Bewildered. Her heart aching

so badly that she thought maybe her mother had ripped it out before she'd left.

"*Duke.*" She turned back to him, tears falling silently on the sheets.

This was the choice? This was how she chose her destiny? Was it really a choice?

"*Duke.*" She projected it loud, using all of her magic to send it into him. "*Wake up! Please! This isn't how it's supposed to be.*" She clasped his hand, wrapping her fingers around his. His skin was so clammy, so cold. "Duke! Wake up!"

But he didn't. Instead he cycled into another nightmare and thrashed, and screamed, and pleaded for her to stop...to stop what? Was she hurting him? Had he conjured some image of her that was torturing him endlessly?

Another hour passed, another revolution of his endless process of terror, calm, then terror again. It was agonizing to watch. His muscles got so rigid, veins popping in his neck, like he was struggling to get himself out of the world that the toxin was making him endure. His eyelashes fluttered as if he was struggling to wake, erratic movement behind his lids suggesting anything but peace. And his breathing was slowing, his mouth gaping with short pants. She laid her head on his chest and heard not the thundering roar of his heart but the soft thud of a dying and withering thing.

He was going to be dead before the day was over. She could feel it. He was too weak to fight. Her mother knew. She always knew what to do, or what had to be done.

And really, Hazel had no choice. When it came down to it. Her life was about sacrifice. That's what she'd always believed. And her mother was right. She owed Duke a life. He'd made a worthy sacrifice so she could have hers even if her mother had gotten part of it wrong. He didn't want her to join the Circle, but if she didn't then he would die and he couldn't die—not when there were so many witches who needed his help, so many tribes he hadn't discovered. He still had so much healing left to do.

She checked to make sure no one was around, then leaned in and kissed Duke on the lips and on the forehead. "It's a worthy sacrifice. For love. I will be selfish for you. I can't imagine this world without you, Duke. I want you to live."

She didn't need to stop anywhere. She didn't need to get anything from her room. When she entered the sacred vaults, she would remove all traces of her old life, don one of the long white robes worn by the members of the Circle. She would be anointed with little fuss and then she would join. No ceremony beyond that necessary. And she didn't want the pomp and circumstance. Her mother would know immediately. All Healers would. Hazel joining the Circle would send a ripple of power out. And then nothing else would matter but maintaining the source of power so that Healers could do their jobs effectively.

So that her mother could save Duke.

The sacred vaults were just on the other side of the building, a bit of a walk, crossing the main stairs that went down to the lower level but conveniently located close to where Duke was. The doors lay ahead, twins in design, with intricate carvings in the dark mahogany wood, warded against intrusion from hostile visitors. They went from floor to ceiling and had huge iron rings that acted as door handles. They would open for her as she approached—she'd tested it before. Like the doors knew who she was and what her purpose would be.

This was her destiny. What lay past those doors.

"Hey, Hazel!" Mahdyia shouted from down the hall. "Wait up!"

Shit. Okay, this was a roadblock. Mahdyia would never understand. She'd never accepted Hazel's destiny. She wouldn't be okay with it. Hazel sucked in a deep breath, knowing what she had to do to keep her cousin out of this decision.

"Hazel, what are you doing?" She grabbed Hazel's arm, intent on spinning her around based on the force and grip.

Hazel armed herself with a spell, ready to jolt Mahdyia back. She began to pivot, with the spell crackling on her fingers.

"Oh no you don't!" Mahdyia reacted before Hazel could fully turn, armed herself with a whopper of a spell and jolted Hazel back. "What the hell, Haz?"

Hazel stumbled backward, more surprised than hurt by Mahdyia's spell as she fought to keep herself on her feet. "I have to go!"

"Go where?" Mahdyia was recasting, arming herself again.

But so was Hazel. "Please, Mahdyia, you don't understand. Mother can save Duke."

"What? Of course she can... So can—"

Hazel sent her spell out, wrapping Mahdyia in a binding of rope that would keep her busy. "I don't have time for this."

"Tate!" Mahdyia shouted. "Stop her!"

Hazel turned, ready to run, and instead met a wall of Tate. *How'd he get there?*

He put his hands on her arms to steady her. Looking down with concern. "Mahdyia thought it might come to this." He winced. "I'm sorry, Haz, but it's for your own good."

And then he electrified her.

Oooouuuuuch.

26

OKAY, THIS WAS DIFFERENT. DUKE HAD GROWN USED TO THE dreadful cycle of his erotic dream with the horror twist. It didn't make it pleasant, especially since he didn't remember the dream itself until it was over. So when he didn't cycle through on cue he felt a little disoriented... Well, more disoriented than he had been for the last...however long he'd been in the hellish loop.

Instead of finding himself in a dream, he was floating...outside of his body.

Cool, astral projection. It was a skill that the humans could do seemingly with little trouble, especially those with familiars but Duke had never before been able to wilfully project his essence outside of his meat locker.

He felt a wave of dizziness when he made the mistake of looking down. His body was there, looking peaceful. Alone. He frowned.

Hazel had been there. He had sensed her at his side.

He glanced around the room. But she wasn't there now.

Nice room though.

Okay, focus, Duke. He was projecting—there was a reason for it. Either he was dying, which by the look of his body, was entirely possible, or his instincts were pushing him out because he had something to do.

He looked around again. He couldn't walk. He waved his arms. He couldn't fly. So what the fuck was he supposed to do?

He strained to remember. The humans had given him a process for achieving astral projection—he just didn't exactly recall all the steps. He was already out of his body, presumably the hard part. Now he needed to move.

Vibrations.

Right.

There were vibrations. Magic waves that he could use to help him move. *Focus.*

He closed his eyes, calmed his mind. Opened himself up to the vibrations. *Show me what I need to see. Take me where I need to go. Help me find the way.*

And then he felt movement. A slight breeze on his face, tickling his scalp, cooling his skin. Fuzzy noise, like wind passing, or conversations buzzing in his ears.

He opened his eyes.

He was moving, quicker than he thought. Floating through things, walls, doors, people. It was only slightly weird. Only freaky if he let himself consider that perhaps this was what being a ghost felt like. Was he that close to death? Perhaps.

But he was flying, fast. Up two floors, down corridors he wasn't completely familiar with. Was he going to find Hazel? Was she in some kind of trouble?

He tried to shake his fear for her. Tried to keep his mind clear. *Help me find the way. Take me where I need to go. Show me what I need to see.*

When he came to an abrupt halt, he was disoriented once again. The vibrations stopped, the white noise that came with it stopped as well. He was in a grand library, shelves stacked with books from floor to ceiling. No, wait, not a library—there was a huge desk, with an ornate chair, red brocade fabric, lion heads on the arms, fit for a king...or queen.

"Will she obey?"

Bridget's voice was clear suddenly, the tone all business. She walked into the room, moving through Duke as she did.

She shuddered, looked back, almost as if seeing him, then shook it off.

Mother Knight was just behind her, looking her usual militant self.

"Of course she will obey," Mother Knight said dismissively. "She's my daughter. She knows what she has to do. It's her destiny."

Her destiny. Duke's stomach plummeted.

"And Duke?" Bridget watched as Mother Knight moved to the other side of the desk, laying some files down before taking her seat.

"I will see to Duke once Hazel has taken her place. I explained that to you already."

"Because the amulet is broken, right? You need her there to bolster you for that reason?" Bridget winced, lowered her head briefly. "Perhaps I can locate another crystal instead. Give Hazel enough time to achieve her training. A year would do her good. She showed such potential, such strength in the field. I just think—"

"No." Mother Knight glared at Bridget, a fiercely dark look that spoke of dangerous things. Mother Knight was frozen in her movements, hands clenching on the top of the desk. "She is a powerful witch as it is and has had enough experience already. You think I don't know what's been going on behind my back? You think I'm not aware that my daughter is in love, or what she perceives as love with that man?"

"I didn't know—" Bridget did her best to look surprised, shocked, mortified.

Nice try, but not even I'm buying that act.

"Well, *I know*, Healer Rose. I know my daughter, I know every move she makes, every thought she thinks is clear on her face. I knew when she was sneaking out to see the humans to participate in their celebrations."

But she didn't know that she'd been sneaking out to be with him. She didn't know everything her daughter was thinking. Duke would dare say, she didn't know her daughter at all.

"I indulged it because I knew I could always call her back if necessary. The amulet gave me that peace of mind. She was keeping herself happy, not going stir crazy, not putting herself in danger. The humans are harmless really and everyone needs an escape. I am not without compassion, understanding." Her expression softened, as much as a hateful stone of a face could. "But now she *is* in danger. The feelings she thinks she has for Healer Hart, those are too dangerous to indulge. She will join the Circle and fulfill her obligation to me... To all Healer-kind. That is her purpose. That is her duty."

"And you will heal Duke?" Bridget asked.

"Of course I will. That is the promise I have made to Hazel and that is what I will do. As soon as she joins the Circle."

So that was what was drawing him there. To learn that Hazel was about to be lost to him and there was nothing he could do about it. He clenched his fists and roared, his frustration making him want to rip his way through the building to find her.

If she joined the Circle she was gone. Forever.

"Now, Healer Rose, I have things to do." She waved her hand at the file in front of her. "What was it you needed to ask me about your patient?"

"Oh, yes, let me show you. I have the x-rays right here."

Bridget turned away, bending to retrieve something from the pack on her hip, then looked directly at Duke, her lips moving soundlessly, her voice suddenly a whisper in his ear.

"I'm buying time. We have a plan. Don't panic. Yet."

❧ 27 ❧

HAZEL FELT LIKE SHE'D BEEN HIT WITH A SLEDGEHAMMER.

"Owwwwch." She tried to lift her hand to her head but found her arms bound. "What the..." Her vision cleared. Mahdyia was standing in front of her in a room she felt she knew intimately. She darted her eyes around. Duke lay on the bed, the rise and fall of his chest reassuring her somewhat.

"Don't freak out." Mahdyia lifted a steaming cup to Hazel's lips. "Drink this. It will help with the pain."

She didn't give Hazel a chance to argue, not unless Hazel wanted to wear whatever was in the cup. She drank tentatively. Tasted peppermint and ginger, something else, but it did seem to help with the pain, taking it down a notch or five.

"What happened?" she croaked once Mahdyia took the cup away. "And why am I restrained?"

Mahdyia sighed as she laid the cup on a table then sat on a stool in front of Hazel. "It was the only way to stop you."

"Stop me from...oh, Mads, I have to go, Duke is dying, I have to get out of here! Mother said she'll save him if I join the Circle now. He's dying, Mads. His heart—it was barely beating...how long have I been unconscious? How long?" She was watching

Duke's chest, couldn't take her eyes off the steady rhythm of his breathing.

Tate was sitting there, partially concealed by a curtain. He leaned forward so Hazel could see and waved. "Guess it wasn't unwanted attention after all, huh?"

Hazel blanched. "I'm sorry...I—"

"It was my lie," Mads said. "Hazel just went along with it. She thought pushing Duke away was best for everyone. She loves him, Tate, she's always loved him."

"He's dying," Hazel pleaded. "We don't have time for this."

"If his heart stops, Tate will zap him."

"That won't work!" Hazel yelled. "His heart can't take it, he's too weak. That will just kill him faster."

"Hazel, please." Mahdyia put her hands on Hazel's knees. "Please, calm down."

"I can't calm the fuck down!" Tears burst from her eyes, embarrassing considering the audience. "He's dying and Mother is the only one who can fix him!"

"No." Mahdyia gripped Hazel's knees harder, digging her nails in. "She's not. She lied to you."

Hazel tried to stomp her feet on Mahdyia's, the words registering on a delay. "W-w-what?" She stopped struggling.

Mahdyia relaxed her grip. "Your Mother lied to you. She wants you in that Circle where she can safely siphon your power. Especially now that the amulet is broken."

"It's broken?" But she knew that. It had broken when they had returned from Scotland, the magic required to bring them all back too much for it to handle. It had shattered in her hand.

"She's not the only one who can save Duke," Mahdyia said. "But she wants you to believe that she is."

"Why?" Her mother had the best interests of everyone else at heart, didn't she? No, that wasn't right...she could be self-serving too. Hazel knew that. She knew that with such certainty before they left Scotland, when she and Duke...

Duke...who was dying. "Why would she lie to me about saving him?"

"Because she's a selfish bitch." Mahdyia coughed. "Sorry, I know she's your mother."

"She is selfish," Hazel agreed, earning a startled look from Mahdyia. "I know she is thinking of herself most times. But she said that the spell Duke needs takes years to learn. She wouldn't lie about that. He's infected with a toxin."

"Hazel." Mahdyia leaned closer. "You really have no idea what you're capable of, do you?"

"I don't—"

"You know what that soothsayer said to me?" Mahdyia snapped, cutting her off. She paused, then spoke more softly. "She said that you would have a choice to make. Duty or love. Only one would fulfill your destiny."

Hazel frowned. "This is duty and love...you must have misheard."

"No, I didn't. I heard it clearly. Duty *or* love, Hazel. She said you'd have to make the choice."

"Why did she tell you? Why didn't she say that to me?"

"Because you're blinded by duty. Because my destiny is to be your eyes. Hazel." She leaned closer. "I have always known your place is here, not in the Circle. Not fulfilling your mother's fucked up sense of purpose. Not to keep *her* from sacrificing her own life to Healer-kind. Think about everything that's happened. Think about everything you've learned. Everything you've accomplished. Can you honestly say to me that you can't save Duke with your magic?"

Hazel closed her eyes. "Mads, I can't take that chance." And that's what it really came down to. If there was a spell she didn't know, if it took years to learn, she would rather hand over her power to her mother so that Duke would live.

"Yes, you can. I have faith in you. Duke has faith in you. Everyone, including Bridget, has faith in you. You can save the love of your life. You can do that. So stop being an idiot and fucking do it."

Could she take the chance? Wasn't that selfish? Cocky? And if she was wrong? If she was denying her destiny in favor of her heart's desire?

Do not be led by the desires of others. To be selfless, sometimes you need to be selfish. Destiny is what you make it. It's never set in stone. The soothsayer's words echoed in her head.

She felt a flutter of something, a whisper of a touch against her cheek. She lifted her head, could have sworn she could feel him. *Duke.*

Stranger things had happened.

"I don't have enough power on my own." Hazel opened her eyes, shocked that she was even considering it. "I can't do it alone."

"You have us to bolster you." Mahdyia released the bonds from Hazel, freeing her from the chair. "You have all of us behind you. Please, Hazel, have faith in yourself like we have faith in you." She called behind her. "Guys, come in here."

And the group filed in. Tate stood to greet them, his face a little red as he briefly glanced at Hazel. Chanda, smiling brightly. Even Bas, who looked sullen as usual, gave a nod to her as he entered.

"We're all behind you. You can do this," Mahdyia said.

"The spell—"

"I have it!" Bridget burst into the room, totally out of breath, a book in her hand. "This is it." She thrust it toward Hazel. "Your mother is right behind—"

"Healer Rose! What are you doing?" Hazel's mother swept into the room.

Hazel sucked in a deep breath, she flicked her eyes to Mahdyia for a second, then she let her breath out and stood up from the chair. Two steps to meet her mother. Eyes locked on hers.

No flinching.

Don't show weakness.

"Mother," Hazel started, straightening her spine. "I am not leaving Duke. I love him."

Her mother's stern look crumbled into one of pity and understanding. "Oh, darling girl, I know you do."

Hazel frowned.

Her mother raised her hand to Hazel's cheek and stroked her tenderly. "He made such a sacrifice for you. Cared enough to give up his life. Felt so strongly about your destiny—"

"No, Mother," Hazel took a step away, creating a pocket of space between her mother's hand and Hazel's face. "That's not what he did. We met, a year ago at Salem Village for the solstice. And we kept meeting, every few months. Sometimes every week. I'd sneak out, I'd meet him. I didn't know who he was..." Her voice cracked. "He didn't know who I was, but we fell in love. Mother." She hated that her voice sounded like she was pleading. "We fell in love. He sacrificed himself to save me, yes, but he doesn't believe that I am meant to fulfil the destiny you have laid out for me."

Her mother's hand curled, along with her lips. "You've been seeing Healer Hart? You've sullied yourself...with this man..." She covered her mouth for a moment. "If you had gotten pregnant..." Fury snapped in her eyes. She flattened her palm and then slapped Hazel full force.

Hazel's head whipped back, her eye felt like it was about to explode. She didn't fall. She didn't dare fall.

"You crazy bitch! What the fuck—"

Hazel stopped Mahdyia from attacking with a wave of her hand, magic flowing like a wall. "No." She made eye contact with her cousin, shared a nod, before straightening herself to face her mother again. "You will never touch me like that again."

Her mother raised her hand to strike a second time and Hazel froze her in place with another wisp of magic. Her mother's expression changed in an instant, realization dawning. "Darling, girl—"

"Mother, be silent." Hazel froze her mother's tongue, then glued her mouth shut. "It's funny, all of a sudden, I feel like I have the surge of power, you know? Almost like for my whole life I've had a drain on me, siphoning off the top, making me weaker than I really am." She moved around her mother's frozen body. "Almost like someone has been keeping me from gaining full strength. And now, just this minute, I've realized how much power I have. Isn't that strange, Mother? Who would do something like that? Take another witch's magic?"

"A selfish, self-serving, bit—" Mahdyia started.

"Oh, yes," Hazel interrupted. "Definitely self-serving. A person who perhaps was scared of what the younger generation may be able to do. A person who feared becoming irrelevant, less powerful, less esteemed." She was back facing her mother now. "A person who would do anything to grasp at immortality, even at the expense of her only daughter."

Her mother's eyes were wide, fear replacing all else there. Her jaw was working, like she was struggling to speak. Hazel let the spell loosen her mouth and tongue.

"You have something to say, Mother?"

"Your destiny... I was only following what was predetermined. You can't hold me responsible. I was only—"

"Oh Mother, things maybe would have gone a little differently if you'd only taken a fraction of responsibility." She nodded toward Mahdyia. "I'm going to need as much power as I can get if I'm going to heal Duke."

Mahdyia moved behind Hazel's mother and gripped her arms. "I'll escort her to the sacred vault."

"What do you mean? I can't go there. I'm the Great Mother. You can't do this to me! You are nothing without me, Hazel. All of your power has come from me! My years of dedication to your training, my blood and sweat to get you to this point. My devotion to all Healer-kind to give up my only daughter so that we may all benefit."

"That was not your choice to make! And you lied to me!" Hazel lashed her mother with another silencing spell. "You lied to me. You told me that I had only one destiny. That I was only fit for one purpose. You didn't tell me you were stealing power from me through your amulet. You didn't tell me that you were controlling me in order to fulfill your needs. Your quest to live as long as you could. Your desperate need for power. The Great Mother who is so highly regarded for charity and strength, for skill and compassion. You lied to me for my whole life so that I could fulfill a destiny that was meant for you. You wanted me in your place so that you could live on. You didn't do that for all Healer-kind. You did that for yourself!"

"You treated her like her only purpose was as a surrogate to you," Mahdyia hissed. "I've watched it my whole life. Hazel being crushed by the weight of your expectation. Your disappointment. Your selfish decisions. She deserves better."

Hazel swallowed the lump in her throat, tears burning the back of her eyes. *Suck it up. Hold your ground.* "Mother, I need your contribution to the Circle. Mahdyia will take you there to ensure you fulfill your destiny. It is always the role of the Great Mother to sacrifice herself when the time is right in order to supplement the next generation of Healers. You know, as well as I do, that the Board has a successor already chosen for you. Despite your attempts to live forever, they are always prepared with a backup just in case—"

Her mother's eyes were tearing.

Hazel's resolve began to shake.

"Oh Mother..." She motioned for Mahdyia to release her then moved in closer so that she could hug her tightly. But only for a second. She pulled back enough so that only her mother would hear her. "The time is right and you will do your duty. You will choose this or I will tell the Board about your treachery. I will share with them, and all who will hear, how you stole magic from your only daughter. I'm giving you the choice, to go to the Circle, rather than go to the Scrub. Which would you prefer?"

Hazel removed the silencing spell once again.

Her mother opened her mouth looking like she was going to rage, then closed it again, then opened it again, was nudged hard by Mahdyia, and closed it again. She gave Hazel a withering glare, closed her eyes, gulped, then finally spoke. "My daughter has laid a charge against me that I cannot dispute. It is my duty to fulfill my obligation to the Circle and join their ranks. I trust..." She cleared her throat. "I trust that Healer Rose will inform the Board of my decision immediately so that my successor can be notified."

She didn't spare another look at Hazel. She didn't utter another word. She straightened her back, squared her shoulders and walked out of the room with Mahdyia right behind her.

There was stunned silence for a few seconds.

"Hazel, the book, the spell." Bridget came toward her, flipping the ancient text open where she'd marked it with her hand. "Here, you need to do this now. Duke's not breathing."

28

DUKE'S NOT BREATHING?

That was news to Duke. He'd been so enthralled by Hazel and the strength she showed, standing up to her mother like that. If possible, he loved her more for finally thinking of herself.

But she wasn't just thinking of herself. She was thinking of him. And now she was doing her best to shove down the panic he could see threatening to derail her completely. He couldn't feel her though, and the lack of her energy playing on his senses was enough to send him into a panic himself if he let it.

He was still out of his body. He could see everything playing out. He had no idea how to get back where he needed to be. In fact, it was harder to stay rooted at all.

Hazel had the book spread on his bed, her finger moving swiftly through the lines of text as her mouth moved silently.

Tate was pumping oxygen into his body, giving him zaps of power that make his body jolt and jitter but did nothing to get things working again. He felt like he was floating for real now. Like he was truly disconnecting from himself. And he was drifting.

Maybe it was too late.

He reached out to Hazel, willing himself with everything he had to be by her side like he had been while she'd stood her ground and defended her feelings for him. He moved slowly, excruciatingly so. Somehow, he managed and brushed his fingers against her cheek, his thumb to her lips, imagining that he was feeling them as she kept up her whispered practice.

When she looked up, it was like she was looking straight at him, the projection of him. Or was he a ghost now?

"I can do this," she said.

He nodded, knowing she couldn't actually see him.

"You can do this." He cupped her chin, then let his hand slide down, her neck, her collarbone, her arm. "I'm right here with you."

She sucked in a deep breath and she drew her blade. "I need our circle, guys, if you'll help me. I need you."

And without a word, each one of the witches in the room, from Bridget, to Tate, to Bas, all pulled their knives and bloodied their hands for her. For him.

They joined, palm to palm, a circle around him, giving him their power as Hazel ignited the spell that was supposed to bring him back.

As she spoke the first string of words, Duke felt himself fade, like the essence that gave him life outside of his body was draining away. He didn't know what was happening or if this was his time but as his eyesight flickered, the image of Hazel going dark, he projected the last of his magic toward her with his thoughts, hoping the message got to her somehow.

"Whatever happens, Hazel, whatever come of this, I know that you're the love of my life, so hold me in your heart and I'll see you on the other side."

❧ 29 ❧

THERE WASN'T ENOUGH POWER. SHE WAS STARTING THE SPELL the second time, having already led them through once and nothing was happening.

"Not enough power!" She pulled and pulled, drawing from not only what her friends were giving her but from her own well, it wasn't enough.

"I'm unifying our magic—it's just not sticking to the spell," Bas growled.

But that wasn't the problem. Their circle was incomplete. Without Duke to help. Without Mahdyia, they just weren't strong enough to defeat death.

"You are the love of my life."

Words echoed to her. Duke's words. His voice. Just there. She couldn't open her eyes. Was he dead? Was he speaking to her from beyond the grave? Had she lost him in that moment?

Duke. Don't leave me.

She needed something more. She couldn't let him go. Not like this. Not right now. She had a lifetime to live with him. She'd made her choice. *Love.*

"I just found my forever," she whispered. "I choose love!"

Who was listening? She, a Promised One no more, was supposed to be able to do anything. She could do anything.

But her hope was fading, along with her magic. Pouring everything into the spell was costing her and she knew it was draining the witches in her circle. Every word she spoke, every invocation of the spell was draining them all.

Had she made the wrong choice?

Please. Please. Please.

"Whatever happens, Hazel, whatever come of this, I know that you're the love of my life, so hold me in your heart and I'll see you on the other side." Words echoed in her head again.

She opened her eyes and he was there. A fading silhouette floating above the bed like a ghost. The look on his face was one of resignation but also love.

"Nooooooo," she heard herself moan, a mournful, pitiful sound that broke her own heart. "Nooooo, Duke, stay with me."

She opened herself fully, willing to give until she had nothing left.

Her heart beat hard and fast, her blood flowed from her hands. She just needed...

Spark.

A spark.

A flare.

A flame.

She felt it. It was there. Like a beacon. She reached out and grasped it, pulling it greedily toward her, infusing her circle with this new power. It rushed up her arms, into her heart, fuelling her.

Mother.

Her mother had joined the Circle in the sacred vault. Her mother had claimed her rightful place and had directed her power toward Hazel. Dedicated power so she could save Duke. Her heart melted all over again.

Mother.

She started the spell again. She tore the words from her

memory, spoke them with a fevered dedication that came with the desperation only a battle with death could bring.

Another jolt came.

"I'm here," Mahdyia said, power in her words. "This party ain't over yet."

And it came in a rush, all the power, all the words, all the magic, came to Hazel, through her, flowed out of her, and reached for Duke. The toxin in him wanted to fight her, wanted to keep eating at his poor body but she blanketed it with the counter spell, making it null as she swept through him, moving it from his cells, from his veins, from his blood and purging it from his system.

She opened her eyes to see the cloud of toxin coming from his mouth, spewing it out like a dust storm. His whole body heaved, a torrent of the stuff. She thought it would never stop. And when the last of it left and she continued to dose him, giving him whatever essence she could, pumping full of magic until he finally, finally drew in a strangled, gasping breath.

"He's breathing." Tate looked shocked, his eyes wide. "He's alive!"

"He's breathing but he's not awake," Hazel said, trying to keep the disappointment from overwhelming her.

"Give him a minute." Mahdyia was on the other side of the bed, holding hands with Bridget and Bas, her eyes closed, clenched so tight it looked like it hurt. "Give him a minute."

Hazel couldn't cry any more. Could she? Was it possible? To get this close and never see those dark beautiful eyes—full of intelligence, full of love—look at her, be aware of her?

Mahdyia mumbled something, her frenzied words a hiss on her lips but otherwise indecipherable.

One blink. Two. A flutter of blinks. Hazel gasped.

His eyes were open.

"Duke!" Hazel unclasped the hands holding hers and shoved

her way closer, draping her body onto his, her lips on his lips, her hands on his face. "Duke, Duke, Duke."

"I'm here," he croaked.

"You're here." She smiled down at him. "I thought I'd lost you. I thought you left me behind."

He shook his head, licking his dry lips and trying for a smile, which looked more pain than pleasure. "Nah, I was here the whole time."

❧ 30 ❧

"I've been meaning to ask..." Hazel had her arm entwined with Duke's as they strolled through Witch City, Salem. "Where'd you learn astral projection? I mean, that's what that was, right? You were there, I didn't imagine that."

Duke chuckled, squeezing her hand as he wrapped it around his forearm. "No, you didn't imagine it. A tribe in Africa taught me actually. Or at least I tried to learn. Hadn't realized I knew how to do it until I was doing it."

"So there won't be a repeat performance?"

"I don't know... I'm not exactly sure how I did it. I think... perhaps we should go there on a field trip see if maybe that's a skill you can pick up."

"Another field trip?" Hazel patted his hand. "The new Great Mother arrives tomorrow. I've heard rumors."

"Ah yes, Mother Stone. I've heard rumors too." Duke winked. "Guess we'll have to see what the new sheriff decides is appropriate for a first year intern."

"Hey, I *am* the Promised One."

He swept her up in his arms, halting their walk in the middle of a throng of tourists. "No, sweetie, you *were* the Promised One. That job has been filled for another fifty years at least."

He dipped his head down, pulling her closer into his body, loving how she fit there, snuggled in close. He kissed her softly, tenderly, lips pressed to lips, opening himself and giving her all the love in his heart.

She sighed as she pulled away. "I could do that forever."

He tucked her under his arm again and moved them forward.

"Where are we going?"

With everything that had happened, Duke and Hazel hadn't had much time alone together. And with the new Mother on her way, Duke had a feeling things were going to get hectic again before they settled. So he wanted to take Hazel somewhere special.

"Remember that place I told you I found?" He moved them down one of the side alleys, bypassing the crowds.

It wasn't as busy in the city this time of year as it was around October, but there were still more people than usual. Probably because of the excitement of what was happening at White Willow. Despite the fact that the witch world was shrouded in secrecy, most of the Pagans knew exactly what was going on. Rumors flew faster than magic most of the time. They were flocking in to celebrate the arrival of new leadership and he knew that there was a hope, perhaps farfetched, that this leader would be more open to the humans rather than shunning them as Mother Knight had.

"The fairy place?" Hazel asked, her hand on his chest as they strolled. "It's around here?"

"It's not a fairy place." He chuckled. "But yeah, it's here and it's special. I think you're going to love it."

He turned them down another cobbled walkway. It had taken him some time to hunt it down. Over the years he'd found veils separating these little bubbles of space in many different places. Sometimes in forests with sparkling waterfalls, sometimes at the edge of a desert where an oasis with crystal clear water and shady palms existed. This time, as was fitting for Salem, it was a little crooked house, nestled between two buildings.

"Do you feel that?" It was a tickle against his skin, like a warning but without the trepidation.

He'd stopped them just where the front door was, a gaping black maw between a spell shop and a bookstore. Completely concealed if you didn't know what you were looking for.

"It's here?" Hazel was grinning. "It feels heavy with magic. Is this it? An alley?" She winked at him.

He waved his hand, opening the veil. "Not an alley."

The house was one story, basic design, with two steps leading to the front door. It matched the architecture surrounding it, like the magic had adapted to its surroundings, building this space to fill a need, or used the magic that was hanging around. It implied sentient magic, thinking on its own to adapt to the surroundings and use the magic stores that were floating around. It was an interesting concept and something to explore, study perhaps, but not now. Now was all about Hazel.

"Want to go in?" He didn't wait for a response, instead moving them both up the steps and opening the front door.

Inside were creaky wooden floors, a wood stove that already had a fire burning, giving off warmth and a muted light that made the space feel cozy and welcoming. There was a huge bed in the middle of the room, with piles of fluffy pillows and a duvet that Duke knew was plush and soft. The mattress you could sink in. But the centrepiece of the place was a grand window at the back that somehow had a complete view of Salem forest, despite the reality of being in the middle of the city.

"How is this even possible?" Hazel was clearly awestruck, gaping as she moved toward that window, her hand out to touch the bedding as she walked past. "You think there's some kind of time shift?"

He'd guessed that was going on when he first started discovering these places. Like the magic shifted them back in time somehow, when the forest surrounded Salem and the city itself had been just a small cluster of houses.

"It's magic." He gathered her up in his arms. "And it's ours."

She stared up at him. "No one else knows about this place?"

"I've been finding these magic spots for years, and never have I encountered another witch or human here. It's possible that it's our little secret, at least for now. Empaths are rare. Maybe it speaks only to my kind of magic."

"And no one can find us here." Hazel hugged him then, pressing her face to his chest. He sighed into the hug, his arms wrapped tightly around her waist. "I can't imagine a better place to be."

"Me neither." He pressed his lips to the top of her head.

"I know I was awful," she whispered, her voice almost lost in the folds of his sweater. "Spoiled, ignorant, wilful."

He shifted back a bit, using his fingers to tilt her head up so he could look at her. "All those things." He smirked, then kissed the tip of her nose.

"Thank you for not giving up on me, on us." She lifted her hand to his cheek. "I love you, always have."

"I would have chased you until the end of time. You're my soul mate, Hazel. You don't just walk away from love like that."

He lifted her to the bed, before settling her down so he could crawl up her body, loving how she giggled, how her hands ran up and down his arms, how hungry her lips were when he kissed her.

They took their time removing clothes. Pants off so he could kiss the inside of her thigh, shirt off so she could lick her way over his stomach, her fingers trailing down just to the edge of his jeans. He loved how delicate her skin was, flawless and smooth. He couldn't touch it enough, teasing with feather kisses until she giggled more.

She sighed as he settled between her legs, breathing in her sweet scent as he spread her pussy open to his tongue. Kissing her clit before licking and flicking, eager to make her writhe as she did so prettily.

She had her hands on her tits, stroking herself to the peaks before pinching her nipples. She was watching him too, her head bent to the side so she could see what he was doing to her. He loved that.

As she shuddered through the first rise of her climax, he released her from his mouth and moved up so that he could slide his aching cock home. The feel of her pussy clamping down hard on him, her moan as he stroked her climax so that it would build to an explosion for only him made every second of torture worth it.

"I'll never get enough of you, village girl." He kissed her smile, sucking away the groan as he pounded into her fiercely until they were both crying out with sudden and complete release.

❧ 31 ❧

HAZEL WAS SEATED IN THE INTERN'S LOUNGE, DRINKING HER latte and wondering where the others were. They couldn't be late. This was day one of Mother Stone's rounds. Hazel had yet to meet the woman but she'd heard things...

"There you are." Mahdyia walked through the door, her arms loaded with boxes. Before Hazel could get up and help, she'd dumped them on the floor. "New uniforms, apparently."

Hazel nudged one of the boxes closer. "Have you seen her yet?"

Mahdyia's eyes darkened and she snagged Hazel's coffee from her hand and took a sip between words. "Yeah, from a distance." She cringed.

"That bad?"

"You got enough sugar in this thing?" Mahdyia laughed, shoving the empty paper cup back at Hazel. "Ick!"

"Mads!" Hazel tossed the cup in the garbage. "How bad is she?"

"Well, she doesn't look anything like your mother. Her hair is red and curly. Kinda wild actually. And she has a crowd around her. Someone with hair like that can't be bad."

"Don't be so sure," Hazel said. "I'm sure she has all the usual ass kissers trying to get in good."

"No." Mahdyia's tone was doubtful. "It didn't look like the usual bunch."

"Are you guys ready?" Chanda and Tate burst into the room, Chanda's words rushed and urgent. "She's coming!"

"Who's coming?" Bas stepped out of the bathroom with a towel wrapped around his waist and a *who gives a shit* expression on his face.

Hazel didn't buy it. They all knew who was coming.

And suddenly there she was. Mother Stone standing in the doorway, her eyes moving purposefully over the crowd of them, only to settle on the boxes practically blocking the entrance way.

Tate and Chanda scrambled to move them.

"I see the shipment of uniforms has arrived." Mother Stone's voice was cool but her smile was bright. Her skin was freckled and her hair a vibrant red with corkscrew curls that framed her face and came to jagged halts just past her ears. Her eyes were dark, maybe blue, but Hazel couldn't tell. "Open the box please."

Tate thought she was talking to him but when he went to do it, someone else moved forward. A person in a blue cloak, hood covering his or her head, who'd been standing behind Mother Stone, stepped forward to follow her orders.

Mother Stone moved farther into the room, allowing for her entourage to come in as well. There were six in total, including the one currently opening the box.

The magic signatures were unique. Hazel detected...humans?

"Interns, I've heard great things about you all." She motioned for her helper to pull out one of the uniforms. "These will be your new clothes for the duration of your training."

Black. Cotton looking. Hospital scrubs?

"The color was chosen on purpose. Black, as I'm sure you know, acts to absorb and nullify some magics. The cloth as well as been infused with rosemary and hawthorne to protect against energy attacks."

Hazel tried to keep her expression neutral. Herbs and colors? That was human magic.

"Is this for real?" Bas blurted, taking a step forward as if to argue with the Great Mother. "Human wards?"

Mother Stone turned her head slightly to address him, her smile not fading but her eyes narrowing. "Bas Frank." She continued before he could answer. "I knew your mother."

And that was all she had to say to shut him up. With wide eyes, he stepped back to his place.

"And Hazel Knight." She gave Hazel a once-over, seemingly not impressed. "You have quite a reputation to overcome."

Hazel startled, not expecting those words. "I do?" *To overcome?*

"I've always found..." Her smile turned wistful. "That the bigger the ego, the more there is to learn. And you, dear, what with your history, have quite an ego to shed. Not to worry though. I plan to dedicate myself to improving your skill."

Mahdyia shot Hazel an *ohhhhhh shit* look that was part horror, part comedy.

"Yes, ma'am, I'm honored." Which really meant *fuck me*.

Mahdyia snickered silently, covering her mouth as she did.

Seemingly satisfied with Hazel's response, Mother Stone turned her attention to the rest of the group. "All of you have learning to do. These"—she waved to her group—"will be your secondary mentors. Answering only to Healers Rose and Hart, here are the Sin Eaters, and you will abide by their instruction. They will teach you how to be humble."

Sin Eaters? Hazel wanted to cringe. Some of the others did but quickly, and smartly, fixed their expressions before anyone noticed.

Sin Eaters were human witches, one of the oldest and oddest clans that existed in literally every country. Nomads, they were drawn to Pagans and magical tribes to offer their services as Sin

Eaters. Doing exactly as their name suggested, they consumed the sins of others. Taking in their wrong doings, absorbing the ill will of anyone who asked them to, cleansing curses and dark magic.

Sin Eaters were both revered and cherished because of their service. Their willingness to take on the sins of others, including magic gone wrong, was a sacrifice that cost them hugely. Sin Eaters were deformed, diseased, and ultimately always in a constant state of pain. The cloaks worn by all of them were meant to not only mark their purpose, but also hide their deformities.

Hazel flicked her gaze to the hands of the one holding up the scrubs and noticed that his knuckles were gnarled, his thumb missing. She could only imagine what lay underneath.

"You will abide by their teaching," Mother Stone repeated sternly. "And add their knowledge to your repertoire of skills." She nodded to the group. "Now, interns, get changed and get to work. Today marks the first day of your probationary period. Disappoint me and you will be asked to leave the program."

And with that, smile firmly in place, Mother Stone left the room, her trail of followers on her heels.

"Oh my—" Chanda started.

"That's what I'd heard," Hazel said. "I didn't want to believe it but I'd heard it. She's a strict leader."

"Well, this is going to suck." Bas looked suitably freaked out. "What do you think that meant? What she said to me?"

"That she knew your mother?" Mahdyia shrugged.

"Yeah, like in a bad way?" Bas frowned. "It could be worse... I mean, she clearly doesn't like Hazel."

Hazel winced. "Yeah I picked up on that."

"She wasn't wrong about your ego—" Bas snickered.

"Enough. We're all up shit's creek with this one. Sin Eaters? Really?" Mahdyia said. "I've heard they can be brutal."

"Tough teachers," Tate added. "But we'll learn a lot. I'm not scared of the challenge."

"At least we're in this together, right?" Chanda said. "I mean, we're a team."

"We are a team." Hazel picked up one of the scrubs, a pungent smell wafting. "And we're here to learn. We can do this." She wanted to believe it but the smell of the scrubs was making her slightly nauseous.

"Go team," Mahdyia cheered. "Barf. Well, what doesn't kill us makes us stronger, right?"

Hazel could only hope that whatever came next would indeed make her stronger.

"It'll be an adventure." Hazel tossed the shirt to Mahdyia. "Let's uniform up and get started. We have healing to do."

The End.

ACKNOWLEDGMENTS

I want to thank the usual crew of cheerleaders, beta readers, proofreaders, overall awesome friends I have in my life: D.B. Reynolds, Michelle von Enckevort, Dianne Waye, and Tammy Crosby, Anna Sotiropoulos, and Kate Riddell. Thanks also to Holly Atkinson, my forever editor who keeps making sure my books aren't full of crap. And thank you to my husband who bought me some noise cancelling headphones and my kids who are noisy almost all the time but who also help me come up with magic ideas so I guess I'll keep them around.

A CONVERSATION WITH ANGELA ADDAMS

What inspired you to write The Witches of White Willow?

Well, probably not where you'd expect, actually. A couple of years ago I discovered *Grey's Anatomy* and became addicted. Like, seriously, became obsessed with the show. My husband and I binge watched every episode until we were completely caught up and then I went through that weird withdrawal you get when you have to wait forever for a new season so you can reconnect with all your fictional friends. While I was waiting, I started thinking about the things I really loved about the show, the characters, the drama, the love affairs and I thought—well, I love all of that but you know what would make it more interesting? Witches!

You set this in Salem, which I know you recently travelled to for a book signing. Any particular reason why you chose that location?

I love travelling to Salem. I went there for my honeymoon and it inspired my first witch novel (one that will likely never see the light of day, EVER). I set up the book signing to celebrate the rerelease of my *Order of the Wolf* and *The Dark War* series and while

I was there, ideas started really taking shape for the setting of *The Witches of White Willow*. Salem has such a rich history when it comes to witches and witchcraft. A terrifying history in a lot of ways but it's also a place that I find infused with creative energy, both dark and light. I did take some fictional liberties with the locations in the story because it's a world of magic and alternate dimensions in some ways but I did capture the essence of my experience when I go there.

*You've written a complete werewolf (sexy werewolf and badass hunters) series but this is the second series featuring witches, (*The Dark War *would be the first, which we are all waiting on a sequel for, hint, hint). Do you like writing witches more than other paranormal creatures?*

First things first, the sequel to *The Dark War* has been written, praise chocolate, and I know it's been a long time coming. It's tentatively called *Fortune's Fool* and it takes place ten years after *The Dark War* ends. I'm not going to go into too much detail about it here but keep an eye out for some news soon (signing up for my newsletter would be a good way to keep in the loop).

Writing about witches is totally a passion of mine. If I could choose a paranormal creature to be, I'd have to go with witch. The power and magic that comes in a seemingly innocuous form is most appealing to me. Witches can blend in with society and hide tremendous power to heal or harm. They can walk in daylight and don't rely on blood to stay alive and powerful. They aren't governed by the changes of the moon and don't transform into beasts (unless they want to) and much of their power is not only innate but also skill-based that can be honed and manipulated. I also feel very drawn to the persecution side of things. The fear that actually still exists surrounding the idea of witchcraft fascinates me. Being an outcast or other is something I identify with and often strive for in a lot of ways so writing about witches feels like a natural thing to me.

Will there be any crossover between The Dark War *and* The Witches of White Willow?

No. These are two very separate worlds despite the fact that they are both about witches. *The Dark War* series is definitely darker, grittier and more in the vein of urban fantasy where *The Witches of White Willow* is straight up paranormal romance, complete with the promise of happily ever after.

Let's talk about themes. I noticed that you tackle the idea of identity, discrimination, and self-sacrifice in this book. It always amazes me how a sexy paranormal romance can hold such deep explorations.

Paranormal romance isn't just about hot sex (I mean, don't get me wrong, I always enjoy the opportunity to write some super sexy scenes.) Often, in paranormal romance, there's a lot of topics that parallel things we deal with in our real world. In *The Witches of White Willow*, there's a lot of racial discrimination happening between the old school pure witches and their feelings toward the human witches. Hazel has a different view of humans than her mother and is more open to working with them because she knows they have a lot of natural power and honed skill that the "pure" witches don't understand. She sees value there where her mother, and some of the other interns, don't. So this book attempts to tackle some of those issues. Hazel also struggles with her own identity and the role she must place in the future of her people. She has to learn that sometimes self-sacrifice isn't about giving all the parts of yourself away in order to be the hero— sometimes it involves keeping a lot of those parts for yourself so that you can be strong for your people.

What are your plans for this series? Any hints of things to come?

Oh, I have big plans for this series. The next book is

underway already and it's going to feature bad boy Bas Frank and his quest for redemption. He's got a dark history that's going to be explored in his book, as well as a really naughty sexual appetite. After that I have plans to continue the series by following the interns as they make their way through their Healer training. They've got years ahead of them and many things to learn along the way.

ABOUT THE AUTHOR

Every day is Halloween for author Angela Addams. Enthralled by the paranormal at an early age, Angela spends most of her time thinking up new story ideas that involve supernatural creatures in everyday situations. She believes that the written word is an amazing tool for crafting the most erotic of scenarios and has recently started down a dark path to disturbing thrillers and erotic horror.

Her Order of the Wolf series, featuring kick ass Amazon warriors and their mates, and her Dark War series, set in a world of witchcraft and war, are available from Entangled Publishing.

She is an avid tattoo collector, a total book hoarder, and loves anything covered in chocolate...except for bugs.

She lives in Ontario, Canada in an old, creaky house, with her husband, children, three cats and a couple weird guinea pigs.

Visit her website or sign up for her newsletter for more information!

ALSO BY ANGELA ADDAMS

Witch Hospital Romance
The Witches of White Willow

The Dark War Series
The Dark War

The Order of the Wolf
Cursed
Wolves' Bane
Spell-Weaver
Valiant Heart
Beast Rising

Single Titles
Burning Kiss
The Temptress
Assassin
Ghost Bride